To Mila
Fantasy fuels the

Enjoy!

Julie

SECRETS OF THE HOME WOOD

The Sacrifice

by Julie Whitley

FriesenPress

Suite 300 - 990 Fort St
Victoria, BC, Canada, V8V 3K2
www.friesenpress.com

ISBN
978-1-4602-5527-8 (Hardcover)
978-1-4602-5528-5 (Paperback)
978-1-4602-5529-2 (eBook)

1. Fiction, Fantasy

Distributed to the trade by The Ingram Book Company

Dedicated with love to Pierre and
Jennifer and my Mom

CHAPTER ONE

Jonathon

Where could she be?

Morning sun streamed over him through the mullioned panes as he sat folded into his bedroom bay window. Jonathon felt turned to stone. The eyes of his favourite baseball and hockey players stared down on him from posters that papered his walls. Photographs of his parents and grandfather sat on his dresser. He saw none of them. His mind's eye snagged on the image of his mother, smiling at him, hugging, teasing him until the space between his ribs that held his heart smouldered.

Why hasn't she called?

A movement in the lane beneath his window caught his attention. His dad, work backpack slung over his shoulder, moved quickly, as if he was late for work at their James Farm Produce store in the village of Dunston Mills. But when he glanced up at his son's window, his face wrenched with an emotion that chilled the heat in Jonathon's chest. The sight of that bleak expression yanked Jon back to the phone call his dad had made at breakfast time.

1

Jonathon had been sitting with Gramp at the table in the large farmhouse kitchen, but they could still hear his father's voice in the hall.

"Hi Debbie...uh...could I please speak to Sarah?...Oh, she isn't... She didn't? She did *what*?!" The receiver hit the cradle with a bang and he'd seemed to stumble as he came around the corner into the kitchen.

"David? How is Sarah?" Gramp Matthew's deep bass voice rumbled like thunder.

"Dammit, Dad, I don't know!" The unexpected roar of his reply had startled them all.

Seeing the expression on his father's face just before he veered from the lane and into the Home Wood brought Jonathon to his feet. He slipped on his windbreaker, grabbed his backpack and raced down the stairs.

"Jon? Where are you off to?" Gramp's tone slowed his step. Jonathon thought quickly.

"Just going to Michael's."

"Michael on the next concession?"

Jonathon nodded his head, unwilling to double the lie out loud.

"Here, take this with you. You didn't eat all your eggs." Gramp Matthew thrust some fruit and a power bar into Jonathon's backpack and patted his shoulder. Jonathon gave him a quick one-armed hug in thanks and raced out the backdoor, catching the screen door before it slammed.

"Jon, wait! Can you bring up the mail? I just heard the mail truck."

Jonathon groaned. *Gramp and his bat-like hearing.*

He rode his bike like a madman to the end of the lane and grabbed the bundled mail. The address of the top letter hooked his attention. Mrs Sarah James. The type font had a cold, official look. His mother usually got hand-written mail, and the weirdness gave him a chill. He dropped the stack on the hall table and refocused on his original task.

Follow his dad.

He took his bike with him as far as the path into the Home Wood and tucked it behind a bush. He couldn't put words to the *why* of it, but something twisting in his gut told him he had to find his dad.

The sun had already filtered its heat through the last of the early morning mist, but under the entwined branches of the forest trees, coolness still clung to the shadows. The Home Wood stretched far back for a hundred acres both beside and around the James family farm.

When he was little, one of Jonathan's favourite tales—how he loved to hear it over and over again—involved his Great-great-great (and at least a couple more greats) grandfather, William James, a United Empire Loyalist who had carved this farm out of the forest more than two hundred years ago, and how his assistance in the War of 1812 had earned him more land near his holding. William left a portion of the forest alone as a buffer between his and the next farm and gave it the name that stuck: the Home Wood.

Jonathon's father, David, built the James Farm Produce store in the village where he sold the apples, peaches, cherries and vegetables grown on their farm. From midway down the long lane from the house to the Concession 2 Road, a path led into the Wood. The path meandered through acres of trees older than William until it crossed a creek and continued into the dark heart of the Home Wood. Jonathon had heard how, when David had disappeared for a whole day and night twenty-four years ago, Gramp Matthew called it the last straw and forbade anyone to go past the creek. Even now his Gramp's bushy eyebrows trembled with emotion whenever the woods were brought up.

There was a secret hidden in these trees. Some in the family even called it a curse. In the week between last Christmas and New Year's, Gramp's brothers and sisters, ten of the original twelve, came for dinner. The family discussion became heated. Jon heard several of his uncles and aunts, goaded by Great Uncle Jeb and his sniffy wife, Aunt Euphemia, declare that the only way to deal with the evil of the Wood was to sell it for condos and smart centres. After all, the village of Dunston Mills was looking to expand, so why not get in on it?

Jonathon had boycotted the rest of the evening and plugged his ears with his pillow against the vulture shrieks of the dispute that circled up the stairs and pierced the peace of his room. *What would the loss of the farm mean to them? Nothing. They were sell-outs, comfortable in their homes in the village. What did they care?*

He knew it didn't matter to them that *his* branch of the family loved the farm and the Home Wood. Or that his dad looked more stressed every day and his parents had barely spoken in weeks and that his Gramp had taken up more of the chores again.

It all came to a head three days ago.

He'd been sitting on the front porch and heard the fiery voice of his mother.

"All I asked for, David, was a little support!"

There had followed a muttered reply from his dad but all Jonathan had caught of it was, "...waving self-righteousness like a banner."

"You know what? That's it. I'm going to Debbie's, and before you ask, no, I don't know when I will be back. I have a lot to think about."

If his father had a reply to that, Jonathan hadn't heard it.

What had followed was three days of silence.

Jonathon approached the grassy creek bank and stopped. The tops of the trees met in an arch above water that burbled and splashed over smooth-edged stones. The rich smells of decaying leaves and new growth suffused the air. A woodpecker hammered a tree trunk for breakfast, and a cardinal trilled to his mate. The farmhouse seemed in another land. He saw the fresh imprint of a running shoe on the other bank.

Dad crossed over!

What was he going to do? His grandfather said no one was ever to cross, but Jonathan knew he had to follow. His dad had been so agitated the last three days, his moods swinging from glum to crabby and back. Jon forgot about his own hurt in the family's division caused by his dad's baffling attitude towards his mother. His stomach cramped with indecision, but worry for his dad won out.

Jonathon crossed the creek.

He slipped on the slick verge of the creek but caught himself before he slid backward into the water. As he took the first steps into the deeper heart of the wood, another story surfaced in his memory: his dad taking him to see Great Aunt Louise at the Shady Oaks Rest Home in Dunston Mills village before she passed away. Some of the family, led by Aunt Euphemia, called her Loony Louie behind her back. All Jon had seen was a sweet faced, white haired woman whose tiny body barely lifted the covers off the bed. She'd smiled at him and offered him a mint.

"Would you mind taking your sketchbook in the hall? Draw something for me while I talk with your dad."

The youngest of Jonathon's twenty-two cousins was ten years older than him. Growing up surrounded by adults allowed his solitary, curious, imaginative nature to roam free around the farm and the part of the Home Wood near the house. That curious nature had got the better of him as he sat beside Great Aunt Louise's open door, his sketchbook blank as their words painted a picture in his mind. They'd talked about a giant oak in the Home Wood. They'd talked about "going through" and whom they had met. They'd talked about her brother Frederic who had "gone through" and never came back, and they made identical noises that suggested he couldn't have been that bright. Jonathon had peeked around the corner and saw their heads close together, each holding what looked like a medallion. A knowing look passed between them, one that hinted of a shared common experience and a secret.

Now, as he moved closer to the heart of Home Wood, Jonathon knew he was approaching that secret. Maybe he would see his father there and they could finally talk about it. The birdsongs were hushed. The sudden brightness of the clearing hurt his eyes after the deep gloom under the trees. In the moment it took for his vision to clear, he thought he saw his father sitting in the cave-like shadow created by a huge broken oak, long ago cracked in two.

"Dad!"

Jonathon called out, but when he blinked and ran forward, the leafy seat under the oak was empty. He dropped to his knees and felt all around on the ground. There was still a warm spot on the spongy cushion of fallen leaves. He sat back on his haunches and rubbed his eyes. The telltale warmth told him the truth. He had seen his father—just for a second. He'd been holding something pink.

What was that? And how could he have just vanished?

Jonathan was unsure whether to simply go back to the farmhouse and confess to his grandfather. He had to think. The emotional seesaw he had been on left him feeling drained. He found it strange, but his eyes grew almost too heavy to stay open.

I'll just sit and think for a few minutes. This is so quiet. So peaceful. Is this the place Dad and Great Aunt Louise talked about? Is this where they "went through" whatever that means? Could my eyes have been playing tricks on me? Why am I so tired all of a sudden? I just...need...to...

Jonathon's eyes popped open like window blinds. He was disoriented. He hadn't fallen asleep during the day in years. As his eyes adjusted to the light again, he felt a shiver start at his shoulders and trickle down his arms and spine. The clearing looked *different*. His head swivelled. The broken oak cave was gone. This was not Home Wood.

He took several deep breaths to slow the pounding in his chest and then allowed his eyes to search his new surroundings.

A deadfall replaced the lightning blasted oak. The clearing was larger and round. The ground looked swept except where a trail split the dirt as though someone had drawn a line or dragged a sharp-pointed object. He saw some footprints about his size, but oddly shaped: large toes and narrow heels, and then he saw the unmistakable tread of a running shoe.

His dad's shoe.

He followed the markings in the dirt to a confused dance of footprints. The footprints and dragged object then trailed off the dirt and disappeared along a faint path carpeted with mouldering leaves.

His dad led the way. Jonathon followed.

His Boy Scout tracking skills took over as a snapped branch clued him to veer to the left at a 'Y' in the path, the other track curving in the other direction. A cheerful chirruping in the trees reassured him he was not alone. He continued to follow the path even as it became narrower and more overgrown. Had he missed a turn?

He followed the path for what seemed a long time before he glanced up to see that the sun, filtering its light through the thick leaf canopy overhead, signalled midday. A rumble from his stomach made him wish he had eaten a bigger breakfast and packed a snack. Then he remembered the protein bar his grandfather had thrust into his backpack. He hunkered down and ransacked the pockets. Just as he ripped off the wrapper and took the first grateful bite, he realized that the chittering in the branches around him had stopped. The hairs on the back of his neck stood at attention. He froze.

The faintest shuffle behind him chilled his blood. Something big was behind him. Something menacing. He closed his eyes tight, but even as he did he scolded himself—it hadn't worked when he was three and it wouldn't get him out of trouble now.

First, he became aware of a mild, musky odour, a smell sort of like his dog, Chuck. Then the slightest chink of metal on metal. He moved his eyes and turned his head until the source came into view. Looking down on him was the most remarkable and alarming creature that Jonathon had ever seen. It was man-shaped but had long ears, one cocked up and forward, the other bent and facing back; a pink nose and rabbity teeth, large piercing blue eyes; and huge feet with (Jonathan noticed) large toes and narrow heels. Its body was stocky—Jon guessed the creature to be about half a foot shorter than his dad—and covered with a thick mottled brown fur. It wore a studded woven tunic and a belt bristling with long and short knives and a sword that looked like it could slice through wood. Jonathon swallowed hard.

As their eyes met, the fierce expression in the stranger's eyes turned to stunned amazement. He began a chittering conversation, but Jon thought he recognized one word. And at the sound of it his frozen shock thawed to wonder.

Did he just say "David"?

David

David squatted on his heels in the heart of the Home Wood and stared at the cave created by the huge oak, blasted in half by lightning nine decades ago. His heart rammed against his ribs. He cursed himself for being so selfish and stupid. He reached into the shadows and snatched a soft pink sweater, covered in leaves: it belonged to his wife, Sarah. He tried to take a deep breath, but his lungs would not fill. This was his fault.

How could I let this happen? She didn't know the portal had a siren call that caught the unwary.

Knowing the treatment Aunt Louise had received when she tried to tell the family about the portal, David had kept his experience to himself. He knew his father had heard about his sister Louise's adventure, but Matthew James made it clear he didn't want to know anything more about such nonsense. David's breath shuddered out. Now Sarah had gone through and it was his fault.

I should have...why didn't I just...

He pushed the half-formed thoughts aside. Sarah, he knew, could be in danger. She had no idea what she was headed for. He scuttled crabwise into the cave, the pink sweater clutched to his chest. He remembered the first and last time he had gone through. He had been twelve years old...the day his mother...

No, don't go there!

He had come back twenty-four hours later, bruised and bloodied. Sarah had no idea what was on the other side. But he did.

Sarah

[three days earlier]

Even before she opened her eyes, the smells were different. The air was tangy and sharp with pine and the rich smell of earth and of old smoke. Sarah opened one sherry-brown eye, then the other. Thick trees still surrounded her, but the wood had changed. The clearing was now a circle of dirt and the hollow of the fallen oak was gone, replaced by a smaller deadfall that seemed constructed and covered in flowers like a shrine. Sarah felt a chill as she rose and dusted herself off, leaves still caught in her auburn hair. She rubbed her arms and realized that she had left her pink sweater behind. She pictured David handing her the sweater in the morning...*before* they fought. He couldn't talk to her about what worried him, but she had to give him credit: he cared about her comfort and safety. *If only he could support me through this one thing. At least until the results.* She pushed the thought away and kneaded her arms again.

The chill was not just in the early morning air. An icy fear ran its cold, bony finger down her back.

Where the flying heck am I, and how do I get back?

In the heat of her passion after the spat with David, the idea of entering the Home Wood to cool down before going to Debbie's house had made sense, but now it seemed foolhardy. The slyly muttered family tales about the Home Wood had given her pause even as she dismissed them as so much gossipy twitter. The story of David's disappearance in the Home Wood when he was just a little younger than Jonathon had always intrigued her but made her nervous enough to never defy Matthew's ban and explore past the creek. But today her rage led her across and deeper into the wood. Once across the creek, her steps had, it seemed, been drawn forward without her volition until she saw the most enormous oak, split in two, the halves forming a cave of sorts.

Sarah had no idea what drew her to that oak cave. It felt like her feet belonged to someone else and her body had been forced to follow. Inside the cave, the sounds of the Wood had been muted and a sense of peace washed over her and eased up her body like a rising tide. As the muscles in her neck relaxed, Sarah had let her eyes close.

Just for a moment. Then I must be going. I just need a little...time...to...

"Well, standing here isn't going to help me get home."

She said it aloud to calm herself, but a niggle of worry shouldered its way to the forefront of her thoughts again. But where was home from here; where *was* she? Then her long-practiced habit of positive I-can-get-this-done thinking reasserted itself. She would find someone who could help her get back home. She would get back to the Home Wood and...

...I'll cross that stream when I get there.

As she began to walk along a barely visible path, the chirruping of invisible birds followed her, and she took comfort in their cheerful noise.

Sarah continued along the overgrown path for a long time, worried that at any moment it would disappear. Low growing branches reached out and grasped at the hem of her long denim skirt, then a thick root sent her sprawling onto the narrow path, cushioned deep with fallen leaves. The birds hushed. The silence was intense.

The sound of crackling, shushing through the underbrush dispelled the unnatural quiet. Whatever it was, it was heading straight for her. Before Sarah could react, a body burst through the centre of the bush in front of her and blasted full tilt into—and over—Sarah, the two of them rolling entangled like kittens. Sarah grunted with the impact. The stranger squeaked.

11

Squeaked.

Sarah pulled back to get a better look at the same time as her assailant. She stared at what she would have taken for an enormous brown and gold pelted rabbit, except for the decorated belted tunic dress of woven fabric. Her face was framed by long floppy ears, and she had prominent teeth and violet eyes that were large with fright.

Not just frightened. Terrified.

The creature crossed her hands over her heart and spoke. A feeling of dreamlike unreality washed over Sarah, but as a teacher of deaf children, she recognized language structure in the sounds directed to her even though she could make no sense of them. She took a chance and signed back she was not a threat and that the stranger was safe. Immediately, Sarah sensed a change. The long ears straightened, the creature's fear-filled eyes relaxed for a moment, and she returned some signs that Sarah interpreted as a greeting.

Then the moment was gone as one long graceful ear twisted backwards, the terrified look returned to the stranger's face. She grabbed Sarah's hand, yanked her to her feet, and plunged them both into a mad rush through the bushes.

CHAPTER TWO

Jonathon

He woke with a start to the smell of woodsmoke. He rubbed his eyes, but the pitch blackness around him defeated any hope of seeing his surroundings. He shook his head to rattle some sense back into his brain. Memories surfaced through muddy thoughts: the rabbity warrior; the secret way through a barrier of foliage disguising a fortress wall and guarding the inner stronghold of the warrior's people; circles of huts, each connected by a single roof with a broad overhang. Then Jonathon remembered the low-walled dwelling into which the warrior had led him; an earth-toned living area with a well-oiled table of hewn wood surrounded by sturdy benches and a smokeless wood fire in the centre of the room. The bed. Soft, warm. His eyes heavy, his limbs like lead. The last thing he remembered, he had crawled up onto the bed and fallen asleep in an instant.

A torch flared in the darkness. Jonathon could hear a few twitters of birds outside. Dawn wasn't far off. He raised himself on an elbow and looked around in the flickering light just in time to see the warrior disappear into a back room and emerge with an object in his hand. He gestured for Jon to sit up.

What is that?

It looked like a medallion—not unlike the objects he remembered seeing his dad and Great Aunt Louise compare—a round disk within a disk, with the edges of the inner disk intricately designed in a way that reminded Jonathan of a watch, but with more divisions. The medallion hung from a braided rope that the warrior put around Jonathon's neck. He twisted the inner disk and tilted his head, one long ear bent forward listening. Tufts above his eyes waggled in concentration as he continued to twist the inner disk with increasing intensity. Finally he released the double disk on Jonathon's chest, and made a gesture as though snapping a twig over his knee and stared into the boy's eyes. Jonathon had learned sign language from his mom, so he hazarded a guess.

"It's broken?"

He repeated the gesture, but wondered what the medallion could do. The warrior nodded his head and spoke the words in his language. When Jonathon copied his sounds, the warrior's large rabbity teeth appeared in a grin and his blue eyes twinkled in unmistakable delight. He went around the room pointing—to furniture, windows, the floor, weapons—and had Jonathon repeat the words. The warrior made movements like running and crouching and sitting. With his knack for mimicry and languages, Jonathan repeated the sounds perfectly again and again. A light of excitement and hope glowed in Jonathon's blue-green eyes as understanding struck tinder. If he could communicate, he could convince his new warrior friend to help find his father.

He pointed to himself and said, "Jonathon." The warrior frowned in concentration and his mouth moved, but no sounds escaped.

Jonathon laughed, and pointed to himself again and said, "Jon." His teacher nodded and repeated the name drawing out the vowel somewhat. Then he tapped his own chest and said, "Pugg." Jonathan held out his hand. Pugg looked at him blankly, so Jon grasped the warrior's hand and pumped it a few times.

"Pleased to meet you, Pugg!"

Pugg led the way to the door of the hut and made a sweeping gesture of his arm towards the circle of huts, and up to the brightening sky.

"Sanigglan." A string of words followed as he looked around with pride, and Jonathan translated to himself.

Welcome to Sanigglan, my home.

As Jon looked around the grand circle of adobe walled huts, a prickly feeling tingled his skin, a feeling of intense scrutiny. No. More than intense. Fierce. His gut sent him an unmistakable message.

Danger.

David

His limbs grew heavy with the burden of returning consciousness, but his eyes were still unwilling to open. He struggled, against the portal's sedation, to remember why was he there. He needed help for something important...

His mind's eye could see the trees, weighty and bent with age, leaning towards each other for support. He reached out with his other senses to examine his surroundings and stimulate his recall. Oh, he remembered this feeling. He had felt it when he was twelve and awakening here for the first time. The smells and sounds were full of memories: the rich, old forest growth, centuries of fallen leaves cushioning the glade, the chitters of small creatures in the branches...

Wait, where are the sounds?

The silence was profound.

He sensed a furtive intrusion. Leaves rustled. They rustled closer. Again silence.

A stealthy, stalking quality to the sound teased its way to the forefront of his awareness. He eased one eye open to peek and almost choked with the next breath. A rough-edged bubble of something like laughter caught in the back of his throat like a chicken bone. David struggled to raise himself on one elbow and keep a solemn face, but the end of a razor-sharp spear, pointed just below the hollow of his throat, discouraged further movement.

The shaky, double grasp of a belligerent young warrior held the spear. Stout legs wide, he stood astride the shadow of the fall of deadwood that dominated the clearing. He was clothed in a studded charcoal black battledress years too large and banded at the waist with a belt laden with knives, short sword, and bow. A high squeaked command and fierce glare were at odds with the gentleness of his grey-furred rabbity face.

David listened to the chitters of the small warrior for a moment before he realized that something was wrong. He pulled back a few inches from the spear's point and held up four fingers of his hand, palm out, in the gesture of authority he remembered from his trip through the portal so long ago. He ignored the squeaks of indignation and reached up to his neck to lift out a medallion from its hiding place under his shirt. He had kept it safe since it had been given to him on his first visit and guarded it so that not even his father was aware of its existence. It gave him the gift of communication.

David showed the young warrior the medallion and motioned for him to speak as he made some fine-tuning adjustments to its complex inner circle. His focus blocked out the reaction of his captor. On the farm, as a boy, when he knew he was alone, he would take it out and turn the inner circle until the airwaves crackled about his head like high voltage static.

The young warrior, still jumpy and mistrustful, gave David's shoulder a small jab with the spear.

"Ouch! Stop that."

Startled by David's thundering command, the young warrior backed up, tripped over the trailing end of the spear and landed with a thud on his plump bottom. David knew then that the medallion still worked. He rubbed at the pinpoint of blood that beaded on his collarbone. The youngster sprang to his feet, fumbling to regain control of the spear and his apprehension.

"You're my prisoner."

As David considered him, the rough-edged bubble again tickled the back of his throat, but he kept his expression grave out of respect. He needed this young warrior to guide him to real help.

"I'm yours. Take me to your leader."

For a moment the young warrior hesitated. A look of uncertainty clouded his large, dark eyes. The rigid warlike ruff of his fur smoothed briefly, then he scowled, bristled his ruff and poked David, none too gently, in the shoulder with the spear's point.

"I warn you. Don't try to trick me! Just because I'm young." He strutted a step and preened. "I'm not brainless." His pupils contracted so that David could see their vivid blue irises, undimmed by age or failure. "I'm a San warrior of Sanigglan."

Snugglum was the closest pronunciation of the forest kingdom that David could remember from his boyhood visit, but now he heard, beneath the word, a drawing out of the first syllable, a guttural roll of the 'g' and a blurring of the final consonant that he knew his own tongue would never be able to duplicate. For him, it would always be Snugglum.

"Come, prisoner!" The warrior prodded him again. David bowed his head in agreement and gathered Sarah's pink sweater to tuck into his knapsack. He jumped up. His captor's eyes grew enormous. At six two, David towered over the young warrior who couldn't have been more than five feet tall.

"I...I said come, prisoner!" The slight stammer belied his bold command. He turned to lead the way. In a blur of movement, he whipped around to face David again, glaring at him with suspicion.

"Wait a minute! *You* first! Walk down that path." He waved the point of the spear at his prisoner's chest. "Go where I tell you. I'm watching!"

Patiently, David allowed himself to be marched along the paths that twined through the dense undergrowth and strange leafy trees of colossal girth dappled by multi-filtered light. Now and then, a warning jab in the back of his thigh reminded him of his circumstance. After a while, the lagging frequency of the jabs cued David to steal a look over his shoulder. Affection budded for his captor when he saw fatigue sketched in the large eyes and hunched shoulders. David stopped and reached around to steady the young warrior as he thumped into the back of David's legs.

"I'm getting tired," David said. "Do you mind if we have a rest before you take me to your leader?" He didn't wait for permission but sat down on the spot. The young San sank down beside him.

The silence between them radiated with waves of tension. They studied each other, the youth wary and undecided, his captive thoughtful and remote. Sarah's face flashed into David's mind like summer lightning. The portal's anesthetic had now worn off.

Sarah! Where is she now? He wondered if this young San would be able to help him find her.

David broke the silence. "Since we're going to be together, I think we should introduce ourselves." He paused for effect. "I am David, son of Matthew."

He could almost hear the thoughts crackle behind the youngster's bright, intelligent eyes, his agitation reflected in the rapid twitch and flick of his large tapered ears.

"I'm Snuggla, eldest of Snugg and heir to the kingdom of Sanigglan."

David's breath caught in his throat. His head flooded with impressions of long past.

"Many years ago," David said, his voice soft with memory, his expression shaped by respect, "your father was my teacher and my friend. He saved my life."

Snuggla's wide-open eyes threatened to engulf his face.

"You're... you're Daavid of the Legend!" His voice was low with awe.

David bowed his head to hide his thoughts. *Legend?*

Snuggla continued to speak. His stilted words came slowly at first, and then tumbled over themselves in mounting excitement as he relayed the story of the legend.

"Many years afore my birth, a boy be found in these woods on the day before the great Battle of the Forest. Some of the warriors thought him a bad omen, and others thought him a spy. But my father, Snugg, defended him. The boy had a brave heart and wanted to help in the fight to save Sanigglan from our enemies. He fought like a true warrior of the San and slew the leader of our foe with only a spear. But before the leader died, he struck Daavid on the head. My father thought Daavid dead, and all of Sanigglan mourned him. They carried him back to the place where he had first been found and covered him with flowers. The next day, when they returned with more, he had vanished!"

Snuggla finally unwound, stilled by his own wonder.

Self-conscious, David reached up and felt the thick scar hidden by his hair. He didn't know what to say, so he sat immobile and tried to look the part of a Legend, but he felt a bitter tinged laugh deep inside.

A failure in marriage and fatherhood, but a legend in my own time...

Abruptly, David stopped. He realized that for just a moment he felt better and stronger than he had in months, more like his old self.

Maybe that's been part of the problem, he thought. *I misplaced the ability to laugh at myself. Maybe if I had laughed more with Jon and Sarah...*

He remembered reading in the newspaper about a new therapy where people made themselves laugh to feel better. It was worth a try. David took a breath and forced himself to laugh out loud.

"I don't know what's so chucklesome!" Snuggla looked offended.

Smiling, David reached forward and placed a large, square hand on the youngster's shoulder.

"Only laughing at myself, Snuggla." He leaned back against a tree. "Tell me, how is Snugg?"

Snuggla seemed mollified at David's answer, but at the sound of his father's name, he stiffened and his ruff bristled.

"My father, Snugg is...is a *murderer!*"

David leaned forward again.

"What?"

The young warrior blinked and huffed a couple of times.

"Well, she never came back." Snuggla's voice roughened with emotion. "It be his fault."

Sarah

Sarah and her brown and gold pelted companion continued their headlong flight along almost invisible paths. All forest sounds and any sounds of pursuit were drowned out by her heart thumping in her ears. Branches from brush and small trees whipped across their faces and chests as they tore through. Sarah's guide, long ears swivelling to each direction, paused now and then to confirm her bearings before plunging them forward again.

They both breathed heavily, hands to hearts when next they came to a forced rest. The silence of the forest around them overwhelmed even the hammering of their hearts. In response to seeing her companion's eyes grow big with fear, Sarah pivoted in all directions but could see only trees and hear nothing but the profound quiet. Slight pressure from her guide's hand on her arm, signalled Sarah to back up slowly, and in the next heartbeat, the earth fell away beneath their feet.

As they dangled in a coarse net high in the air, a rank odour filled the air, then a rumble of scornful, bass laughter surrounded them.

CHAPTER THREE

Jonathon

At first, in the early morning gloom, Jonathon could only see low walled adobe huts draped in vegetation through the hut's door, but as he focused his concentration, he saw an eye peeking around a door frame, an ear tweaked his way behind a bush. The longer he looked, the more he saw. In the few seconds of his scrutiny, the tension grew, amplified by a low, swelling hum. He looked up at Pugg with apprehension. This didn't have a friendly feel to it at all.

Jonathon and Pugg had arrived in the stillness of deep night to a sleeping village. Vague building shapes were all he had a chance to see before Pugg hustled him into the hut and he fell into exhausted sleep on the cushioned bed seconds later. A thought made Jon's heart leap as he stared at the village compound through the doorway.

Dad might be here sleeping in another hut right now!

Jonathon struggled with how to ask Pugg, but the opportunity shattered as the warrior put a hand on his shoulder and led him up the two steps from the sunken living area of his dwelling into the open again.

The morning shadows beneath the deep overhang of the windowless huts contrasted the daylight in the community's common. Beyond the common, Jonathon could see other circles of huts, like cells of a giant hive, each attached by the overhangs whose edges were disguised with tendrils of hanging vegetation. Clusters of round-headed maples, tall, elegant oaks and sentinel blue spruce graced the junctions between the circles and provided connection to the surrounding forest.

A hum like the sound of a million bees stung his ears. Jonathon felt like he stood in a spotlight in the morning brightness of the common, and even Pugg's nearness could not quell his rising unease.

In less than a heartbeat the clearing filled with furred, long-eared beings that Pugg, with a sweep of his ear, introduced to Jonathon as the San. They crowded close, expressions on rabbity faces ranging from fear and wonder to anger and suspicion. Pugg held out his hand, palm out, to stop the pushing, clamorous throng of hundreds of San villagers and gain their attention. With the other hand, he hugged the boy to his side protectively. He called out to an elderly limp-eared individual with rheumy eyes, clothed in a long leaf green tunic, loosely belted with an earth brown braid. In a high thready voice, the elder answered Pugg.

Jonathon thought he heard his father's name pass between them, the first vowel slightly drawn out. His back straightened as though pulled up by the string of Pugg's voice, and his eyes widened. He wished he knew more of the San language. For now, until he built up his command of San, he would have to make do with sign language. He had learned to sign as a volunteer in his mother's class with three children who were deaf. His mastery helped him read Pugg's frustrated message earlier about the broken translator. Could he modify what he knew of sign language to add to his growing San vocabulary and communicate better with Pugg? Taking a chance, he tugged at the warrior's tunic to get his attention. Pugg looked down with a query in his eyes. Jon pointed to himself, placed his hand on his heart, made the motion of a taller body beside him, then he placed his thumb on his forehead, fingers open, classroom sign language for *father*, and said, "David."

David is my father.

Pugg stared down at him for a moment, then a fire lit his eyes. "Daavid!" he said with an emphatic twitch of his ears. He turned to address the crowd, telling them Jon's revelation in a few excited sentences. The voices of the crowd rose in an ardent cry, joy flamed in their eyes, and the nearest reached out to touch Jonathon, patting him with awe. Jon breathed out, grateful to feel the tension ease and the goodwill of the San rise towards him. Did his father know that his visit had made such a lasting, favourable impression on these people? Was his father somewhere around here now?

Jonathon looked around and saw that Pugg had moved off through the crowd. Under the shade of a regal blue spruce, he talked to three others, all armed in the attire of warriors like Pugg. In his humble opinion, Jon didn't think they could fight their way through fog. One was missing half an arm, a second was bent nearly double with age, and the third—though his back was straight and proud—had one ear a ragged half and an eye covered with a whitish film. Pugg, on the other hand, stood head and broad shoulders above them. Jonathon read his gestures and the expressions of the others. The ragged-eared warrior's gnarled finger punched the air above Pugg's chest, swung to point at Jonathon and then at the forest beyond. Pugg's posture resisted the old warrior, but when the elder joined the group and added his voice, Pugg gave in.

The San villagers, meanwhile, ringed him like iron files to a magnet. They gazed at Jonathon adoringly, patted him as if to ensure he was real, and chattered to him. The villagers came in all colours from grey, brown, gold and mottled. In terms of size, most were at least as tall as Jonathon, but none were as tall as Pugg. Many times over, Jon thought he heard his father's name.

He must be here!

He strained to see over their heads. In their eagerness to be near him, the press of their weight triggered a rising panic in Jonathon. His glued smile turned into a grimace of fear as they continued to push in their great desire to touch him.

This must be what rockstars feel like, he thought.

On his tiptoes to look over the heads of the villagers, Jonathon caught Pugg's eye and knew the warrior could see the stress in his face. Pugg parted a line through the crowds with his strength, to reach Jonathon's side. His voice urged the San back, and with the pressure of his hand on Jonathon's shoulder, Pugg guided him back to the hut.

The moon, still three days from full, set over the trees, its brightness dimmed by the rising sun. The sun's climb had not yet dispelled the murk inside the hut. Pugg added to the wood burner in the centre of the room, and its soft glow chased the shadows into the corners. With gestures and words, Pugg told Jonathon the core of the discussion with the other warriors. Jonathon repeated phrases in San and English and signed back to show his understanding.

Jonathon felt a surge of excitement as he listened and watched Pugg's signs. His father was here! No, no—disappointment twisted his gut—his father *had* been here and had left. With an effort of will, he straightened his drooping shoulders.

It's okay. We'll leave soon to find him. He has to be close; I was practically right behind him.

The warrior opened a pair of carved doors in the back wall and revealed a larder. He pulled out a nut loaf, a wooden bowl of leafy greens and a clay jug of clear water. He signalled for Jonathon to eat. The rumble from Jon's stomach needed no further invitation. He sat on a low wooden bench at a long carved table that dominated one side of the room. He wolfed down hunks of loaf and washed it away with the sweet water. Chewing on a bit of loaf, Pugg picked up Jon's backpack. With an absorbed expression, he turned it this way and that while handling the straps, then poked in the pockets. Jonathon heard Pugg's soft satisfied huffs as he stuffed the backpack full of the gathered provisions.

Jonathon's brain gnawed on his thoughts. His father had been here, not just as a kid but only hours ago. Why had he come back? He wished his grasp of the San language was complete so that he could pummel Pugg with his questions. Jon fretted.

What other secrets has Dad been keeping from us?

A pull on his arm startled him. Jonathon's gaze refocused on Pugg's face. With sign and San words, Pugg urged him to finish and prepare to leave. The warrior handed Jonathon a tan-coloured tunic to put over his clothes. It possessed strength and fit like a second skin, completed with a braided belt. Next, Jon was shown an assortment of weapons, including knives and short swords, from which to choose. He picked up a slingshot by its carved Y-shaped hardwood handle and hefted it, running his fingers over the pocket of oiled leathery bark. He then sighted with it, testing the springiness of the braided rubber strips. He remembered competitions he had had with his dad, shooting targets behind the barn. They were both good shots—but he was better, and *this* slingshot was a beauty. *I'll be able to hit anything with this baby!* He tucked the weapon into the side of his belt along with a pouch to hold rock projectiles and gulped more sweet water to wash down the last of the nut loaf. He picked up his backpack and dropped it again. *Cripes, it weighs a ton.*

Pugg took it from him and slung it over his shoulder as if it were a feather pillow.

At the door of the hut, Jonathon stopped to look around. The air was cool and fresh, touched by floral scents and moist earth. A pat on his arm drew his attention downwards. A tiny San child gazed up at him in awe. His face was almost entirely eyes, and his fuzzy brown head barely reached Jon's waist. The youngster's mother came out of the next hut and, with an embarrassed twitch of one graceful grey ear and a shy smile, corralled her offspring but could not resist a maternal touch to Jon's arm. He signed a greeting to her and smiled at the little one. In a blink they disappeared back into the hut.

Pugg signalled their departure.

The warrior's ground-eating pace through the dappled early morning light soon put the village far behind them. Jonathon quick-stepped to keep up with the San warrior's stride through a tunnel of ancient trees each bending an enormous girth over a well-tended path like a row of old compadres on canes. The path led to the secret gate in the wall. Exhaustion clouded Jon's memory of this gate the evening before. *Wow, the design's genius!*

Closed, it blended in with what appeared to be a solid wall of vegetation. When Pugg activated a mechanism hidden in the bole of a tree, it triggered a well-oiled winch that raised a gate, disguised with thick vines, to form a small archway. Pugg signed with ears and hands that the wall surrounded and protected the community of the San. Jonathon marvelled at what he saw, his eyes round and large trying to take it all in at once. It was like a project he had done for history class, the year before, of the stages of a medieval town except filled with these strange, awesome beings instead of English peasants. They lived simply, but then they had technology like this.

What does Dad think of this place? And why didn't he ever tell me about it?

The latter question stung a little bit.

Even as the gate slid closed behind them, Pugg led him down an overgrown path that contrasted with the tended, crafted paths inside the compound. He signed and spoke in simple San phrases to let Jon know that they were headed along a shortcut to speak to someone. To friends. No. Allies? Jonathon shrugged. Probably with his dad. While their ability to communicate improved with every hour together, some thoughts remained too complex to explain. Jonathon felt a growing desperation to ask Pugg for more about his father.

The paths Pugg chose through the San forests were subtle, almost invisible in the overgrowth. As the sun rose higher, the purple shadows from the many filtered light rays played around them. The crisp smell of dew on leaves tickled Jonathon's nose. Lazy twittering trickled from the trees as birds stretched the wrinkles out of their wings. The pace that Pugg set along the narrow, brush-choked paths allowed Jonathon little time to appreciate the beauty of the San's forest. Catching his breath became the major issue. Several hours on the trail, Pugg relented and signalled for a rest.

Jonathon dropped gratefully to a leafy seat in the middle of the path. Pugg passed him a pouch filled with nuts and dried fruits and then offered him some water from a pale fleshy looking water-bag. Jonathon tried to ignore the cold, spongy feel of the bag that sent a shiver bumping down his spine. He had more pressing thoughts.

"When will we reach my father?" Jonathon's confident anticipation shrivelled with Pugg's signed and spoken answer.

"We're not going to your father."

David

A few stars blinked through the branches of the scrubby plains tree that sheltered David and Snuggla's camp. The banked fire released a trickle of smoke. David shifted position on the hard ground and calculated that dawn couldn't be too far off even though the birds had not yet begun their announcements. A lot had happened since he put his feet on the floor beside his bed yesterday morning. Something told him the roller coaster ride had barely even started. When David first met Snuggla in the portal clearing, he felt buoyant hope the San warriors would help him find his Sarah. Hope crashed into disappointment when they reached the San village yesterday afternoon, only to find Snugg away on his own mission. Now here they were, he and Snuggla, on their own again.

David stretched his spine and ran the events through his mind once more, looking for a different answer to his dilemma. He thought back to Snuggla's declaration the day before and all that followed.

"Snuggla, it's time we talked about Snugg. He—"

"He's a murderer!" Snuggla had smacked fist in palm for emphasis. David raised an eyebrow.

"That's a pretty strong accusation against your father. You better tell me what happened."

During a few moments of silence, Snuggla's twitching ears showed his struggle with strong emotion.

"Well, he might's well have been. It's his fault. Three days past, I woke and heard my maam and da in a wrangle. Maam went out and never came back." Snuggla stared at the ground, his large expressive eyes blurred with unshed moisture. "My...Snugg sent out a tracker who followed Maam's trail to a place where it stopped cold, and the trail of our big-footed enemy, the Grue, began. The tracker came back, and my father did nothing. So, I came out to find Maam meself." His voice trembled, and his large eyes shimmered. Then his voice firmed.

"Instead I found you," Snuggla had said. "I thought first you be my enemy and I'd force you to take me to Maam." The youth looked up at David with a blended expression of hope and newly minted devotion. "But I know now you be Daavid of the Legend. You be brave and fearless. You saved my people. I know you will help find me Maam!"

The chill of fear that had skittered down his spine put an unwelcome thought in David's mind. Three days ago, the lad had said. And three days since Sarah went through the Home Wood portal into the San forest. Could she have run into a Grue ambush, too? Urgency bubbled up into David's throat again.

"I will help you, Snuggla."

Snuggla had started up eagerly.

"But first," said David, "I must speak to your father. *I* need his help, too." The lad sank back on his haunches, his nose wrinkled in disgust.

"He won't do *anything*. He won't help you. He won't help me! He doesn't want her back!"

David had lifted Snuggla's chin upwards until he could look into his eyes. He held Snuggla's gaze for several seconds, willing him to listen—a tried-and-true knack of Sarah's, he remembered with a squeeze of his heart.

"In training to be a leader," he said, "there are many things to learn. The first lesson is there are always two sides. The second, that things may not always be as they appear."

Chastened but unrepentant, Snuggla freed himself, and picked up his spear.

"Follow me."

David's return to the San village had brought back a flash-flood of memories that began with images of the first exhausting walk in the chilled dawn air and a slender human boy struggling to keep up with the swift and silent forest dwellers. The circles of huts in the San village were just as he remembered them. The lines of the roofs, camouflaged by lush elevated gardens of flowers and vegetables cleverly interlaced with bushes, which presented, from the air, the appearance of a natural forest clearing. The long, wide overhang allowed movement between the huts without fear of observation from above. Sentinels, on constant watch, advised with signals when the gardens could be tended and when a retreat must be made. The peace of Sanigglan was fragile. As David and Snuggla entered the circle of huts, with the sun at its apex, the silence stretched deep and eerie. Not a breath stirred in the empty compound. Yet the back of David's neck twitched with the feeling of many hidden, hostile eyes upon him. He sensed that Snuggla's stocky body and giant courage were all that stood between him and death.

When Snuggla had announced in a fluting voice, from the centre of the village common, that Daavid of the Legend had returned, the inhabitants swarmed out of hiding and surrounded them. David felt joy and heard exclamations of hope from the host of San who clamoured for his attention. He thought he heard the word "saviour" whispered here and there. Legend was one thing, but saviour? He hoped he was mistaken.

David had searched the crowd, past furry ears that swayed like long grasses in a breeze, but couldn't see his old friend, Snugg. In truth, very few warriors were in the compound, and their absence seemed to David to have an unfortunate effect on Snuggla's self-assurance. David caught a smug I-told-you-so glance thrown his way by the cocky young San. He wished he could bring Snuggla back to earth and show him he was wrong about his father. But how, when appearances said Snuggla was right? Where was Snugg and all his warriors? There had to be a different explanation. The fierce and determined leader that David remembered would never leave his mate in enemy hands nor would he ignore his son. David's insides twisted with a stab of guilt. Had he been ignoring his own son the last few months? When he got back home to the farm, he would make that right. First, he had to find Sarah and fix his monumental mistakes with her.

He had followed the young warrior into the family hut and assisted with supplies for their quest. As much as the San people loved David (or at least his legend), it was plain there would be no help in his search for Sarah here except from his young warrior friend. Through the open doorway, David sighted a group of four worn-out warriors, huddled together and gesturing earnestly. One of them left the group and with a glance over his shoulder in David's direction, slipped away down the path like a shadow before the sun. Snuggla gave him no time to ponder the scene before claiming his attention.

"Now we may go!"

The winding, narrow forest path Snuggla had chosen led towards the land of the Grue. The shadows changed shape and direction as the sun plied its course. Occasional gleams of light through the thick, leafy ceiling marked their route as northerly. David kept checking behind them. Was his imagination overactive? He couldn't see anyone, but the prickles at the nape of his neck told him differently.

The lush forest had yielded to a rough and sinister mix of terrain: abrupt cliff-like drops into deep swampy ravines, towering trees with long moss covered tentacles that reached out to grab at them as they passed. The air, syrupy with a cloying sweet and sour stench, wafted up from the ravines. David felt the smell envelop him, thick as a verminous blanket, and creep up his nose and under his skin. Doubt reached though his defences and constricted his heart like the moss-afflicted limbs of this God-forsaken wood. This wasn't going to work! They would never make it across this foul landscape alone.

David had looked down at Snuggla's fierce determination and took a deep breath. He reminded himself of the discovery that he had made earlier in the day and knew—not just felt—that he could bring this problem into focus too.

"Snuggla, how far is it to the Grue?" The young San glanced over his shoulder. Did Snuggla see doubt lingering in his eyes? David sighed as he watched flickers of impatience and youthful scorn shadow the respect in Snuggla's face.

"It matters not how far!"

He had grasped Snuggla by the shoulder to halt him in his tracks.

"Snuggla," David said, "if we're to rescue your Maam, *everything* matters! We need a plan. We should have talked about this before. If we're to have the strength to carry it out, we have to discuss things like distance and terrain. If the search takes longer, we'll need shelter and maybe more food. Is the country we're traveling through full of enemies, or are there any allies? If we miss something, it could cost your life as well as your Maam's!"

David wondered if he should tell Snuggla about Sarah: that his personal mission was to save his wife. He decided to keep it simple. A bone-deep hunch told him that the fates of Sarah and Snuggla's maam were intertwined.

His words penetrated the barrier of Snuggla's strong-willed self-importance and stimulated the intelligent core of his young mind. Puckers of thought appeared across the lad's forehead in wavering rows that made his long tapered ears wobble uncertainly.

David's logic was inescapable.

Snuggla had squatted down and, with the tip of a stick, drew configurations in the dusty path. As the lines grew, David recognized a schoolboy style map and leaned forward to watch with renewed interest. Stabbing with the twig, Snuggla pointed to the convergence of two lines,

"We're here, just inside the border of the Grue's land. The Grue live here." The twig traced a course between the two diverging lines towards a third that formed the base of a large triangle. The twig stopped in the middle and drew a fortress surrounded by swamps and ravines. David pointed to the edges of the triangle.

"Who lives outside of the Grue's borders?"

Snuggla sketched the trees of Sanigglan and David saw that the point of the Grue's triangular territory wedged into the forest dwellers' land. To the East, bordered by Sanigglan and the Grue, Snuggla smoothed the dirt to show a flat, featureless area and then drew a tiny square in the middle.

"The land of the Maorrr."

David raised an eyebrow in question. They hadn't fought in the battle that made him legend. Snuggla answered David's unspoken question.

"They were allies in times past but not friends. The Maorrr can be an unpredictable lot."

"Do you think they might help us now?" David had asked. He studied the map. It was clear that the best route into the core of the Grue's land was from the short side, the border shared by the Maorrr.

"They might," said Snuggla, "or might not."

"Well, we can ask."

"Or be eaten!" Snuggla added cryptically.

"What?!"

"That's what makes the Maorrr so unpredictable. Sometimes they help us, sometimes they eat us." Snuggla stood up. The uncertain waggle of his ears belied his bluff. "Let's hope we find them in a full mood."

He had clapped the dust from his hands. David followed suit with only a slight hesitation and closed on Snuggla's heels to take the path that branched off towards the land of the Maorrr. The advantage of their new direction lay in putting this sour land behind them. The second advantage would bring them allies to help then in their quests to find Sarah and Snuggla's Maam. They had camped that night on the grassy Maorrr plain under scrubby trees.

With the sleepy tweets and cheeps in the branches overhead, the dawn of his second day was not far away. As Snuggla roused beside him, David felt a stir of dread. *Where was Sarah now? Was she okay?*

Would they find the new allies full?

Sarah

When the hood was lifted from Sarah's head, she squinted into the thin yellowish light and tried to get her bearings. Her last memory consisted of being swept up into the air like a butterfly in a huge net and an incredibly foul stench before she passed out. Now she saw her companion, blood clotted above one eye, lying limp and motionless on the large filthy flagstones. It was a prison cell. The walls of their cell dripped with moisture. There was a bench seat of stone covered with a mattress of moss, and bars of two-inch thick iron killed any hope of escape. An enormous figure, sour smelling and half-naked, over six feet tall, blocked the cell doorway. He looked like a huge roughly drawn human caricature, and chuckled as he backed out through the cell door and clanged the iron clasp into place. His exposed skin was hairless, coarse and had the almost colourless transparency of a sunless existence.

For a brief moment, the repugnant thing stuck its face back through the bars and released a high cackle, spittle flying from his lips, eyes slit with unholy glee, skin hanging like melted wax. Sarah recoiled in fear and disgust. Another figure, heavily armed, and even taller and broader than the first lumbered forward out of the dark and cuffed the brute on the back of the head. He took a set of keys from his studded belt and locked the barred door. A whiney jabber of complaint from the first accompanied the two of them as they exited the cavern into whose walls the cell had been built.

In the silence that followed, Sarah took a deep shaky breath, slid on her knees across the flagstones, and lifted her companion's head and shoulders onto her lap.

"Come on, my friend, you've got to live! You can't leave me now!"

A sob caught in Sarah's throat, and her sherry eyes shimmered in the half-light. In this terrifying world, her long-eared companion was Sarah's only link to sanity in this moment. Without her new friend, finding the way back to the clearing, the Home Wood, and her family faded to impossible. Time seemed to hang still until Sarah saw her companion's chest rise and fall in shallow waves and her long, graceful ears begin to twitch and flick. Her enormous violet eyes opened, and she looked straight into Sarah's terrified gaze.

"Thank God!" Sarah gasped. "You're alive."

A scrape of wood on stone behind them made Sarah freeze on the spot. A voice. Words. Words she could understand. But how was that possible in this strange place? She turned to the barred door and saw a stooped, white-haired man with basset-hound eyes. Then he spoke again.

"Tsk tsk, young lady. How did you get yourself in this mess?!"

CHAPTER FOUR

Jonathon

"I thought we were going to find my father!" Jonathan paced a tight circle around the San warrior. His eyes beseeched the other's piercing blue gaze. Pugg scratched his nose with the tip of one long ear.

"We know not where your father be for sure," Pugg answered, his words firm and signing brisk. "Our leader and Snugg's heir—named Snuggla in father's honour—led Daavid out of stronghold yesterday. We think Snuggla takes your father to Snugg. We know where Snugg sits, but the path is dangerous." His tone relented. "If you're brave we will find 'em."

A gruff twitch of Pugg's ear signalled the end of their rest break. He jumped to his feet and, after a few strides along the path, paused to look over his shoulder. Jonathon scrambled to follow, but he felt shaken and all of a sudden unsure of himself.

The sun soared well past its zenith when the San forest dwindled and a grassy plain stretched out to the horizon. They stayed in the cool shelter of the trees, the sun blistering straight down on the plains to their right. Within a few miles, the terrain felt far less welcoming.

The trees grew shabby with ragged trailers of moss and rolled over the edges of deeper and steeper ravines that shredded the earth of the new countryside alongside which the pair travelled. Even on the edge of the territory, a foul smell intruded. Subtle at first, the stench seemed to paint the air in a poisonous grey. Jonathon covered his nose and mouth with his hand to breathe.

Where is that coming from?

Pugg moved more cautiously, testing the ground for hidden crevasses rumoured, he told Jonathon, to stretch like evil fingers out into the Maorrr plain, and he checked often that Jon remained right behind him. With an abrupt powerful hand, the warrior pushed Jonathon deeper into the trees. Together, they huddled by a great tree curtained by streamers of long mossy tentacles. They waited. And waited. Pugg stood with infinite stealth and pushed through the veil of moss, first his head then his shoulders, as he looked left and right for the source of the noise. He should have looked up.

Without even a whisper, Pugg was gone, his large furry feet the last thing Jonathon saw as they took flight through the mossy curtain.

What the heck?!

The boy leapt to his feet, all caution forgotten. The San was Jonathon's only ticket to track down his father. Determination fuelled by fear supercharged Jonathon's pursuit through the curtain of moss into the open. He stopped and crouched. A circle of strange trees he hadn't a chance to notice on the way in faced him. Each looked frozen in time, as though caught running away mid-step with huge root feet, boughs raised in supplication and strangle vines muffling their throats. Murky shadows turned day into twilight in a swampy forest beyond the eerie trees. On one side, through the branches of the circle, he glimpsed a shimmer of golden grass in the plains. He searched the branches above and the spaces between.

Where is he?

"Jon, hey..."

The sound of Pugg's voice came from so far up it was almost swallowed by the moss-padded branches. Looking way up, Jonathon saw a long furry ear wave at him through the wide mesh of net.

"Hurry...get up here!"

Jonathon looked around. He tugged on a long rope of moss and it held firm. He tied one end around his waist and, using other dangling ropes of moss for stability, Jonathon began to climb the tree. It was tricky business. In certain places the bark on the tree felt slippery as though oiled. Gradually, with each thrust and grab, the ground fell away and Pugg drew nearer. Jonathon could see the warrior more clearly now through a woven mesh of thick strands. The strands seemed almost *sticky*.

What the...?!

Pugg's efforts to free himself only trapped him more each time he moved. He held a knife in his hand, but his snared wrist rendered it useless. Pugg's fierce expression was tempered with another emotion.

"Hurry!"

A few more feet.

"Hurry!"

Jonathon looked up again and could now see Pugg's wrinkled nose as though smelling something foul. Seconds later, Jonathon could smell it too.

"Here. Catch me knife. Cut the web!"

Pugg opened his fingers, and the knife dropped into Jon's outstretched hand.

Web? Jonathon thought. *Does that mean—*

"Cut, boy! Yer wasting time. Do you want to be dinner?!"

David

A few more twitters floated down to them from the branches of the scrubby plains trees under which they had made camp the night before. Snuggla handed David a thick slice of nut loaf and a half mug of cold tea. Twenty-four hours had passed since he stood by the kitchen table at home.

Where is Sarah? Is she okay?

An intuition like an electric zap travelled from his bones to his brain. The Grue had captured her along with Snuggla's maam. He couldn't feel more certain if he had received it in writing. The congealed mass of nut loaf threatened to lodge in his throat, but David choked it down. Who knew when they would eat next?

Meanwhile, Snuggla packed up their meagre camp gear with quick, practiced moves. The sky lightened into a display of pearly rose and mauve, blended at its height with indigo. A flick of nature's match lit the sun like a candle flame on the horizon. Snuggla pointed out a flat-topped hill on the skyline, aglow in the sunrise, which reminded David of an African kopje. The Maorrr fortress. A thought plunged a shiver down his spine with a mind's eye view of a constructed rock outcrop draped in lions at the local Safari Adventure Park. David pushed the unsettling memory away and carried on.

A fine dew, not yet steam in the rising heat, sprinkled and refreshed them as they passed through the tall grasses towards the distant rock fortress. The grass at first came to David's mid-thigh and Snuggla's waist. The further they travelled, the higher the grass grew, until it reached David's chin and he was forced to lift the young San to his shoulders. As the grass crept higher, Snuggla became their eyes, guiding their progress. An alarm pinged along David's nerves from one of his bone deep hunches.

As he stumbled over a football-sized rock and staggered into a shallow ditch, the alarm rang in triple time. The tall grass cut their vision to half a step as the ground underfoot grew more unpredictable. How could Snuggla guarantee they weren't heading into danger? With his last worry barely formed, David stepped out into nothing.

The sound of a cough brought David back to a red haze of awareness. He realized, as the blackness receded, that the noonday sun was blazing the red onto his eyelids and the cough was wrenched from his own chest. A memory collage played against his mind's eye of swirling currents, Snuggla's weight clamped around his head and neck with the strength of a startled clam weighing him down, darkness spinning behind his eyes, his struggles to rise slowing and his last conscious sensation a mighty yank on his arm.

Exquisite pain. A gush of water spewed from his mouth and traumatized nose and racked David again with a sneezing, spluttering, coughing fit. When it stopped, he opened his eyes to find a grizzled San warrior watching him anxiously. The stocky body shifted slightly, and David saw Snuggla lying head down on the bank, unmoving.

David struggled upright and shuffled on his knees to Snuggla's side. He put his ear to the young San's chest and listened for an anxious moment. A faint lub-dub beat in his ear, slowing. Life was fading. He had to be quick. He stabilized Snuggla's head and sealed his mouth over the unconscious lad's nose and mouth and puffed air into him. He repeated it several times before he paused and watched for a spontaneous breath. Nothing. David breathed into him again and again as he remembered from his CPR training. He was at last rewarded by a convulsive heave of Snuggla's limp body. A gush of water fountained from the youth's mouth. David rolled the young San to his side and rubbed his back. Another convulsion. Another gush. Snuggla dragged in a raspy breath. A few more heaves and his breathing became easier. David sent up a prayer of thanks.

The adrenalin washed out of him and left him weak. He chafed Snuggla's arms and legs to improve their circulation and felt the life return to his own. David looked around in time to see the strange San warrior blend into the cover of the tall grasses a distance down the riverbank. Had he seen this warrior in the village? Was he the one who left the group?

Snuggla's eyes opened. David watched their stunned expression clear and saw them change. In place of the young San's habitual bristle dawned a glimmer of adoration. David felt both humble and uneasy in the glow of Snuggla's emotion. They both owed their lives to the unknown San's quick reaction. He tried on a smile for Snuggla, but the muscles of his face would only contract in a grimace. David gave it up. He made a plan instead.

"We'll rest here for a while and then find a place to make camp."

The old Snuggla struggled to sit up in spirited protest, but the weakness of his still shocked body forced him down again.

"Yes, Daavid," he said.

David was awash in the mix of his emotions: affection, relief... sadness. Had this brush with death tamed and matured Snuggla's spirit, or broken it?

David bundled the young San to protect him against the chill of shock, and placed a mug-full of water beside him. He felt stronger and the need to see the San warrior became urgent.

"I'm going to look around. I won't be far away or gone long. You'll be all right here until I get back." Trust tinted Snuggla's gaze. He nodded and closed his eyes.

They had been pulled from the water on the bank of a deep narrow river, the point of their abrupt descent between two identical, steep, rock-faced cliffs. The tall grass grew right to the edge of the cliff and waved in the breeze like an overgrown crew cut. Snuggla lay on the sandy bank of a small indentation in the opposite cliff-face. David stared up at the rock wall and turned his head to follow it in both directions. To his right, the cliff continued in an unbroken line, and to his left, it tapered down to the water's lip. The grasses met the river's edge about a hundred yards upstream, marking the San warrior's exit. David picked up his backpack and followed the narrow bank to find him.

The heat from the sun blazed down, trapped between the cliff walls and unrelieved by the occasional wayward breeze that ricocheted off the rocks and skimmed along the surface of the water. David's shirt under the tunic was soon drenched in sweat and stuck to his skin.

When he reached the grassy shore, the breeze became more constant. David stripped off the tunic and then his damp shirt and laid it out to dry. The shirt lay suspended by the sturdy stems of grass. He put the tunic back on and buckled the sword around his waist.

A few steps forward. The ground was again smooth, the grass chest high. In the distance and to the north, the rocky fortress gleamed. It shimmered in the hard light and seemed no closer than when they first sighted it. David's eyes watered as he watched its outline expand and contract against the white blue of the sky.

"Heh! Watch where ye be going." Through the glare-induced mist of tears, David looked down and saw the San, feet spread and arms akimbo and stepped back. The warrior's head came to David's armpit.

"Who are you?" The question popped out before David could filter his thoughts.

"That be yer way of thanks for saving yer sorry hide?"

"I apologize," David said. "I am deeply appreciative you saved our lives...er hides."

"That's better." The warrior's ears twitched down once in introduction. "I'm Tugg. Our leader's oldest brother and right hand. I mind you when you been just a lad. Very serious you been then." He peered at David. "Seems still. I be spared to keep Snugg's heir out of danger." He rubbed the tough pads of his furry hands together. "So now what's the plan?"

Though David had wanted to say more about the rescue, the warrior's matter-of-factness pushed aside the need for further gratitude.

"As I see it," said Tugg as though answering his own question, "we be upon the Maorrr anytime now. The moon approaches her full term, the Maorrr be restless. They be on the hunt."

David gulped.

"Did you say...*hunt?*"

Tugg gave him a sardonic look.

"Yes. Hunt."

"Wh-wh-what do they hunt?" David closed his eyes and tried to will the answer his mind most wanted to hear. It didn't work.

"The Maorrr aren't fussy when they're hungry. They'll eat just about anything." Tugg paused for several heartbeats of silence and then, with the superiority of a seasoned warrior, he laughed. He peeked at David's face through scrunched-up eyes, doubled over, hooted and slapped his thigh.

"You should see your face! I swear you be as green as a Saniggle-pea!" Gusts of mirth shook him. Only lack of breath forced Tugg to rein in his glee. David's face was no longer green but fiery with the heat of embarrassment, annoyance and a tickle of amusement. He sensed a master pulled his leg. He just didn't have time or energy right now for the stocky warrior's quirks.

Tugg regained his wind and explained with a shrug.

"I overheard Snuggla tell you about the Maorrr. The Maorrr be herders and warriors. Not hunters. 'Tis a childish tale we tell the young ones to keep them from wandering away."

"That hardly seems fair to the Maorrr," David said. In his experience, this philosophy had a fatal flaw.

"Oh, they understand. They tell their young the same about us. The Grue be friends to none and enemy to all. To protect our young, we teach them to rely first on their own kind. When they are grown is time enough to learn how to tell friend from foe."

David shook his head. A frown furrowed between his brows.

"But don't they feel betrayed when they find out it's a lie?" He thought of Jonathon's reaction when an older neighbour boy laughed at him for his belief in Santa. It was not quite the same, but the twist of fact and trust was close enough. It had been all David's idea to foster Jonathan's belief. Each year he went to great lengths to build the excitement and magic with the help of two old friends who each had a child—Marly and Michael—the same age as Jonathon. They carried it off a couple of years past the age that most children still believed. When the bubble burst, none took it harder than Jonathan. Marly shrugged as though she had known all along, while Michael was distracted by a new snowboard. Not Jonathan. Sarah had insisted David talk to him. He tried. He talked and talked to soothe his son's feelings of betrayal and to comfort him. But for weeks, Jonathan wouldn't speak to him. Sarah took over. Although Jonathon accepted the spirit of the season, David felt he never regained the full measure of his son's trust. He came to realize that it wasn't the loss of the fantasy that wounded Jonathan, but the abuse of his intelligence that offended him.

The similarities between Jonathan and Snuggla made David sure of Snuggla's reaction to the tale of the Maorrr. His anger would be fierce and his hurt deep to have his intelligence deliberately misused.

David struggled to explain his thoughts to Tugg. Though the warrior huffed and denied any need for worry, a waggle of ears exposed his concern.

"The telling may not be needed yet. When we meet up with the Maorrr, Snuggla'll work it out."

The whole thing didn't sit well with David. Could Tugg be right? Every cell in David's body screamed, no! Jonathan's face appeared in his memory, angry and hurt, and David relived the moment when his son found out the truth about his role in preserving his belief in Santa. David's gut twisted. He had promised himself never again. When David's mind saw his son's face fuzz over and his ears grow long and tapered and Snuggla stare at him in accusation, he knew beyond a doubt what he needed to do. Snuggla had a right to know the truth. Now.

David's frown cleared. That settled it. No more secrets.

"Come back with me, Tugg. Now. I won't allow Snuggla to go any farther with the fear of the Maorrr." His hand dropped onto Tugg's shoulder and he half led, half dragged the warrior along the path.

They re-entered the oven heat of the riverbank between the high cliffs. It beat upon them in waves. David was glad he had left his shirt off. He worried about the effect of this intense heat on Snuggla's recovery. He wiped his streaming eyes and peered ahead.

Where is he?

They should have been able to see him bundled up on the riverbank by now, where David had left him to recover from his near-drowning. In spite of the heat reflected back by the sand and the gorge walls, David began to run. His legs pumped hard against the shifting sand. His hands alternately reached out, fisted and pulled back to his side as though grasping at the heavy, overheated air to drag himself forward. Frantic and spent, he reached the spot where he had left Snuggla.

Tugg caught up to David and grabbed his arm.

"Where's Snuggla?" Anger and fear sparked from Tugg's eyes.

Stunned, David shook his head and pointed to the smooth sand. Not even a ruffle betrayed where Tugg had dragged them to the bank, where David had knelt at Snuggla's side and breathed life into him, where he had bundled him and left the cup of water at his side.

Panic melted his paralysis. David swung around and lifted the startled Tugg off the ground and shook him as though he weighed less than a rag doll.

"Who's got him! Who took him, Tugg!" Marbles of air rattled in the back of Tugg's throat as he struggled to speak. Shamefaced, David recollected himself and set Tugg on his feet again. The stocky warrior staggered a step and regained his balance.

"Hoo, that sure rattled the trap." He put his hands to the sides of his head and squeezed as though to push back into place whatever had popped loose. David's quick flare fizzled, but the fear still lingered. Tugg's powerful hand gripped David's forearm and pulled him down, with a jerk, to sit on the sand beside him.

"Well, as I see it, there be only two possibilities. It be either the Maorrr or those sneaking Grue that nabbled the young'un the way they did the Maam."

Both David and Tugg looked up at the sheer walls. The same question teased them but the cliffs guarded their secret.

Finally, David roused himself from the lethargy of despair that threatened to overwhelm him.

"We can't do anything on our own if the Grue have him, so we might as well go on and find the Maorrr."

Tugg agreed. They made their way, for the last time, out of the heat trap of the gorge and breathed deep of the cooler air of the grassy plain. From the vantage of his greater height, David indicated the direction of the rocky fortress. He read, in the San's easy acceptance of David's assumption of leadership, content in his life-long career as his commander-brother's valued right-hand. The subordinate role came naturally to him.

David just wasn't sure about the gleam in the San's eye.

Sarah

"Who are you?" she asked the old man.

Something about him looked familiar. He stood in the spot by the cell door where the foul cackler had harassed them. He put his finger to his lips and peered over his shoulder into the shadows. He was dressed in ragged pants belled at the bottom, a short-sleeved shirt with an odd swirled stain and wooden clogs on his feet. He shivered in the dampness of the cell's cavern. Sarah's companion looked from one to the other of them in confused amazement.

He crept close to the bars of the door and held out his hand to beckon her closer. Sarah released her friend and went to the old man, staying just out of his reach.

"Who are you?" she asked again.

"I think I should ask you that question." His eyes were hot and intense, but his voice ended on a quaver.

"I'm Sarah," she said. "Sarah James."

"JAMES?"

"Yes," she said. His response pulled her nerves even tauter.

"Who do you belong to, Sarah James?"

She pondered the oddly phrased question for a moment. She didn't 'belong' to anyone! What was he looking for? Who could they possibly know in common? A touch of exasperation flamed the sherry in her eyes.

"My husband is David James."

"Who is *his* father?" His second question almost trampled her answer. His body seemed to vibrate with tension.

"His father is Matthew." Sarah raised an eyebrow. What was going on?

The old man sat down as though the air had been punched out of him. Within a blink, he was back on his knees at the bars. His hands clenched the damp metal, his knuckles turning white.

"I'm *Frederic* James. Matthew's older brother!"

Sarah forced her gaping jaw to close.

Oh. My. God! How can this be? And yet, here he is.

She had heard stories in the family about her father-in-law's brother disappearing when he was a young man. There was a lot of speculation about his whereabouts—San Francisco being a favourite since it was the Flower Power days. No one came close to knowing. Although she suspected now that perhaps Great Aunt Louise and David may have had a good idea. Her insides felt like jelly.

"Has the family finally come for me?"

Frederic reached again through the bars, his hand palm upward, his eyes entreating. Sarah looked around at her surroundings and at the intervening bars and felt a wave of sarcasm crash against her clenched teeth. She took a deep breath and rattled the barred door between them.

"I'm sorry... uh, *Uncle Frederic,* but I'm in a bit of bind, myself."

"Oh, my dear, how foolish of me." He shook his head until wispy locks of white hair fell over his forehead and he met Sarah's bemused eyes with a self-deprecating laugh. "Of course, you're on the wrong side to help me now, aren't you?" He reached through and patted her hand reassuringly. "It's okay. I may look a little wild, but I'm not completely crazy."

Sarah looked at Frederic more closely. She had thought he was wearing rags, but could now see that, while they had been repaired many times, they were clean and his clothes still bore a faint resemblance to the bell-bottomed jeans, tie-dyed tee-shirt and Birkenstocks they had once been. He had long white hair tied back with a leather strap. Heavy white brows long enough to braid sheltered eyes that were so similar to his younger brother, Matthew. He was definitely one of the James clan. Those basset-hound eyes were as good as a DNA test. Could he help them? Sarah decided to ease into that question.

"How long have you been here, Uncle Frederic?"

"Let's see now, it was June first, nineteen sixty-eight at nine o'clock in the morning. I was eighteen and two days old." Sarah couldn't suppress a smile at his detailed memory.

"Oh my, Uncle Frederic!" She moved a little closer to the barred door. "How did you get here...and what do you do?"

"I guess you know about the portal since you're standing there." He paused to pull on a couple of scraggly hairs that dangled from his chin. "When I came through, it was a time of relative peace between the three countries: Grueland, Sanigglan and Maorrr. The Grue found me wandering on their border with the San and brought me here. They taught me their language and put me to work. I'm sort of a Steward/butler/housekeeper." He passed a self-conscious hand down his body. "I came through in these clothes, but they're my cleaning clothes now. I have a nicer outfit for my other jobs." Uncle Frederic's expression became thoughtful.

"Over the years, the Grue have changed, and it's much harder work these days." He paused to study Sarah. "You know what? I could sure use your help!" He hesitated and chewed his lip. "If I could just get you out." Then his brows waggled with excitement. "I know, man! I'll say we're related!" He slapped his thigh. "Cool! That will do it! I'm trusted. I'm part of the walls, I've been here so long. "

"Do you really think you can get us out of here, Uncle Frederic?" Sarah glanced back at her rabbity companion, resting in the centre of the cell. Frederic followed her gaze.

"Ohhh."

"What?" asked Sarah.

"That's the San creature I've been hearing talk about. She's the mate of the leader. The Grue have big plans for her, and letting her out isn't in them." Sarah didn't like the sound of that.

"What do you mean, Uncle Frederic? What are they going to do with her?"

CHAPTER FIVE

Jonathon

Do I want to be dinner? Cripes, what kind of question is that?

Jonathon passed an assessing glance over what held Pugg fast. The world, at that moment, consisted of Pugg's alarmed face and an intricate trap the size of a bus woven between the branches of the tree. Jonathon's heart thudded against his breast bone. He drew in a breath and began to slash at the sticky web. He struggled to maintain a determined focus as he sawed with all his strength on the hawser-sized strand of the web that kept the warrior captive. Jonathon blocked out Pugg's tension and the hissing, clicking sound from the higher branches. *Clicking?* It sounded like giant castanets. He cut harder. With a grunt he was through. Another down. He moved to the next while trying to stay clear of the sticky strands himself.

The clicking grew closer. Jonathon avoided looking at Pugg's face and continued to hack until he had made a hole large enough for Pugg to drop through. The boy grabbed one of the warrior's legs to guide him. He pulled hard but Pugg didn't move.

Jon looked up. The web had stuck under one of Pugg's arms. The warrior's eyes were huge and black, pupils fully dilated, as he cast a quick glance down at Jonathon. Jon followed the direction of Pugg's stare. Two enormous hairy legs pushed aside the leafy branches above him and revealed the clicking's source.

The razor fangs and mandibles of a black spider smacking together in ravenous anticipation, red eyes aglow.

The beast was the size of a bull elephant. Jonathon screamed out loud and with all of his strength pushed out from the trunk of the tree while clinging to Pugg's legs. His added weight finally freed the San and together they fell through the curtains of moss and the branches until the rope of moss around Jonathon's waist pulled them to an abrupt stop a few feet shy of the ground. The force of gravity ripped the larger warrior from the boy's grasp and Pugg hit bottom with a thump.

"Get up. Get up. Get up! We have to get out of here!" Jonathon cut the moss rope from around his middle with a single swipe of Pugg's blade. He helped the warrior to his feet, and together they set off through the circle of frozen trees towards the grassy gold promise of the plains. Pugg took the lead. In a much shorter time than it took them to enter, they were back out of the sour forest and wading through the grasslands skirted earlier in the day because of the intense heat.

Pugg set a swift pace. Jonathon was in no mood to disagree. They would both feel safer, he decided, the more distance between themselves and the spider's dinner table. Despite the heat, the plains grass made an easier traverse than the deep ravines. Jonathon felt the miles melt under them as they pushed through the tall grasses. The sun sailed well past its peak, but they still had lots of good travel time ahead. Pugg signalled for a brief rest. Jonathon fell to the ground, more spent than he had realized.

"Where are we going now, Pugg?"

"We seek help from the Maorrr. That route not safe for you." His ear pointed back the way they came. "Too much danger to go to Snugg's camp just us two. The Maorrr will lend their muscle. Here." He handed Jonathon a bit of nut loaf and the bag of sweet water. "Keep up your strength."

What's he mean by 'not safe for you' Jonathon thought. *Who saved who back there?*

He jumped to his feet, ready and eager, when Pugg again signalled to move on. The grass crept higher, until it was over Jon's head. He pushed to keep up to the warrior even though the ground grew rougher. If they lost sight of each other now, they would lose precious time.

The sun sank lower in the sky. Jonathon felt his restlessness grow. He sensed that Pugg had slowed down. They needed more speed. They had to keep going, move faster. Another night was crashing towards them, and his father was still out there somewhere. He pushed himself in front of Pugg.

"Come on, Pugg. Let's not stop till we have to. Let's keep moving. We're getting close to my dad, I can feel it. We can go faster can't we? It's only gra—"

With a lightning reflex, Pugg grabbed for Jonathon's arm as he tumbled over a grass-edged cliff. Far below at the bottom of a gorge the swift current of a deep, narrow river severed the plain.

"Hold onto the roots!" Pugg yelled. Jonathon looked down at the protruding rocks thirty feet beneath his dangling legs.

"And don't be looking!"

Jonathon raised his eyes and stared into Pugg's grim face.

"Don't let me go."

"Hang...on!"

Jonathon wrapped the fingers of his free hand around the thick grass roots. His legs swayed over the rocks and rushing water. He stretched to dig his toes into the side of the cliff, but it curved inwards away from him beneath the grassy edge and offered no purchase. The grip of his fingers, greased with fear, slipped. His heart pounded as a scream ripped from his throat.

"I'm gonna fall!"

Pugg still had hold of Jonathon's arm. The warrior adjusted the wrap of several sturdy stems around his arm, tested for support then he leaned further over the edge. With a mighty, lightning fast heave, he changed his grip from Jon's arm to his belt and hauled with all his might just as the boy's slippery hands lost their grasp. Jonathon somersaulted over the warrior's shoulders and landed on his back on the uneven ground. His breath left his lungs with a huff.

Jon lay for a few seconds until his oxygen starved body screamed for air. He gagged and wretched as he tried to suck in a breath. Pugg heaved him upright and rubbed his back. A trickle of air entered his throat followed by a bigger breath until soon he breathed easily again.

Pugg allowed him to lie still to gather his wits. Precious moments passed as he drew in and savoured one sweet breath after another. A sharp punch in the arm startled him back to the present.

"Hey!" He pushed himself up onto his elbow.

"Come Jon." Pugg gestured with his ears for Jonathon to get up. "Surely you be better now. We need to move!" His scowl sent a stern message straight into Jonathon's eyes. "This time *follow* me!"

Jonathon nodded, subdued but unrepentant.

"Let me look first, Pugg. I have to see."

On his knees, he parted the grass at the cliff's edge and looked down. Pugg joined him. The river was fast but not very wide at this point. A little further down, on the opposite side, they could see a sandy area beneath a steep rock face, which declined to a ford crossing several hundred yards up. Pugg pointed to the churned up sand on the beach and along the river's edge.

"Someone been there, Jon. Not too long ago. We go this way." He pointed in the opposite direction. "Find another way cross the river."

"But what if it was my dad?"

Pug shook his head. "Can't know. Not safe to check." He strode away, one ear pointed towards Jonathon.

Not safe to check with me along is what he means. Jonathan's thoughts were sour.

Backs to the sun, they followed the cliff's edge from a safe distance. The terrain changed again. The grass became shorter and the brush thicker as they reached the source of the river and crossed over. Before long, on the other side, the ground turned rocky and scrub replaced the tall grasses. The sun had a quarter of its arc left before another day would be behind them. Jonathon thought about his dad. Where could he be in this huge strange empty land? What if those tracks had been his dad's and now they were going in the opposite direction? How would they find him?

An eerie cry keened out of the blue sky and interrupted Jonathon's thoughts. Pugg crouched in a wary stance. Jonathon scanned the sky again and, from the corner of his eye, saw Pugg lunge for him. The breath was again knocked from his abused lungs as the weight of the warrior punched him into the ground and pinned him down.

Before Jon could react, his ears were buffeted by a jet loud whooshing sound and Pugg's weight was ripped away from him.

David

The sun descended well past its peak but still beat without mercy on their backs. Protected by his fur, the forest-dweller was more affected by the heat and less by the sun than David who felt the back of his neck and arms sizzle under the fierce rays. He pulled on his shirt over the tunic. Without breaking stride he tore a strip from the bottom of the shirt and tied it around his head with the tail hanging down to protect the nape of his neck.

David stepped up the pace. Too much time had been lost. It was imperative to reach the Maorrr before nightfall. Not only was Snuggla's safety at stake, but also the longer the Grue had Snuggla's mother—and quite likely Sarah—well, he couldn't bear any deeper thought right now. It was bad enough his bones told him Sarah's safety was somehow tied to her San counterpart. David's pace quickened.

Mid-afternoon, David and Tugg stopped only long enough to swallow the last few mouthfuls of nut loaf washed down by tepid water Tugg carried in a skin bag at his belt. David tried not to look too close at the fabric of the skin bag. Its texture made his flesh crawl. It was like touching the cold, dead arm of a human. He caught Tugg's sly look, but David refused to comment. His temper was too raw to handle the warrior's wicked humour. David stood up and set the pace, Tugg close behind in a tireless trot.

After hours of punishing effort, the fortress, at last, loomed before them. They were able to pick out a few features, but nothing that looked like an entrance. As the distance closed, the walls towered higher and more intimidating until they stood at the base.

David stopped and looked down at Tugg. He then glanced back up at the soaring heights of the fortress. The warrior stood waiting for David's command. The rampart surged in both directions. He fought against the squeeze of hopelessness and exhaustion.

We have to find a way in.

"Let's circle and see if there is a path or a gateway or something."

After a mental coin toss, David pointed in the southerly direction. The warrior shrugged and followed.

They picked their way around scrub brush, scree and enormous scattered boulders, one eye scanned the heights, the other on the ground. The grass here was coarse and short, but the ground it covered was treacherous and uneven and made for ambush. A defending Maorrr might not ask questions first.

David stopped and pointed out a thin path that wove through a stand of scrub up to the wall. It was the first sign with any promise. Shallow, almost invisible steps ascended the wall in a gradual slope.

"This looks like a way in," David said. Tugg shrugged again and offered to scout the path up the stairway.

David kept up as well as he could. The warrior's compact body was better suited to the narrow staircase. Several times the stair all but disappeared—leaving him clinging to shallow handholds and groping for the next narrow step—only to reappear a few feet further. The higher they climbed, the more the staircase began to resemble a ladder with rungs missing. David had never climbed any higher than the middle branches of the oak trees in the Home Wood. He willed himself not to look down, but when they stopped to catch their breath, his eyes strayed over the dizzying height. The plain stretched out before them, the grasses looked like a smooth carpet with dark stains of scrub trees here and there. The lowering sun gave the air a soft, rosy clarity. The baked rock under his hands hissed as it cooled and gave up a floury, warm bread smell that caused David's empty stomach to cramp and growl. He ignored it and reached for the next rung. The entrance to the Maorrr stronghold had to be close now.

Ahead, the stair had disappeared again, but Tugg continued to progress well, climbing from one precarious hold to the next. David saw the warrior, twenty feet above, glance down at him between braced legs.

"There's a ledge here," Tugg called down. Heartened but tired, David redoubled his efforts and ignored the discomfort in his hands, scraped raw by the rough stone surfaces, and the cramp in his feet from the strain of holding up his weight in tiny toeholds.

Tugg's legs dangled over the ledge just above David's head. The warrior reached down a hand. A loose rock tumbled past David's nose. He flinched back, and his feet slipped from their hold, and he found himself suspended, hundreds of feet above the ground, by two fingers hooked into a shallow depression.

An internal scream filled his head and deafened him to Tugg's calming advice. Desperate, his feet scrabbled for and failed to find purchase. His free hand flailed the empty air as his finger hold weakened. Eyes squeezed shut, David flooded with relief as the warrior's vise-like grip clamped onto his wrist. Another strong hand grasped the back of his tunic collar. David felt light and limp as a newborn puppy as the hand hauled him over the rim of the ledge. He gulped in a breath and opened his eyes, only to explode the precious air out of his mouth in a terrified huff.

Two-inch, razor-sharp fangs in a blood red maw gaped before David's face. Through a darkening haze, he heard growled words.

"Why did you not come to the front gate?"

Sarah

"What are they going to do with her?"

"Well, it is just what I overheard, understand, but the Grue have to go to war to defend themselves against the San. The Grue have some really complicated rituals, see. They need a guarantee of success against the San. The sacrifice of this creature gives their guarantee."

Frederic looked through the bars of Sarah's prison cell, his tone seemed flat, almost indifferent. She couldn't name his emotion. There was something off with his explanation.

"They're going to sacrifice her on the night of the full moon," he said. "Six days from now."

Sacrifice?

Sarah recoiled in horror and retreated to her companion's side. She took hold of the San's hand and looked back at Frederic. She wanted to rail at him and tell him that the San wasn't just a creature: she had a life and a family. Something in Frederic's expression made the words stick in her throat. He gazed at Sarah with affection but looked through her companion as though she did not exist.

"I will get you out of here, Sarah. Not to worry. You'll be all right." He hurried away into the gloom.

Sarah felt a gentle pat on her hand. She looked down at her companion and locked with her intense violet gaze. Even without words, Sarah could tell. Her friend understood the situation.

"Save yourself." She signed to Sarah. The human and the San held hands, speaking with their eyes. A large tear rolled down Sarah's cheek.

"I will get you out of here. I promise!"

Within the hour, Frederic was back with the enormous gaoler, who jangled his keys at them through the bars. Sarah covered her nose as his foul odour punched through the opening ahead of him.

With a creak, the barred door swung open. Frederic gestured to Sarah to come out. Sarah gave a last squeeze of her San friend's hand, got to her feet, and hustled to Frederic's side.

"How did you do it?"

"I told them you're my daughter. They're not very good at math." Frederic chuckled to himself as her led her away. As the distance widened, Sarah heard the gaoler cackle and torment the San through the bars. Only silence answered him.

Frederic had changed his clothes. A purplish brown collarless tunic ended at his hips and overlapped a pair of matching trousers. A dingy white shirt peeked out at the neck and sleeves of the tunic. And over all, a fawn-coloured multi-pocketed apron tied around his neck and his waist protected his outfit.

They took narrow stone steps up towards the light and away from the dank dungeon. Sarah felt conflicted, for though she was sad to be leaving her friend behind, she was grateful for every step that took her away from the horrible cell. The strangeness of everything that had happened to her since she woke up in that clearing was over-whelming. And nothing was more strange than meeting Frederic James of all people.

Can this rumpled old man, who looks so like a pale version of Matthew, help me get home?

One set of stairs led to a studded locked door and then several more sets of stairs until they stepped up into a large hall with tall archways leading off in different directions. Frederic continued to chatter to her, but she heard hardly a word as she took in her surroundings. The castle had been built almost entirely of stone. It was cold and damp even up here, and the drafts swept through the endless hallways. How would she ever find her way back to the forest portal from here? Would she see her family again, or was she destined to remain trapped to the end of forever with Uncle Frederic, serving these foul-smelling people? She hoped they didn't all smell as bad as the gaoler. Sarah bit down on the inside of her cheek and folded her negative thoughts away. This line of thinking was not productive. She would learn all she could about these Grue. She would help her friend escape, and she *would* get back home.

Yes, that's all there is to it.

With a mental dust of her hands, Sarah determined to memorize everything she saw.

Frederic led Sarah down again, but only a short flight this time, to a huge kitchen checkered with wooden tables piled high with unidentifiable foodstuffs—or what Sarah took to be food. Much of it was still in its natural state of fur and feathers. One wall was dominated by two enormous fireplaces perched, each large enough to walk into and set up housekeeping.

"Raise your chin, girl, you're going to catch flies!" Seeing that flies buzzed around the pile on the tables, it seemed altogether possible. Sarah closed her mouth.

"What am I to do here, Uncle Frederic?"

"You're going to serve the food to the Grue. And if you're really good at it, you may even serve the King himself, Cragmire the Third."

CHAPTER SIX

Jonathon

Jonathon leapt to his feet. He ducked just in time to avoid the sweep of the eagle's wings as the mighty bird thrust at the air to gain height with Pugg captured in its talons. Jonathon's chest tightened with fear. Pugg struggled to slash his way free, but his broad sword looked no bigger than a cheese knife against his target. Jonathon gathered several rocks at his feet and loaded his slingshot.

His first shot struck the eagle in the chest to no effect, but then he followed it with an explosive second shot to the side of the head. A screech split the air as the bird turned in a reflexive arc to see who harassed him. The third rock caught him square between the eyes. The eagle shrieked in anger and stretched his talons into attack position as he came around again.

Pugg fell free and landed on his feet. He yelled an order to run. Jonathon dodged around the eagle's dive. He felt the graze of the talons brush his head as they snapped shut too early. He converged with Pugg and together they raced across the uneven shrub-covered ground in search of shelter.

The flap of wings and huge eagle-shaped shadow chased them. The beat of their feet almost matched the rhythm of Jonathon's heart. Pugg nudged Jon to signal a change in direction towards a conical sand hill three times his height.

The shadow wings, the size of a farmhouse, were almost upon them.

The warrior dropped to his knees and began to dig into the side of the hill like a dog. Breathless, Jonathon joined him just as the eagle's talons exploded the top of the hill and covered them in its debris. Pugg didn't flinch. He continued to burrow until he uncovered a small cave-like opening into which they both tumbled just as the eagle's shadow made another pass.

Pugg pulled a second sword out of the armoury around his belt and handed it to Jonathon. Each pointed their weapons out through the opening of the cave and waited. The shadow passed again, but this time did not seem as large. They waited. Then nothing. It was cool inside the dirt cave after the heat of their race across the scrubby ground. A good place to rest for a few minutes.

"Ouch!"

Jonathon yelped and smacked at his ankle. His hand came down with a crunch on the carapace of an ant-like creature the size of a rat. Pugg beat at his feet and then grabbed Jon and dragged him from the hole. A stream of angry ants followed and fanned out around them, moving fast to close the circle.

Pugg and Jonathon yelled at the ants, making noise to keep the swarm at bay. Back to back, the San warrior stabbed at the advance guard while Jon swung the sword Pugg had given him. Then he plucked up some rocks and heaved them just short of the leaders to keep the circle from closing. The huge black ants clacked and clicked their displeasure at the intrusion, lifting and pointing with front legs.

The pair sidled out of range as quickly as their uneven strides would allow. A hundred yards out, the ants lost interest in the duo and stopped their advance. They remained in a watchful phalanx as the intruders turned and hurtled side-by-side across the rocky terrain.

On the northern horizon, a square edifice glowed like gold in the setting sun. Pugg pointed at it with one ear.

"We go there."

Jonathon nodded, weary in every bone. "Can we make it tonight, Pugg?"

"No. We'll get closer, then camp. We be there early in the morning." The sun slid faster towards the horizon. Small islands of trees dotted the plain. Pugg made a choice and set up camp. With practiced ease, he created two places for them to sleep and a small smokeless fire on which to heat some water to make broth. He threw in a few dried vegetables from a pouch on his belt and served up a cup to Jonathon.

"Will we find my father tomorrow, Pugg?"

"Yes, lad, almost certainly, with the help of the Maorrr." Conversations during the long hike and surviving multiple disasters seemed to have cleared away any debris of language barrier left between them. Jonathon could now understand most of Pugg's words and signs.

"Tell me about the Maorrr, Pugg."

"They been good allies in the past. They'll help us now."

Jonathon swished the broth in the bottom of his cup. He had so many questions.

"Pugg, did you know my father when he first visited Sanigglan?"

"I been just a wee-un when your father visited us. He arrived the day before the great battle. Just a lad himself no bigger than you."

"What did he do here? Did he really kill the enemy leader?"

Pugg chuckled.

"Many questions, little patience, lad." As he gathered up the cooking supplies and tamped down the fire for the night, Pugg continued his story.

"Your father was known to us as Daavid and after the battle he became Daavid of the Legend."

"What legend, Pugg?"

"Patience, lad!" The warrior admonished him with a flick of his ears. "Where was I? Ah, Daavid been found in the forest by my older brother—our present leader, Snugg—when Snugg been just a young captain. Our father was leader and groomed Snugg to take over." Pugg paused and the subdued glow from the fire gleamed in his eyes. He settled into a storyteller's posture.

"The Grue had grown ambitious and wanted to spread into Sanigglan. Cragmire the Second had cruel reputation, and it be whispered that he might-a had something to do with the death of his father, Good King Cragmire the First. The night after Daavid came, the Grue struck deep into the forests of Sanigglan. It been the first real test of Snugg's leadership. Against Snugg's orders, your father followed the warriors into battle. Your father picked up a lance from a fallen Grue and yelled to draw the King's attention from an attack on Snugg who had fallen. Cragmire turned to him. Big he was even for Grue. A giant of a tyrant. Snugg heard Cragmire's cruel laugh and saw him head towards Daavid with his sword raised for a killing blow. Snugg ran to save Daavid and sliced the hamstring of Cragmire's leg. Cragmire squealed like a kit but still charged forward onto your father. The rest of the Grue fled the battle in confusion when the King did not get up." Pugg drew a breath.

"The warriors thought Daavid be dead, crushed beneath the Grue King. When they toppled the body of Cragmire away, they saw

Daavid had stood fast and brave with his lance and when Cragmire fell, he been skewered upon it through his black heart." Pugg looked across the fire's remains at Jonathon.

"Daavid been not crushed after all, but he did not move when Snugg tried to wake him. Much blood came from a large wound in his head. All thought him dead. To honour him, the San took him back to the place in the forest where he first been found and covered him with a blanket of flowers. When they returned the next day with more flowers, Daavid was gone and his legend born."

Words failed Jonathon. His dad had faced a giant's attack! His dad had killed the enemy and been injured in the assault. No wonder he never talked about it. At least now Jonathon knew how his dad had gotten the scar on his scalp.

Wow! Dad a hero at my age. A legend!

Jonathon felt a stirring of familiar feelings for his dad that somehow seemed new.

"Sleep, lad. We must be up and out early tomorrow to get to the Maorrr stronghold."

Jonathon curled up by the fire's remains and continued to replay Pugg's story in his head until it faded into the dark. It seemed only moments later when Pugg shook him awake again and held one furred hand against his mouth for silence. As they waited, Jonathon became aware of a vibration coming from the ground. The vibration grew until it pulsed against every part of their bodies in contact with the earth.

"What is that, Pugg?" Jonathon asked through Pugg's hand.

"Shhh." Pugg held his ear to the ground. "Many feet, going west. An army on the move!"

David

In the predawn darkness, Tugg and David followed two hundred Maorrr troops. The air was still cool. Since David's ungraceful arrival at the Maorrr fortress the evening before, much had happened. The best part was he felt different and the feeling was a good one he resolved to keep. He mulled over when the tide had turned as he huffed to keep up with the night-sighted warriors. Perhaps it was his first meeting with Maorla, the leader of the Maorrr warriors or more correctly, his *second* meeting with her after he regained conscious-ness inside the Maorrr communal area and Tugg had introduced him properly.

"This be Maorla, the Maorrr commander...she saved your furless hide." Then he'd muttered something about *gratitude*.

David had sensed that, when he screamed and passed out on their arrival, he had fallen low somehow on etiquette, but he couldn't help it. His heart slammed his ribs like a jackhammer every time he looked at the Maorrr leader. He didn't have a lot of memories before the age of twelve, but David would never forget that, when he was nine, on a visit to his friend Tim's farm near the Safari Adventure Park, he encountered—and barely eluded—an escaped cougar. The reality of the appearance of the Maorrr brought his worst nightmare to life.

"I... uh, I apologize for... for my lack of m-m-manners." David had said. "I am indeed g-g-grateful to you."

Maorla gave a close-mouthed smile and dipped her chin to her chest with feline grace. Her eyes were tawny gold, striated with green around vertical oval pupils. She had fur the colour of ochre, and rounded, alert ears perched above her face and broad nose.

"What was that about a front gate?" David had kept his eyes on her as he turned to ask Tugg. "Why didn't you tell me?"

Tugg gave David an inscrutable look. "You didn't ask," he said followed by a noise that sounded like *Phhhht!* and stumped off on a mission.

Leadership lesson number three, a humbled David had thought. *Ask*.

He'd watched the San warrior go and, with immense effort of will, forced his taut, cramped muscles to slacken and slouch. In darting glances that betrayed his residual nervousness, David inspected his surroundings.

Maorla and David sat on a bench padded with grass stuffed cushions. The bench, tucked in an alcove, overlooked a cavernous vault lit by the flicker of a hundred torches, the distant ceiling bruised by shadows. David allowed his gaze to wander. He became aware of the bustling activity of the Maorrr community in the flickering light. The vault seemed to be a communal meeting area. There were groups in active discussions, individuals dozing, and youngsters roughhousing amongst patient adults who tended the fires and prepared meals. David closed his eyes and tried to control his breathing as he looked out over the hundreds of replicas of his nightmare. His heart beat so hard, it felt ready to explode. How was he to survive this trial and find Sarah? Maorla distracted his attention.

"I understand, Daavid," she said in a low, guttural voice. "I sense a mix of unease and deep sadness in you. I feel the sadness has three prongs, one greater and older than the others." She placed a large, furred hand on his arm. "My father, Memgarr, is a healer and has trained me in some of his arts. Would you allow me to help you?"

He didn't known what to expect and barely stifled a scream when, in one swift glide, Maorla landed on light feet behind him. She began to knead the cement-like muscles in his back and shoulders until his neck and head lolled loosely.

The knots in every sinew melted like ice before a fire. But it was more than just relaxation. His tension receded, the pain in his head eased, and best of all, he felt a calm strength infuse his tissues.

David became aware that Maorla had stopped and moved away. He faced her gratefully, astonished that the fear that seemed an elemental part of him was now gone—like it had never existed. The feeling of being in tune with himself had also grown stronger with the Maorrr leader's ministrations. Her father, the healer, taught her well.

"Rest awhile longer, Daavid. I will bring you food." Before he could respond, she was gone, and the feeling of emptiness left in her wake surprised David.

A while later, rested and fed, his injuries tended, David looked up to see Maorla, standing at the entrance to the alcove. She watched him with feline patience and judged the moment when he was ready.

David smiled when he met her eyes. He still felt no trace of his old fear. In fact, it seemed that Maorla's magic touch had kneaded out most of the negative emotions that had plagued him in various ways since he was twelve. The oldest and deepest feeling that she had read in him...that stemmed from his mother's leaving...he took a deep breath against the catch in his chest. Nope. He still wasn't quite ready for *that* one. Better to concentrate on why he was here. To find Sarah and bring her home.

Maorla was taller than David by three inches and dressed in an intricate ceremonial robe. She'd led him through the now deserted vault of the communal living area towards a black opening in the back wall guarded by two massive gold and black striped Maorrr warriors. A wide stone staircase rose from the floor through the opening and ascended out of sight. Low murmurs floated downwards. The two warriors stared unblinking over his head. David turned with a question in his eyes and Maorla, solemn, gestured him onward.

The stone steps were smooth as silk, worn into a curve in the centre of each riser by generations of ascending Maorrr feet. The murmur grew louder and could soon be distinguished as a chant, with deep, hypnotic, skin-prickling, soul-stirring undertones. In subtle gradations, the air took on a luminescence. They had reached the summit. An outdoor amphitheatre on the very top of the fortress.

There, an astounding scene unfolded before David. The Maorrr gathered, thousands en masse, beneath a tapestry of stars, bathed in the silver-blue light of a moon just a shave less than full. Weighted under the immensity of the sky, David felt like a tiny speck in the universe of moon, stars and Maorrr. David's greatest sense of wonder stemmed from the realization that his heart no longer pounded in fear, but swelled only with awe at the beauty of the night sky and the palpable dignity of the Maorrr people.

Maorla led David through the masses, plentiful as plains grass, to a raised dais. On a carved stone chair sat a Maorrr elder, open hands at rest on the arms of the chair, hoary head bowed but golden eyes fixed on David's face as he was brought forward. When the chanting ceased, the silence stretched out and David felt his nerves stretch with it. The ancient one's voice boomed with low, vibrating power.

"Bring forth the warriors from Sanigglan."

Warriors?

David kept his gaze on the ancient one's face and sensed a shuffle of feet behind him. In a moment, silence again. He spared a quick glance downwards and saw Tugg's stern face and, behind him, *Snuggla*. He was here! The Maorrr had found him. The young San met David's joyful look with a mischievous grin. David wanted to hug him.

The elder raised his arms to the stars, his eyes fixed upon the moon as though in prayer or invocation. David watched him with a thrill of expectation.

"Mother Moon approaches her full and perfect roundness." His voice rolled over them like summer thunder. "A time of birth, and celebration, of sacrifice and battle..." He paused for dramatic effect. "...the Grue once more grow strong, and revenge swells their bellies, against those times that our friends and allies, the San, had defeated them. The Grue have nursed their hatred and their revenge and fed it to their fledgling leader with his mother's milk. He thinks himself full grown now. He plans the Grue ritual to make a sacrifice to the first summer full moon with the belief this sacrifice will give strength and fortune to his army over the San. The Grue have been without teeth since their powerful King, Cragmire the Second, died in the great Forest Battle, twenty-four summers ago. Cragmire's son has his father's vile ambition." The wise one lifted his head, the blaze of his golden eyes heating the blood of his people.

"The time is now for us to aid the San and send this foolish son to his father's fate." The blood-chilling roar that rose to the stars left no doubt about the strength of Maorrr support.

Throughout the elder's oration, David had a feeling of déjà vu but the stirring conclusion had the opposite effect on him. His heart collided with his stomach.

Crap! It's started again!

This time, he *and* Sarah would be caught in the middle of an all-out war!

I have to get her out of here, but I don't even know...how am I going to find her?

The ancient one stood then and gestured for the visitors to follow. Maorla trod silently in the rear as they rounded the stone chair and descended a steep, narrow staircase that opened in its back. They entered a circular room lined with drying herbs. A laden worktable took up most of the rounded back wall, and in the centre on a waist-high stone platform was a smokeless fire. The elder moved about the room, touching and lifting objects as though searching for something. Maorla stood tall and proud, waiting.

A triumphant huff of breath punctuated the elder's success. His cupped hands hid the fruit of his search as he turned and approached the fire. He gestured with a sweep of his tail for David to draw near. His fingers then opened like the petals of a furry flower and revealed the glow of a sphere.

It radiated a cool heat and colour like the mesmeric brilliance of a blue-white diamond, its surface smooth yet swirled with the nature of mist. As David watched, pictures formed and reformed in the swirl until a familiar image that made his heart ache took shape.

Sarah's face.

She looked back over her shoulder, her usually well-kept auburn curls unruly, and the expression on her face showed determination. She held something in her arms that looked like a platter. She looked forward again, the angle in the sphere following her like a camera lens, and her eyes widened in fear. The mist closed in, and she was gone.

The Maorrr and the San had watched the play of emotion across David's naked countenance and waited with varying degrees of understanding and patience. Seeing Sarah's image, on top of the message of the elder's speech, David's feelings were barely under control.

What is happening to her? What has my fearless Sarah so afraid?

His legs itched to run and run until they found her. Maorla rested a calming hand on David's forearm as his mind continued to spin with urgency.

"Daavid, the image crystal does not always tell all, especially to the uninitiated. This is your Sarah?" Maorla asked.

David nodded numbly. *How could Maorla know? When did I say Sarah's name out loud?*

"It could be that the crystal felt your distress and showed it to you. In addition, it could be something that is happening now, has happened or is about to happen. Because it is your uncontrolled intent that caused the image to appear, we have no hint of its meaning."

"I thought I saw rock and a torch behind her when she turned. Could that mean something?"

David felt like he was grasping at wisps of air, but his bones told him the image had significance. He looked into the swirl of the mists straining to see Sarah again. This time, however, David saw his own face: his hair standing on end, dark shadow of stubble on his square chin, his green-blue eyes ablaze with fierce emotion and he clutched what seemed to be a round weapon in his hand, then his image disappeared as many battling bodies flowed around him. The mists billowed and the scene dissolved.

Oh, crap! It keeps getting worse!

The ancient one closed his hand around the crystal. Maorla turned to him, bowed her head once and then turned back to David.

"This is my father, Memgarr. He is guardian and healer of the Maorrr spirit." As tall as he was, even David had to look up into Memgarr's golden eyes. The all-knowing compassion in them soothed David's apprehension.

"I do not need the crystal, David, to see that your Sarah is not in danger at the present," Memgarr said. "I feel her energy and know that it is her own wisdom that keeps her safe. However, even with her strength, she needs you, David."

Startled, David realized that Memgarr had pronounced his name properly. What other powers did the Maorrr healer have?

"I will find her and bring her home." As David made his promise aloud, he'd felt his heartbeat steady with his resolve. Memgarr's next words didn't seem in reply.

"Many hidden truths will be revealed before this is over."

"We must leave this for now, Daavid," Maorla interrupted, "and discuss our strategy to aid the San. There is little doubt, since Mother Moon has yet to reach full term, that Snuggla's mother is still alive and meant to be the sacrifice of the Grue. We have two days to plan, enter their territory and aid the rescue. Time is short." David again felt a wash of relief to hear Maorla's assurance added to Memgarr's.

Time may be short, he thought, *but until it's too late, it's still on our side.*

Maorla led them out of the circular chamber through a side door. A series of tunnels chiselled through the rock brought them to a long, narrow room, its length bisected by a table and benches filled with Maorrr officers. Maorla strode to the head of the table, David and the two San at her side, and addressed her officers.

"Maorrr, you heard Memgarr. We have only a brief time to plan. Before dawn we must be on our way. We will stand beside our San friends and allies in our common cause to tame the Grue once and for all."

David had watched and listened. Maorla's leadership skills impressed him as she guided the discussion and at the same time delegated tasks for weapons and supplies to be gathered and packed before they left. She was masterful. He hoped she was as accomplished in the field under fire as she was at the planning table, because despite the image of himself in Memgarr's crystal, he was less sure about himself.

The great Battle of the Forest was the only combat he had ever experienced and other than the indelible memory of the Grue King standing over him, he remembered little else. The war games schoolmates played hadn't interested him as a boy. Baseball and art were his passions, encouraged by his father. David represented his school three years in a row, and won top prize for his realistic portrayals of animals and people and landscapes. At that moment, he thought, if he could go back, he would trade his pencil for at least one lesson with the bow and arrow. The slingshot contests with Jonathon were the closest he came to handling a weapon. Throwing a baseball with pinpoint accuracy was his only other skill. Where was that going to get him now?

The silence made David look up. Everyone in the room stared at a spot on the table in front of him. He followed their gaze and realized that his fingers had found a piece of charcoal and he had been doodling while his thoughts wandered. His son, Jonathon, stood in mid-toss with his slingshot, and Sarah's beautiful, determined face looked up at him from the rough surface of the wooden table. David flushed under the silent scrutiny of the Maorrr officers, their faces unreadable.

Memgarr had come into the room behind Maorla. He watched David with interest and speculation and broke the hush with a gesture and a command.

"David, come with me."

Tugg stayed with Maorla to complete the plans while David followed the healer back through the tunnels to the circular room beneath the throne. Once again Memgarr shuffled through the clutter on his workbench, muttering to himself as he searched.

When at last he turned in triumph, he uttered an exclamation that may have been the Maorrr equivalent to "Eureka!" The grizzled hands held a long, narrow cylinder of bark. He opened the end of the container then and slipped what looked like an ordinary piece of artist's charcoal into the palm of his hand.

"I invented this, but no one here has the skill to use it properly, so I put it away. Draw for me a bird, David."

On a piece of parchment, David sketched a sparrow, tiny beak open in silent song. As the last wing feather took shape, the room echoed with a tweet. David's jaw dropped in astonishment as his creation blinked back at him. Then it stretched out its wings and took flight. It skittered on the scant air currents until David stuck out his hand and it landed on the tip of his finger. Memgarr chuckled at the speechless artist.

"This will be a far more useful weapon for you, David, than the bow and sword you wear so uneasily." David flushed at that.

Does this old one know everything about me?

"Yes," Memgarr had said, "your naked face hides nothing from me."

This time, David grinned as one hand rasped over the day old stubble on his chin. It seemed like everyone had been reading his face since he arrived.

"Do you mean in a few days there's hope I can keep my thoughts to myself?"

Memgarr nodded, a smile crinkled his wise, golden eyes.

"From everyone else but me."

He shuffled to David's side and offered a perch to the sparrow, who hopped to it without fear.

"The only caution, David, is that you use the charcoal shrewdly. This is the only piece. Your arsenal is limited." Memgarr paused and looked into David's eyes.

"Trust yourself, David. You will know what to do with this charcoal to help your Sarah when the time comes." Memgarr wrapped the charcoal piece in wadding, replaced it in its bark cylinder, and handed it along with pieces of parchment back to David, who laid it away in his backpack.

"Thank you, Memgarr." David took in a breath and grasped onto the feeling of calm strength that Maorla had gifted to him earlier. "I will try to trust myself...no...I *will* trust myself. Sarah is my life."

In his alcove, David had settled to have a nap for what was left of the night. He awoke a short while later to a now familiar tug on his arm, and opened his eyes to Snuggla's grin.

"Daavid, I have much to tell you." And with that, Snuggla launched into his story with characteristic enthusiasm while David used the bowl of water that had been left to wash away the grime and sleep residue. It seemed by his tale that Snuggla's rescue at the riverside was like a dream sequence in his semi-conscious state but he remembered arriving at the fortress and being cared for by Maorla until he felt strong again.

"Those old stories about the Maorrr be not true, Daavid," Snuggla said in exasperation. "When I'm Chief of the San, the Maorrr's story'll be changed and they'll not be wronged." David smiled to himself. Huh! So *there*, Tugg! A few moments later, the San warrior and Maorla arrived at the entrance to the alcove.

"The troops are ready," Maorla informed them. "If you are also, Daavid, we will join them." Snuggla jumped down and stood beside her.

"I'm ready, too," Snuggla declared. Maorla and had Tugg looked at him with expressionless faces, then the Maorrr leader leaned down to his level. "You are to stay *here*, little one. A battle is no place for you to be." A multitude of arguments swelled in Snuggla's eyes,

David could see them, but the telling one emerged through his clenched teeth.

"I am *not* a 'little'un', I am a *warrior* and I *will* be there to rescue my Maam!"

"You will *stay here*," Maorla waved then to an amply built Maorrr matron and instructed her to keep close watch on the feisty San.

There were no more protests from Snuggla, but David had a different read on the craft in those vivid blue eyes.

Sarah

Sarah glanced around at the little lop-eared kitchen helpers as they bustled around the fur and feather laden tables and swept the uneven flags of the stone floor.

"I'll do my best, Uncle Frederic. How do I tell when the mealtimes are and where will I take the food?" *Serve the King if a good job is done, he'd said. That might be helpful,* Sarah thought.

"Right this way, my girl! I'll take you on the grand tour!" With an obvious sense of pride, Frederic led Sarah up out of the kitchens and back through the long drafty halls. She saw his pride wobble as though he now viewed his domain through her eyes. The walls were made of stone, smooth blocks mainly, but here and there rough stone patched crumbling areas with poor skill. Smokeless torches lit the hallways in uneven bands. The treads of the wide stone staircases were chipped and worn. Frederic stopped before a broad wooden door, carved in relief of a stag standing on a rise, front leg lifted in anticipation of flight. In the background, under a tree's canopy, stood an archer, bow drawn. Frederic pulled open the door.

"Here is the dining hall for the warriors," he said.

Sarah saw a high-ceilinged room with flagstone floors striped by rows of wooden tables and benches. Light was provided by fat, round candles stuck into metal candelabra that hung above the tables. A bent creature scrubbed at the tables, each movement arthritic and slow. It looked like a smaller, lop-eared version of Sarah's San friend. Sarah wondered about this creature, but Frederic ignored its presence. The little worker seemed oblivious to them, too.

They moved on to the back of the room.

"This is the King's great room." With a flourish, Frederic pulled aside a heavy damask drape that may have been beautiful for a generation long gone. The table was old but the detailed carvings in the legs and around the edges declared great skill. The table's top was crisscrossed with scars from a bored leader's blade. The wood had not been oiled in a long time. The King's chair was equally intricate and equally abused, the seat once padded but now in shreds.

"The King doesn't visit this table much anymore. His deputy, Worl, uses it." A cloud crossed Uncle Frederic's face but lifted before Sarah could question him.

A shadowed balcony overlooked the dining hall and great room. Frederic gazed proudly around the hall as though seeing it in all its original glory.

"Ah, if these walls could talk! The feasts held here in the old days! King Cragmire's grandfather, Cragmire the First, was known to friends and allies alike as Cragmire the Good. He was a great King. He was kind and wise. He loved to eat and entertain. The dancing and singing that went on." Frederic gave a gusty sigh. "Those were the days."

"So, what happened, Uncle Frederic?"

"Shh!" He seemed to recollect where he was and looked cautiously from side to side.

"We don't want to be overheard. I'll tell you later." In a louder voice he said, "Come, I have more to show you."

As they climbed and descended a multitude of staircases, Sarah tried to get a feel for the layout of the castle; she also tried to piece together the Steward's shifting attitudes. *Why was Uncle Frederic so skittish and careful about what he said?* The maze of halls and stairs made developing a rescue-escape plan difficult, she would need to learn as much about these people and their castle as she could.

Frederic led her through a narrow doorway to a poorly lit gallery. As they moved forward into the light, Sarah realized that she was on the balcony that looked down on both the dining hall and the King's great room. The walls of the gallery had discolourations, some square and some rectangular, all old and dim under layers of grime and soot. Sarah imagined that this had been a picture gallery at one time. *Where could those pictures be now and why had they been taken down?* Further down the gallery, Frederic opened another door and stepped aside to allow Sarah to enter.

"This is the war room," he whispered even though they were alone. It was an enormous room with tall ceilings invisible in shadows, dominated in the centre by another of the intricately carved tables—this one in better condition. The carved chair had a well-padded cushion, also in good condition. A dozen chairs lined the wall facing the table. Two of the three walls were mounted with lethal looking weapons. The back wall was covered, floor to ceiling, in grey gauze. It looked so soft that Sarah reached out and touched. It was thick and heavy and...stuck to her fingers.

It's not gauze, she thought. *It's made of cobwebs.*

Her jaw dropped open as she contemplated how long the curtain had been here and the size of its builder. *No, don't be silly*, she thought. *It couldn't possibly be spiders.* She reached to pull it back to see what was behind.

"Hey, let that go!" Frederic yelped in fear. "We need to get out of here."

"But wait, Uncle Frederic. Just a second. Tell me, how long has that curtain been there?"

The steward two-stepped towards the door as he answered.

"Since the King's father, Cragmire the Second, took the throne. He ordered it built and to remain untouched on pain of death."

"That's a bit severe, isn't it?" Sarah said to the back of her uncle's head and received no response. *What makes that curtain so special, just what is it hiding?*

Frederick hustled her from the room and along the gallery to the stone hallway before she could even draw breath, then he led the way up narrow stairs to a long dark hall. He pushed open a door.

"This is your room. I have to go and check whether the hunters have returned. I will come and get you soon to show you what to do with the meal." The door swung shut behind Frederic. Sarah was alone for the first time since she had raced through the forest with her San companion. Her new room was spare with a narrow four poster bed, thinly covered, and a small table that held a wash bowl and ewer. The sliver of window looked out over a jungle of untended garden surrounded by fieldstone walls.

Sarah paced a restless pattern around the small room. *I must get back into that war room*, she thought. Her line of thinking continued to tumble. Her practical side steered her thoughts away from examining the weirdness of this world she had dropped into. It was fruitless. Or was it? Could the achievement of her main goal rest on figuring out what was going on here?

Little goals first. What is behind that curtain? There has to be a clue to these people hiding behind that curtain of cobwebs. If I can find some answers and learn something about the sacrifice ritual, maybe I can figure out how to help my friend.

Then her thoughts circled back again. Her final aim, her raison d'être, was to get back to her son and husband. Maybe she could bring Uncle Frederic back with her too. And wouldn't *that* put paid to all those snide comments by Aunt Euphemia?

The James family would be whole again.

Frederic returned to lead Sarah back to the kitchens. Tension radiated from him.

"What's the matter, Uncle Frederic?" Sarah asked, putting all other questions aside for the moment. Concerned, she laid her hand on his arm.

"The hunters were unsuccessful. The cooks will have to make do with what we have." His glance at Sarah held more than worry. "As their server, I'm afraid it won't be easy for you if the warriors go hungry."

CHAPTER SEVEN

Jonathon

The vibrations under their feet faded away in the predawn darkness. Pugg stood up under the branches by the trunk of the scrub tree. The ends of the branches swept the ground providing the perfect cover. His agitation melted with the fade of the rhythms through the ground.

"What *was* that, Pugg?" Jonathon asked again. The warrior cleared up the evidence of their camp with swift, economic moves.

"An army heading towards the Grue's country. We must get to the Maorrr fortress fast."

Jonathon looked around. He wanted to help but the work was already done. No one would ever know that someone had slept and eaten in this spot during the night.

"Was it the Grue?" Jonathon asked.

"A lot of bodies and they be big." Pugg motioned for him to follow. "We'll find our answers when we reach the Maorrr stronghold."

The warrior set a brisk pace through the long plains grass, and Jonathon doubled his effort to keep up. The going became easier as the sky brightened. The sun's appearance created a colourful display of red and mauve. Jonathon wondered if his dad saw it too. In the distance, the stronghold of the Maorrr glowed.

"How much farther, Pugg?"

"Two flicks of Maam's ear," he said with an amused twitch of his whiskers. Jon stared for a moment and then chuckled in return. He was beginning to catch on to Pugg's quirky sense of humour. As the sun glowed against the fortress, his excitement grew. He could hardly wait to catch up with his dad. He kept his eyes on the stronghold as their pace ate up the ground, but it seemed to remain distant until almost between breaths it loomed over them in a massive sheer wall of golden rock.

"How do we get in?" Jonathon asked, glancing over Pugg's back.

"Follow me, lad. There be a gate on the far side."

The warrior wove around the large boulders strewn at the base of the towering wall. With a quarter of the sun's journey done, the crisp dawn air had warmed steadily, and heat bounced off the wall. Jonathon tugged at his collar to loosen it as sweat trickled down his face. Pugg looked back with sympathy in his eyes, although his pace never slackened.

"We'll be there in two thumps. It be just around the bend."

Jonathon believed him—until many thumps had passed and the bend still arced before them.

"Hey, Pugg, just around the bend?" Jonathon asked in exasperation. One of the warrior's graceful ears tweaked backwards and the tip bent in acknowledgment.

At last, the final bend curved before them. A pair of splendid columns of red marble rose twenty feet in the air supporting a stone portico above the entry recessed into the rock wall of the fortress. The carved stone around the entryway displayed bas-relief figures of sun, grasslands, Maorrr warriors, herd animals and community scenes. Two tall feline creatures, armed with lances and swords, guarded the entrance. Each showed tight scowls, large fangs and eyes fierce with a sentry's challenge.

Pugg greeted them silently. Jonathon interpreted the unfamiliar signs as a passcode between allies. His heartbeat marked the passage of time as he waited beside the San warrior. Pugg sensed Jon's mood and waggled his ears and whiskers at him, a message Jonathon interpreted as, *lighten up, it'll be okay*. He raised and lowered his eyebrows back at the San warrior in answer. He and Pugg had become close over the last two days.

What felt like many hundreds of heartbeats later, another Maorrr, smaller and leaner than the sentries and dressed in a simple tunic with no weapons, appeared and led them into the dim interior of the fortress entryway.

Through the gloom of the tunnel leading from the entryway, Jonathon followed sounds ahead of padded feet shushing on stone floors. The tunnel opened into a small torch-lit anteroom. They continued across the room into a smaller tunnel. The switch from light to dark once again blinded Jonathon, but before his eyes could make another adjustment, they entered a room whose size Jon compared to two football fields, side by side, hewn from the rock and lit by hundreds of torches. No wonder they could see the fortress on the horizon and the perimeter hike to find the door took forever. It was enormous inside. Furred creatures, all variations of the feline sentinels, performed tasks throughout the living area. His eye caught on weavers who worked huge looms.

Their guide led them through the communal chamber to a steep stone stairwell, risers worn smooth. Halfway up the stairs, a landing announced the presence of a doorway, outlines faint against the rock walls. With a push, the door swung open.

"Welcome, San warrior and son of David."

Jonathon's feet felt glued to the stone doorstep. He tried to swallow, but his throat thickened with apprehension. A huge Maorrr, even bigger than the guards at the gate, greeted him. Over his gold pelt, he wore an elaborate robe with intricate designs of moons and galaxies. His head, heavy with an enormous black and gold mane, nodded at Jonathon, once, then twice. His eyes were his most remarkable feature. They were kind and wise and seemed to read into Jonathon's mind. It took a few seconds for him to realize that, for the first time, he had heard his father's name pronounced correctly. *David. Of the Legend.* Jon's tension eased. He smiled to himself. His dad was here!

"Come in, son of David."

Jonathon's head swivelled to take in the amazing room filled with alchemist tools: a pot bubbling over a small smokeless fire; bunches of herbs hanging upside down from the rafters and myriad mysterious implements that lay scattered on every surface. Jon looked to his friend for direction. After travelling together and saving each other's lives, Pugg had become sensitive to Jonathon's unspoken queries.

"This be Memgarr, Shaman-leader of the Maorrr, lad. He'll help us."

Jonathon turned to the Maorrr eagerly.

"Where's my dad?"

"He has gone."

Jonathon's hopeful smile collided with lines of disappointment. Memgarr took immediate pity on him.

"He was here but left with our army before daybreak. They plan to meet with the San and help them rescue Snugg's mate, Meeri."

Jonathon's brain buzzed with the information. His dad *had* been here! He left with the army, the one that vibrated the ground when they were camped on the plains. His dad had passed so close to him just hours before. The frustration of another miss fizzled along Jonathon's nerves. Then, like an echo, the rest of Memgarr's information played in his head...*who is Meeri? A rescue?*

He didn't care about that. He just wanted to find his dad. As though he had heard Jonathon's thoughts, Memgarr placated him.

"Peace, lad. All are linked in the Universe. You will be taken to David. My warriors will take you." Memgarr turned and beckoned Jonathon to follow him further into his lair. "But come with me first. I would talk to you about where you are going."

Jon, feeling a tingle of unease, looked back at Pugg. The San motioned him forward with a flick of one ear. A long blink and slight nod said it would be all right.

Jonathon went alone with the enormous Maorrr Shaman.

Memgarr led him to a wooden table flanked by chairs carved out of stone. Wall sconces cast light and shadows into the round room sculpted from the rock and lined with colourful tapestries. Memgarr lowered himself on the cushioned chair with a sigh and motioned Jonathon to take the other. Jonathon eyed the stone seat for a moment. He was tall and gangly for his age but still had to knee up on the chair and then turn around to sit. His feet dangled like he was three years old.

"My bones are much older than yours, lad. I need a little ease in these years of my life." Memgarr pulled a round globe from a deep pocket in his robe and handed it to Jonathon.

"I will show you the enemy." He pointed into the misty globe. "And give you some ammunition for your trials ahead."

"Gaze deeply," Memgarr instructed. "See the people you will face on your journey to find your father."

Jonathon watched as the milky swirls in the globe parted and the ugliest being on the planet strode through the mists. Jon, used to the sight of the San and now the Maorrr, felt his perception slip sideways with his first sight of a Grue warrior. He looked almost human—more so than the San or the Maorrr—but freakishly big with skin a muddy paste furled in vertical rows from eyes to chin. On one cheek a deep scar pulled down the corner of his eye and wandered in stark, puckered flesh to the side of his mouth. The warrior's eyes were wild, restless and fierce as though in search of a target for his hatred. Long, greasy plaits swung loose from hair pulled back. Muscles bulged under a leather tunic and trousers. He held a broadsword in one large fist, a round shield drooped from the other hand.

Jonathon shuddered. He had a strange feeling. Great Aunt Euphemia would have said a goose had walked across his grave. Then he realized what he sensed. Evil oozed out of this Grue...deep, consuming evil. This guy's ugly came from the inside out.

"Ahhh. You may be repulsed by this creature, but do not be fooled. He is a dedicated warrior of the Grue." Memgarr shook his head. "They were once a proud and beautiful people. They were skilled in art and music and had the most wonderful feasts to which they invited the neighbouring kingdoms. They were a great people accomplished both in the arts of beauty and in the art of combat. Often, our peoples would engage in contests of skills, and the Grue often won for they were truly gifted. They had a vision enhanced by the roundness—the fullness—of their lives." Memgarr paused and drew in a deep breath. His eyes closed briefly.

"With the death of their good king two generations ago, all contact with us ceased. The new king and his wife, and in turn, their son craved ultimate power and dominion over their neighbours. To achieve this goal, all arts but the art of war were forbidden. They banned all skills but those of battle. While they have lived each day to become better and better warriors, the heritage of their forefathers has been lost and, with each day, they become more unlovely." The Maorrr leader narrowed his eyes as he leaned towards Jonathon.

"It is the mockery of life that, as the Grue became more dangerous as warriors, they won battles but lost wars. And as time went on, they have not even been able to defeat the tiny San. It can only be due to the loss in their lives of the roundness that makes life whole." Memgarr patted Jonathon's shoulder.

"You thirst, young lad, and I forget my manners. You will eat and drink while my warriors prepare, and then you will follow in your father's footsteps."

David

The Maorrr marched silently through the darkness. When the sky behind them lightened to vivid rose and lavender and a blood red sun leapt above the horizon, murmurs from the battle-hardened Maorrr around David told him they saw it as a favourable sign. David felt less sure.

They marched through the growing heat of the morning in a single file that allowed the plains grass to spring back into place behind them. As one body, they changed direction and at noon, again as one, the Maorrr sank down to rest in whatever shade they could find. If it had not been for Sarah, David would never have been aware of the subtle commands telegraphed down the line.

Sarah had taught both Jonathon and David to sign. Their son could sign before he could talk. On school career days, David would come into her class and have simple conversations with the children about the farm and the store. He mixed up the words as he described the animals—his dogs clucked and his horse barked—and made them laugh and roll in their seats. Through Sarah's influence, David recognized the refined gestures of signalled orders that otherwise might have passed unnoticed.

Maorla materialized at David's side, her expressive tawny-green eyes questioned his condition. He nodded to indicate he was able and ready even as he tried to ignore the aches in his feet and calf muscles and the strain in his back. Physical stresses hadn't been a concern the last time he came through the portal. He could still feel his determined twelve-year-old self inside, but the aches and pains reminded him that his shell had grown older while disappointments and distress had made his heart more fragile. Or was that true? Wasn't his heart stronger now because of Sarah? A niggling memory struggled to surface. He was twelve and had been called to the summer camp office. The solemn look on the counsellor's face, hand placed in comfort on his shoulder, his heart about to explode—

No, no. No. Not yet. Not now. Later maybe.

It had been buried too deep and too long. He couldn't face that memory just yet. First he had to find Sarah.

They ate and drank lightly, and when the sun passed its highest point, they pushed on.

The nature of the land changed as they trudged northward through the long plains grass. The sun's slanting rays caressed the left side of David's face, and ravines, marshy creek-beds and twisted trees began replacing the plains. At a quick pace, the sun approached the horizon. The long line of marchers came to a halt and dispersed into small groups. They made camp. David appreciated their speed when, within two blinks of time, the sun touched the horizon and was sucked out of sight, leaving them in total darkness. Soon, smokeless campfires winked like fireflies, and the night rustled with the soft sounds of the warriors settling into camp.

Tugg and David stretched out by their own cook-fire. Tugg held a hooked stick which suspended a small pot over the glowing coals. A faint spicy aroma teased the air. The warrior chuckled as David's stomach rumbled loudly. "It be coming soon, hungry sir," he promised. "Hang on to yer gap." As good as his word, David soon held a wooden cup brimmed with a stew of herbs and chunky roots and bits that reminded him of 'tofu' bean curd. It smelled better than it looked. He lifted the cup to his mouth. Mid sip, an eerie sight drew David's attention. In the darkness beyond the fire, two floating green circles reflected the ember's glow. The orbs drew closer until the subdued light of the coals revealed Maorla.

"This is for a warrior's energy," she said. She offered him a tidbit half the size of his hand. "You will need all your strength in the days ahead." She turned away and melted into the night. David took a bite of the offering. It was meat of some kind: tender, juicy, lightly seared. As he finished it, he looked up to see Tugg watching him, nose wrinkled in disgust. David felt a twinge of guilt at his enjoyment. He picked up the cup again and raised it to Tugg before downing the contents in a few gulps. The broth was tasty but he hid the chewier bits when Tugg turned away.

The moon rose, and its light threw deep shadows across the camp. David thought about the sacrifice. *Memgarr said it would take place in three nights on the full moon. With one night on the move, that leaves one night to rendezvous with the San and plan their rescue of Meeri, before the ceremony took place. Is there enough time? Will we find Sarah when we find Meeri?*

From this distance, the task seemed immense. The night settled a heavy silence over them.

David kneaded what tight muscles he could reach and then curled up in his blanket. Fatigue ensured sleep was not far away. As his consciousness spun down into the depths, a nudge snatched him back. Wide awake again, his arm snapped out and grabbed the culprit. A familiar squeak triggered a suspicion, and David ran his fingers over the face of his captive in the darkness. Snuggla. How did he escape the Maorrr matron? David angled one of the young San's long ears towards him. "Sleep! We'll talk in the morning." He felt the lad snuggle against his back for warmth and comfort. Soon they were both asleep.

Sarah

"Uncle Frederic, what do you mean that it won't be easy for me if the warriors go hungry?" Sarah asked.

She stood with her hand arrested on the doorknob of the room that had become her bedroom. She pushed down thoughts of her own beautiful bedroom at home with its lacy curtains, white wicker chair and rosewood sleigh bed. A spill of late morning sun through the dirty mullioned windows cast yellow stains of light across the flagged floor and right up to her hand. This was her first day on the job, and for her own sake, she didn't want to start off on the wrong foot.

"Well, the warriors have been known on these rare occasions to take out their, shall we say, displeasure on the server bringing them their meal."

Sarah did not like the way Uncle Frederic shuffled his feet and avoided her eyes.

"And *displeasure* means...?"

"Well, a while back, they beat a server into a coma, and the Ahman could do nothing."

Sarah stared at Uncle Frederic for a moment.

"You're not kidding, are you?" More statement than question. She already knew the answer before Frederic even nodded his head. His eyes stayed riveted to the floor.

"Uncle Frederic, look at me. We have got to get down to the kitchen and assess what there is to feed these guys. I am not going to be their next casualty!"

Sarah's haste dragged Frederic with her. In the kitchens, a cavernous high-ceilinged connected series of work areas, the workers—all smaller lop-eared versions of Sarah's San friend, captive in the Grue dungeons—milled around in distress. The tables nearest the door were still laden with furred and feathered masses.

"What is the problem with what's on the table, Uncle Frederic?"

"It won't be enough, my dear. The Grue warriors are ravenous eaters, and they only eat meat. This catch will barely feed three quarters of them." He wrung his hands.

"Do you mean they never eat vegetables?" Sarah asked.

"Not since the old King's time."

"Is there still a vegetable patch?"

Frederic looked at her with confusion and then dawned on him what she was asking.

"You want to feed them *vegetables*? You will die for sure, my girl!"

"I plan to be a little more subtle than that, Uncle Frederic. Can you ask these workers if they have some large soup pots?"

"What are you planning to do?"

"I'm going to make my famous meat stew."

Shaking his head every couple of minutes and muttering under his breath, Frederic led Sarah out to the gardens. They were in a sorry state. One would be hard pressed to even call them gardens as they had become so wild and overgrown in the intervening years.

There were still fruit trees, nut trees, and the hint of row upon row of squared, low-fenced beds. Sarah loved her own gardens and was a knowledgeable herbalist. She began to search through the overgrowth and clumps of weeds. She found dill, oregano, basil and chives. Sarah looked deeper for root vegetables and tubers. Frederic continued to trail behind with a basket to which Sarah added periodically. Farther back in the gardens, she discovered purple carrots and sweet potatoes and parsnips and squash. Sarah was surprised that not all the vegetables she found were perennials. Some needed to be planted each year. Someone had gone to a lot of work to make a working garden look untended. She said as much to Uncle Frederic between grunts as she pulled up more.

"The kitchen workers keep the garden," he said. "But I asked them to make it look neglected. They cannot eat meat, you see. Cragmire the Second hated vegetables, and his first act as King was to ban them from his castle kitchen and forbid his warriors to eat them."

Sarah added a few more questions to her list to ask Uncle Frederic later. *What about the present King? Couldn't he repeal the act? And the Deputy...what was his name? Worl?* Frederic's agitated hesitation when he mentioned Worl hadn't gone unnoticed.

When Frederic staggered beneath the laden basket, Sarah decided they might have enough. She led him back to the kitchen and set to work organizing the kitchen help. She allotted the tasks of chopping and dicing. While they hunted for vegetables, the piles of fur and feathers had become chunks of meat. With Frederic's aid, Sarah found more utensils. Over the fire, she seared the chunks and placed some of the bones in huge pots of water to make a broth. When the water came to a boil, she added the vegetables, diced very fine. She worked hard and pushed her helpers to create a stew that would satisfy the biggest appetites. While her ultimate goal was to escape, her immediate task was her own survival—and according to Uncle Frederic, her survival right now depended on satisfying the Grue warriors' stomachs. She planned to feed them to the best of her abilities. That's the way she did everything.

Sarah gave a whoop of glee when she came across—literally *fell* across—bags of coarse flour in a forgotten cool-room off the kitchen. This would help to fill up those bellies! With some improvisation of materials and ingredients, Sarah created mounds of dough left to rise before baking. The huge oven beside the open fireplace had not been used in decades. Sarah set another crew to scrubbing it clean in preparation for her doughy creations.

Before long the smells in the kitchen were mouth-watering, and Sarah could see Frederic begin to relax.

"This just might work, my girl!" he said as he helped stir the thick, meaty stew. Not a vegetable in sight. The aroma of baking bread brought tears to his eyes.

"It's been a long time since I've had bread like this. Could we keep a small loaf for the kitchen, do you think?" he asked her, earning a smile of gratitude.

"Let's get these...*people*" –Sarah picked her words carefully– "fed first, Uncle Frederic. I'm sure we can make something tasty for ourselves later." She supervised the transfer of the stew into large serving bowls and the golden loaves arranged in pyramids on platters and led the parade to the dining hall, carrying a platter herself.

Uncle Frederic opened the door to the hall and stepped back out of the way allowing Sarah to enter on her own. She caught her breath in a gasp. The stench of all those bodies nearly overpowered the delicious aromas her helpers were bringing in with the platters and serving bowls. Rows upon rows of unfriendly, hostile eyes watched her as she directed the placement of the dishes.

Sarah's heart raced with unleashed fear. Would her plan work, or was she their next victim?

CHAPTER EIGHT

Jonathon

The Maorrr warrior-in-charge had spared Jonathon and Pugg two of his warriors. The pair followed these warriors across the grasslands, the sun mid-morning high and several hours in the wake of the Maorrr army and his dad. Jonathon thought of them as the *Tweedles*. They reminded him of characters in a story that his dad had read with him a few years before. They lacked the imposing stature of the guards at the entry gate. It wasn't the pudge that bulged above their bristling weapon belts or the hint of waddle that tainted their stride. There was a missing element of warrior assertiveness. Dee and Dum suited them perfectly, Jonathon thought. He glanced over at Pugg and noticed a derisive twitch of his friend's whiskers. It looked like the San shared his feelings. Jonathon felt a twinge of anxiety about these two. Would they be able to help him find his dad? Jonathon couldn't drum up much confidence in them.

Memgarr had promised them an escort to help them catch up with the Maorrr contingent that had departed before dawn. He left the choice of the warriors, though, up to the warrior-in-charge. This warrior, Jonathon guessed, resented giving up any more of the troops left behind to guard the stronghold and therefore chose the two he could spare.

The Maorrr shaman and leader had impressed Jonathon. He seemed to be able to read the boy's every thought. Before he'd departed on the next leg of his mission, Memgarr had told him about the Grue's history, that they had once been a great and very beautiful race until cruelty and war took over their lives. Jonathon twirled, between his fingers, the talisman that the Maorrr leader had given him. It had powers, Memgarr had told him, to help him blend in where needed. Jonathon could activate its powers in two ways: rub its smooth, slate-like surface over whatever part of him would help him blend; or turn it over and whisper his command into the ear-like folds on the other side of the talisman. Memgarr demonstrated the first power by rubbing it over Jonathon's hand as it rested against the wood table. Jonathon's jaw dropped as his sleeve seemed to gape open, unsupported. The boy jerked his arm away and his hand reappeared.

"Cool!"

Memgarr raised an eyebrow.

"Is it so?"

Jonathon reddened.

"No, I mean, that was amazing!"

Memgarr nodded wisely. "Now whisper a command to it. Ask it to allow you to hear." Jonathon did as he was bid. At first he thought nothing happened, but then it had been as though his ears had opened wide. He heard a youthful giggle, a firm command to behave, bubbling broth, the snap of a weaver's loom, a flutter of wings, the shush of cloth against stone. As he looked around Memgarr's room, it was obvious that none of these sounds were generated near him.

They must be coming from the communal living area. The ancient leader sat still and watched him. Jonathon focused on the small flame that heated a suspended pot on the workbench against the wall. The flame roared with a blast out of sync with its tiny size; the liquid in the pot snapped and crackled like a cauldron at full boil. Within moments, all sound returned to a normal volume.

"How long does this give me its power?" Jonathon asked, his voice an awed whisper.

"You can learn to control that, son. This is a very special blending talisman. It will help you when you get where you are meant to be." Memgarr's words had puzzled Jonathon.

He continued to tease out the Maorrr shaman's meaning as he followed Dee and Dum through the tall prairie grass. His brain buzzed like a hive full of bees with all that had happened over the last two days since he followed his dad and came through the portal into this strange world: his adventures with Pugg; the Maorrr Shaman who impressed his socks off—*he had so much cool stuff*—the talisman he couldn't wait to use; hoping and crashing time and again as he came so close to his dad. And last, the Tweedles. Were they taking him where he wanted to go or where he was meant to be?

The way seemed easy to track at first—where some clumps of grass refused to stand up or tips were broken. If the indications continued like this, they would be able to follow easily. But when the sun set, he felt more than uneasy. He had not seen signs of a previous passage for hours. The Maorrr set up rough camp under plains trees. They ate a cold meal and curled up in an uneven circle for warmth.

Even though he was exhausted from all the trekking over the last few days, Jonathon had trouble falling asleep. When he managed to drift off, Memgarr awaited him in the mists of his dream. Wordlessly, he led the boy back to the stone table and chairs, bade him sit and again held out the milky sphere to him. Jonathon looked into its depths, expecting to see a Grue when, instead, his mother's eyes gazed back at him. Her eyes were full of love. Her mouth moved but he could not make out the words. As she moved away from him, deeper into the crystal, a wall of large quarried stone became visible behind her as well as a sconce belching smoky light. She still seemed to be trying to tell him something when she turned and hurried away down a long corridor. Jonathon shook the milky orb to try and bring her image back but instead the likeness of a fortress rose through the mists surrounded by twisted trees and ravaged terrain and then, it too, disappeared. He looked up at Memgarr and the shaman stood and pointed. The vision faded to black as a voice intruded on the silence of the dream.

"Jon, wake... we must start."

Jonathon's eyes flew open in alarm and rested on Pugg's trusted face.

"My mom, Pugg...my mom," he stumbled over his words as the dream faded. "I had a dream that she was here, with the Grue!"

"Nay, lad." Pugg shook his head but he offered no other comfort.

They were ready before the sun rose, no urging needed from the Tweedles to break camp and continue on. In his anxiety, compounded by the dream of his mom, Jonathon almost trod on the heels of the Maorrr as he hurried behind them.

David

At the first hint of morning, David felt the stirrings of the San and Maorrr around him. The camp was broken down, and they all stretched and flexed while waiting for the order to proceed. Tugg was stern but said nothing when he woke and saw Snugg's heir by the remains of the campfire. Maorla came down the line and stopped short when she saw the young San in David's camp. Her tail switched back and forth in displeasure. David bowed his head in acknowledgement and signed he would take responsibility. He reached for Snuggla.

"Stay close to me. Do. Not. Stray." David instructed firmly. He sensed—rather than heard—Snuggla's acquiescence. He felt the tension rise and then ebb away as a silent command passed through the masses like a sigh. Time had reached a critical point. Only one more night remained until the full moon... to the sacrifice of the San leader's mate, Meeri. In Memgarr's image crystal, David had seen Sarah against a stone wall. Was she with Meeri?

Snuggla attached himself to David's side as Tugg protected his other flank. The march began in noiseless precision. The sun struggled to send out pale yellow fingers through a grey haze, but soon its efforts failed. Only the slight lightening of the air around them suggested that the sun had risen at all.

The terrain continued to change. The ravines became deeper and more treacherous to cross and smelled of unhealthy rot. The trees were twisted and grey like the air and draped with long dreadlocks of moss. The speed of their advance slowed as teams of Maorrr created bridges to aid their smaller allies across the steeply trenched landscape. David worried that the three of them hampered the advance of their forces, but he pushed the thought aside. What else could they do?

The sky grew darker as they headed further north into the gloom and stench of the Grue forest. An order came down the line, and the Maorrr crouched down into the cover of a steep ravine. Maorla appeared at David's side.

"This is as far as we can go until we have spoken to Snugg. We need now to coordinate our forces," she paused and touched Tugg on the shoulder with the tip of her tail. "The San are entrenched just ahead of us. You must find Snugg and bring him to us."

David felt Snuggla wriggle and heard him snort but not speak.

Tugg saluted the Maorrr leader with nonchalance.

"I be back before you can twitch a whisker!" He winked at David as he disappeared into the murk.

For David, time passed like pulled taffy as he waited for Tugg's return. The Maorrr meanwhile gathered fallen branches to build camouflage over the ravines in which they had taken cover. Others climbed into the trees to act as lookouts and snipers with long bows and supplies of arrows.

When Tugg reappeared in the ravine he was alone. Snuggla poked at David, a scornful expression on his face. Moments later the young San's eyes opened in shock. Snugg, the San leader, let himself down the side of the ravine by handholds of rocks and roots until he stood beside them. He was filthy and haggard. He looked as though he had not slept in months. David pushed through the warriors to face his old friend and reached out to grip the San's shoulder. David's mouth opened and closed. The words of joy mixed with feelings of distress and urgency jumbled together into confusion. *How to start? With the basics....*

"I've missed you, old friend."

Snugg grasped David's forearms, his hands strong as a vise.

"And I have missed you, young master Daavid." His whiskers twitched with emotion. "I feel your presence will bring us success just as it did before."

David felt a tremor in his gut but his heart beat more stalwartly.

"I will do all that I can to help you, Snugg," he said. "What's your plan of attack?" At that moment, David felt a pinch on the back of his leg and looked under his arm to see Snuggla peering around him. In the same moment, Snugg realized that his strong-willed heir stared at him from behind David.

"Come forth, child, and greet your father!" He said gruffly, with just a hint of amusement in the twist of his ears. He hugged the young San to him and then bent down until they were eye-to-eye.

"What you be doing here, Snuggla?"

"I come to save my Maam." Defiance sparked in his eyes. His father's ears twitched and went still. He looked gravely at his heir.

"My child, that's why we *all* be here." He stood up and turned to Maorla and David, an arm around Snuggla's shoulder.

"It pleases me to have you here to aid us," he said to the Maorrr leader. Maorla dipped her head. As leaders in their respective communities and armies, Snugg and Maorla were on equal footing but the circumstance of Meeri's capture put the San in charge of the whole.

"So. Our time is short," she said. "Let us make the plan solid."

They crouched down together while Snugg drew a map in the dirt. A rock in the middle represented the Grue fortress.

"There been no sign of the Grue since they took my mate, Meeri. Not even of hunters. It be as if they locked themselves inside. We cannot attack unyielding walls of the fortress." He gazed off over their heads as though in study of the walls. "We must get them to come to us."

A distant alarm raised the hackles on the warrior leader's shoulders.

"What goes?" Maorla threw the question at her deputy. He dipped his head to her and hurried away. Moments later he returned.

"Someone comes and comes fast."

Sarah

The stench of the Grue warriors combined with the tension in her stomach made Sarah want to run gagging from the dining room. Instead, she held her ground and looked back at the scowls of the warriors, her hands gripped around the platter's edge. She handed her burden to one of the little workers and folded her hands together at her waist to hide her nerves.

The scowls turned into growls and fists hit the tables making the dishes rattle. Uncle Frederic warned her they were expecting platters of chunks of meat. Would her meat stew subtly thickened with diced vegetables pass muster? One huge warrior, easily eight feet tall, with a scar that stitched one side of his face into a permanent grimace advanced on Sarah, his swordlike dagger carving the air. Uncle Frederic had described him. The King's Deputy, Worl. Fear held her incapable of movement. Frederic said Worl's reactions were unpredictable, and she could feel waves of antagonism radiating from him. He lived for violence. She could read his body language. Sarah didn't want to provoke him. She felt her heart clench into a tight fist of muscle. Even though on the inside she shrank away from the pressing Grue Deputy, on the outside she stood straight and proud.

A roar brought the Deputy to a scowling stop just inches from Sarah's face. He glanced back and saw another warrior holding up a loaf of bread sopped in stew. A huge bite was missing and the warrior was speaking through the mass in his mouth. There was bliss in his eyes and he gestured for the Deputy to try it. Worl held his dagger before her face and the other hand gripped her forearm as he backed up to the table. He released her to bring a sop of bread and stew to his mouth. Then he turned his back to her with a growl and grabbed a steaming bowl.

Soon, all in the room followed suit and the only sounds to be heard were grunts and burps. With the attention off of her, Sarah backed away towards the door. As she stepped over the threshold, the door closed as if of its own volition, and Sarah saw Uncle Frederic sag against the doorframe.

"You did it, girl!" Uncle Frederic's voice quavered with relief. "You fed them, and they look happy! You actually fed these warriors some bread and vegetables with their meat."

And survived. Sarah could hear the unspoken words hanging in the air. Now that the moment of truth was past, Sarah could feel her knees tremble and raised shaky hands to her face to compose herself. This was crazy! She had to get out of this place. She just couldn't go through that again!

"I'm so proud of you," said Frederic as he led her down the corridor. "The others can take care of the rest now." He turned wondering eyes on Sarah. "You were amazing. You stood up to Worl!"

"Stood up? Where was I to go, Uncle Frederic? The Deputy almost ate *me* for dinner! Where were you?"

"Oh, my dear..." Uncle Frederic quibbled, "I... I uh, I just knew you didn't need me in there."

Sarah paused in their headlong flight down the passage away from the dining hall. She stared at the old man in disbelief and then shook her head.

"Let's keep going," she said. The close call with the cruel Grue Deputy made Sarah even surer that no time could be wasted in finding a clue to help her San friend and herself escape. And what better time than when they were all at dinner? She pulled Uncle Frederic along even as his feet began to drag when he recognized the direction Sarah was leading him.

"No. No! We can't go there!" He pleaded with her.

Sarah never wavered. The clue she needed was close; she could feel it. They tiptoed across the dimly lit gallery above the dining Grue warriors to the back door of the King's war room. The heavy door opened with a squeaky protest. They paused and looked over the rail, but the noisy eaters below heard nothing. Uncle Frederic eased the door closed behind them. The huge, carved table stood as before in the middle of the room. This time its surface was not bare. An enormous book lay off-centre and opened. She approached the book and reached out a hand to touch it. The pages were heavy parchment. The open page displayed a gory coloured illustration of armed warriors around a stone altar. A single circle in the upper half of the page represented the full moon. The altar was not empty. Behind its splayed occupant stood a feather robed Grue with a curvy knife held aloft in joined hands. Sarah turned the page. Weapons, defensive postures, illustrations of strategies.

This is a book of war.

Sarah could feel Uncle Frederic breathing behind her. He stared at the pictures with a look that was both fascinated and appalled. Hadn't he seen this book before? He reached out to touch the book himself.

With Frederic's attention momentarily occupied, Sarah sidestepped around the old man and went to the cobweb curtain. Using both hands, she lifted up the edge to peer behind. The curtain was heavier and stickier than she thought it would be. All she wanted was just one quick little peek...

"What are you doing!"

In response to Uncle Frederic's panicked yell, Sarah jerked and whirled around. The curtain seemed to come to malevolent life as it stuck to her hands and wrapped itself around her. It began to tear away from the ceiling with Sarah's frantic struggles to keep her balance. She twirled and quick-stepped, then landed hard on her knees all but cocooned in the sticky web.

Frederic danced beside her; his nervous hands making fluttery arcs as he uttered twitters like a bird. In other circumstances, his antics would have made her giggle but bundled like a burrito on the floor of the King's war room, all she could feel was queasy dismay. There was nothing the least bit funny in the contagious panic that the old man passed along to her.

"Please help me, Uncle Frederic. I can barely move."

He pulled and yanked at the gluey strands around Sarah and wiped his hands together distastefully to dislodge cotton candy sized clumps before attacking more of the confining web. At last, Sarah was free and the two stood looking at the damage aghast.

A whole swath of wall was revealed, shelf upon shelf of dusty, skillfully bound books. Set in the middle like a jewel, a portrait of a handsome man and beautiful woman, robes richly furred and embroidered, stared regally into the room. "Cragmire the Good," Sarah thought she heard Frederic say under his breath. The painting was exquisitely crafted with precise detail. Other shelves contained intricate carvings of elegant people dancing, delicate flowers and laughing children playing games. Sarah stretched out a hand to pick one up and examine it more closely.

A ferocious roar filled the room and rattled what little composure Sarah had left. She turned to see the King standing by the table. He stood legs apart in an aggressive stance right out of the book of war. He thrust his hand at the wall and streamed a flood of words over his shoulder at his Steward. Although she could not understand a word, the King's anger needed no interpretation. Sarah moved only her eyes to find Uncle Frederic. That man is a genius at disappearing, she thought. Then she felt a tug at her waist and realized that her mentor was crouched behind her and trying to coax her towards the door.

Step by step, they backed up.

Straight into the arms of the King's vicious Deputy.

CHAPTER NINE

Jonathon

Trapped!

Alone under a bush beneath some squat trees, Jonathon felt shock creep upwards and paralyze his limbs. Where was Pugg? He looked back in the direction of the ravine edge where he had last seen Pugg and the Tweedles, but the brush now blocked his view. One moment he had wandered forward to get a better look through the trees at the cliff rising in front of them, and the next, chaos broke out.

He remembered his derisive comment to his San friend just a few hours ago, as they crossed the boundary between the Maorrr plains and Grue forest. "I think they're lost, Pugg... I don't think they're taking us the right way."

"What makes you say so, lad?" Pugg had cocked an ear at him.

"They keep looking at each other, and I've watched them signal with their hands and tails; they're asking each other which way they should go."

"Aye, lad, you may be right, but we not be far off the right track, and at least they have us on the easier going of Maorrr land instead of through Grue swill. We'll catch up."

Jonathon had to give the Tweedles their due, they trekked hard. As the grasslands changed and became sparser, Pugg signalled Jon to be more cautious. His unease was evident in the swivel of his ears and the constant checking of their surroundings. Jonathon remembered the last time he and Pugg had left the grasslands and he kept a nervous eye on the treetops. Ravines, each steeper and more foul as they progressed, criss-crossed their way and slowed them down.

They came to a deep rift. Dee stood on the bottom and, with brute strength, pushed Dum up over the edge. Next Pugg stood on Dee's shoulders while Jonathon climbed them both like a ladder, then Dum reached down, grabbed his arms, and pulled him up and over. When they were all standing together once again, Jonathon had a quick look around. The ground had levelled off and the trees seemed taller and straighter. A thin cladding of brush skirted the trunks. Through the trees, at a little distance, across a rocky clearing, they could see the rise of an enormous cliff that extended in both directions away from them. Something about the rock face of the cliff struck Jonathon as odd. He moved away from the others to get a closer look.

From that moment, the rest of Jonathon's recollections became a blur. He heard a whistling sound and then a thunk, like a hammer hitting meat. Dum lay spread-eagled on his back, the feathered shaft of an arrow sticking out of his chest. Dee tried to pull his companion into shelter but was struck in the shoulder and knocked off his feet. From under the cover of some low brush, Jonathon's guts twisted in fear as he watched Pugg race out in the hail of arrows. The San grabbed Dee by his good arm, dragged him to the edge of the ravine and dropped him over, then crouched at the ready as his eyes and ears scanned all corners and back to where they had last stood together. Jonathon tried to yell out to Pugg, but it came out in a tight croak that even his own ears could barely hear. Pugg gathered his haunches to leap forward when another volley of arrows stitched the ground around him. Pugg jerked back and disappeared over the edge of the ravine.

Jonathon was alone. Trapped under a bush. Night was not far off. What now?!

The rain of arrows stopped with the departure of Pugg and the wounded Dee. The remaining Maorrr warrior lay in the dust and his own blood.

On his hands and knees, Jonathon backed further into the cover of the brush, away from the exposed ravine edge, his mind repeating like a mantra—*gotta stay back, stay back, stay back*. As he inched along, he realized he had been moving parallel to the bottom of the cliff. He peered through the thinning upper branches of the trees.

Not a cliff!

Jonathon's stomach knotted like his great aunt's macramé as he stared up at the crenellated outer wall of a huge fortress, topped with turrets and a bartizan at the near corner. He had thought the Maorrr stronghold enormous! How did the Tweedles not know they were leading them directly to the Grue? What was he going to do now? Without Pugg?

Jonathon couldn't see anyone between the crenels of the wall, but after what happened to the Tweedles and Pugg, he didn't want to take a chance. He flattened himself under cover of the brush. He only had himself to rely on now. The thought firmed his trembling insides a little. Gramp Matthew's voice sounded in his head: *in times of trouble, stay calm so you can hear your own advice*. He really missed Gramp right now! But not as much as he missed his mom and dad.

Over the last two days, he had been surfing huge waves of emotion as each time he seemed about to catch up to his father only to discover he was either too late or off course. Jonathon felt a longing tug at his insides—to close his eyes and find himself on the safe side of the creek in the Home Wood again. To hear his dad's off-key singing and smell his mom's strawberry rhubarb pie. Instead, all that circled him were the weird, smelly trees of the Grue.

Smelly or not, he hugged the trees and crawled beneath the bushes, memorizing everything within view. The ground dipped in front of him and became softer. Then muddy. A small stream trickled past and flowed into a still pond. The stream seemed to come from beneath an indentation in the side of the large wall. Jonathon stared at the quarried stone of the wall. It looked familiar. A heartbeat later he remembered.

The dream. It looked like the wall behind his mother in the dream.

Jonathon took out the gift from Memgarr and held it in his hands for a moment. Then he lifted it to his lips, whispered his command and held it to his ear.

At first he heard nothing, like the deep silence of midnight when birds are asleep and no one stirs. Jonathon shook the talisman. Then he gave his head a mental knock. *What good did it do to shake a rock?* He put it back up to his ear. The crash of steel on steel rang through harrumphs of effort and dull thumps. He caught twitters of words he had heard when standing in the middle of the San village. Then deep gruff roars that had the shape of commands. In the midst of the cacophony of sounds that buffeted his ear came the clear bell-like tones he knew so well, raised in a question that made no sense to him,

"Can I help you with this, Uncle Frederic?

David

David and the group of allied leaders were huddled together around the sand map in the ravine camp when the scouts raised the alarm. Branches woven together created a camouflaged roof over the ravine, and a small, smokeless fire gave light to their deliberations and brightened the mid-afternoon gloom. In less than a heartbeat, swords materialized in the hands of the Maorrr warriors. Snugg stood with a short sword in each hand while Tugg protected his flank. David gripped Snugg's heir by the shoulder and drew him further into the shelter of the curved ravine face.

Unspoken concern twitched the keen ears of the Maorrr and San as they followed the trace of sound headed in their direction: snapping twigs, swish of branches—something being dragged?—and then the punctuation of low moans.

With a flick of her tail, Maorla motioned for three of her warriors to advance on the intruders and cut them off. The rest of them waited in suspense as the sounds ceased. David felt his heartbeat build into a tattoo and his breath paused.

Who or what is out there?

The three warriors reappeared at the edge of the ravine and signed for help. It was then that they could see, in the gloom, a fourth Maorrr warrior being supported and next lowered to the bottom of the cut. Scrambling down the side to join them was a San warrior.

"Pugg!" the San leader exclaimed.

Pugg gasped for breath and sagged to the ground. David looked from the exhausted blood-soaked San to the stricken Maorrr. The broken end of an arrow protruded from the Maorrr's shoulder. David overheard the Maorrr scouts report that they had found the San carrying the injured warrior and he marvelled at the San's strength to carry the wounded Maorrr twice his size.

What did Snugg call him? Pugg?

Snugg turned to his warrior and asked again.

"What you be doing out there? You were with the village guard!"

"We be...bringing...the son of Daavid...to join his father."

David's heart stood still.

What?! Jonathon? Jonathon was here? Here! He dropped to his knees at Pugg's side, his fists clenched to the white of bone.

"Tell me where he is!"

Pugg, dumbstruck, stared at his hero, Daavid, the Legend of the San, slayer of the cruel Grue King Cragmire the Second. Snugg joined David in his entreaties.

"Speak! Tell us what occurred."

Pugg swallowed, his gaze seared with pain and remorse, and took another steadying breath before he began. He could not meet David's eyes.

"I know not where he be, now." The words seemed wrenched from his throat. In response to a signal from his brother, Pugg started his report from the beginning, "...two Maorrr warriors accompanied us. We travelled along the border between the Grue and Maorrr territory but stayed on the Maorrr side. By sun's decline, we entered Grue land. We went too far and came sudden upon the Grue fortress. Before we could move, arrows flew; both our Maorrr friends took wounds. There been no help for the one. I looked to find Jon but could not see him for the arrows rained upon us still. I dragged this one into cover—I looked again but could not see Jon so then brought this warrior as far and fast as I could go—until you found us."

"You left my son behind?" David's heart crashed against his ribs and fell into his gut.

Oh God, no! Jonathon came through the portal! He could be dead with an arrow in his chest. Oh God! Dad was right—the Home Wood is cursed. It claimed his brother, almost claimed me, and now Sarah is missing and Jonathan! Jonathan could be dead!

With deep breaths and a monumental effort of will, David forced himself to focus on the moment. To focus on the San in front of him. But anguish still vibrated in David's throat. He felt a firm hand grip his forearm and looked into the eyes of his old friend, Snugg. Behind stood his older brother, Tugg.

"What are we going to do?" David asked, his desperation barely coated with a layer of calm.

"Whatever we do, it will be together as before." Snugg looked him in the eye for a quiet moment then tapped David's hand with purpose. "And with both my brothers to join us, we'll be an even stronger force!"

Both brothers? David looked from Snugg to Pugg to Tugg. Although Pugg was tall and lanky, Tugg, stocky and bow-legged, Snugg dignified—it was plain now. They had the same expression in their frank blue eyes and peculiar double twitch of their ears. Snugg returned to his battle plans in the sand. His posture spoke to the necessity of their mission and his goal to rescue his mate before the full moon. That was David's mission, too.

David saw again Sarah's swirling image against the stone wall in Memgarr's image crystal, and a bone-deep hunch shouted in his head. Sarah was somewhere within the same walls that trapped Snugg's mate. Now was the time to share his personal mission...a mission that had just expanded to include his son. David stretched out his hand to gain attention and, in tense short phrases, told Snugg and his brothers about Sarah's disappearance in the Home Wood and that the Maorrr Shaman's crystal had shown him evidence his heart told him was true. Sarah was also somewhere in the Grue fortress. Snugg bowed his head in acknowledgement and empathy. His brothers knelt and told David, each in his own way, that they would help him reunite his family. In the next beat, Snugg returned to the plans with vigour.

"No time to be lost! We must somehow lure them out. We have no hope against those walls. As you see, they can sit up top and pick us off one by one. And we have only until tomorrow night. Their—" Snugg caught himself before saying the word sacrifice "—*ceremony* will be at the full moon, and then they will attack."

David picked up on Snugg's own shallow composure in the slight double flicker of his ear. The risks were high, and they both had their family's lives at stake. When David shoved his hands into his pockets, his fingers touched the wrappings of the gift from Memgarr. He heard again the shaman's words as David's charcoal drawing of a sparrow took flight off the parchment. The gift, Memgarr had said with insight, was a weapon better suited to David's skills.

David took the shaman's gift out of his pocket and held it in his hand. Snugg caught the movement and looked at him with curiosity.

"What have you there, my friend?"

"It is a secret weapon from Memgarr. It may just be our Trojan horse."

David smiled at Snugg's quizzical look.

"It is a myth from my world. An army gave what seemed to be a gift of a large wooden horse to their enemy, the Trojans, who were protected behind thick, impregnable walls. The Trojans took the horse into their stronghold and admired it as a wonderful gift. Then they went to sleep. Late that night, a few warriors hidden in the horse's belly let themselves out and opened the gates for their army. The Trojans were defeated."

Snugg and Maorla nodded their heads and uttered sounds of admiration.

"But what could we produce by tonight that the Grue would think be a gift—large enough to hide warriors?" Snugg asked. He looked around at the others and then rested his eyes on David.

From his knapsack, David took out the large piece of parchment that Memgarr had also given to him and stretched it out on the ground. He twiddled the charcoal around his fingers like a miniature baton as he pondered his creation and the answer to Snugg's question.

"Perhaps not for warriors... but something large enough for one. Me."

Sarah

The exposed wall of portraits and bookshelves in the King's war-room seemed to look out onto the room in mute accusation. Sarah's ears still rang, and her heart shuddered with King Cragmire's angry roar. He stood with his legs apart and one hand fisted around a large ceramic stein, the other jabbing a long finger to punctuate each word. It was Sarah's first view of the King, and in the next fraction of time, as he continued his harangue, her senses made a swift assessment. First, he didn't smell like the other Grue and his foul deputy. He was enormously tall as all the Grue were, but Sarah guessed that Worl had a few inches on him. Everything about Cragmire looked cared for. He wore a clean eggplant-coloured tunic and trousers with embroidered edges over a snowy white shirt and had dark curly hair to his shoulders and a trimmed beard that followed a square jawline. Sarah glanced at the portrait. Was there a resemblance? The King noticed her glance. His brown eyes closed in angry slits.

From behind, the Deputy's vicious hold around her arms yanked her back to her predicament. Frederic squirted out between them like a watermelon seed and stood exposed to his King. Cragmire directed the tirade, with narrowed eyes, at his Steward and his pointing finger swivelled like a canon towards Sarah. Frederic tossed a sideways glance at her then gulped and translated.

"Um...He wants to know why you are here."

Sarah gritted her teeth to distract her from the freak-out zapping along her nerves—*focus! focus! focus!*—and forced her thoughts to speculate on the great deal left unsaid. Perhaps something about the consequences of exposing the wall? She doubted that was it or at least not all of it. There seemed to be an undercurrent to the King's reprimand. Her sensitivity to body language told her there was an unease not just anger in Cragmire's reaction. His performance reminded her of someone, something...that's it! Performance! He reminded her of an actor on stage. *But who was the audience?*

Sarah's mind raced in too many directions. *Focus!* Time was running away on her and her friend in the cell. That was important. The King's issues had nothing to do with her. Despite the ferocity of his glare and the roar that rattled the bones in her ears, Sarah did not feel afraid of the King—well, okay, not entirely true, but at least not in the way the Deputy frightened her. Why did Uncle Frederic seem so petrified of the King? She had picked up a different sense of Cragmire but that analysis would have to wait until later. The idea of analysis felt like balm to her jittering nerves.

The whole sprint of Sarah's thoughts, from the King's roar to Uncle Frederic's translation, took only the space of two breaths and firmed just as quickly into a plan for her next step. Was this moment her best chance? Not just to find answers for her growing list of questions, but to instigate a change of direction for the march of events. She would never get home if that didn't happen.

Why did she ever run away from the argument with David and go into the Home Wood? Why didn't she wait for the report? She pushed away the despair that threatened to swallow her whole. She must be strong. From where she stood at this moment, she was the only one who could make the change happen that would get her home again and save her San friend from being the Grue's ceremonial sacrifice.

Where to start? She needed to be sensitive, diplomatic. Her natural curiosity, though, quivered to know the significance of those beautiful, regal people in the portrait. Evidence of the loss of a wonderful culture? How had that loss brought the Grue to this sad present? That would be a little harsh to start with. She would soften her investigative goal with diplomacy. At least that's how she interpreted her rashness later.

"Please tell the King, Uncle Frederic, that it was an accident. I apologize with my whole heart." She raised her arms as far as the Deputy's grip would allow and clasped her hands in prayer stance and bowed her head. She grimaced and let her numb, bloodless hands fall back to her waist. Her arms felt almost squeezed in half by Worl's brutal grasp. His undirected malevolence terrified her spit-less. The Deputy did not seem to need a reason to hate. He had placed a mark on her back when she first served him dinner. The only thin protection she had was Uncle Frederic and the unknown warrior who savoured the fresh bread first at dinner and distracted Worl from giving her from an unearned beating. She paused for a few beats of time and then took in a breath, but what came out of her mouth next was not the tactful, subtle question she had heard in her head.

"Ask him for me," she continued, ignoring the terrified waggle of her mentor's head, "who are the people in the picture?" With the look of someone about to leap off a cliff without a parachute, Frederic turned to translate her question.

But before the Steward could open his mouth, Cragmire's wrath detonated and the huge ceramic stein in his hand exploded as he slammed it onto the table. The shards flew like shrapnel. The King cried out and stared down at his arm. Blood flowed over his wrist and open palm.

A high sound like a keen escaped from Frederic before he clamped his hand over his mouth and rushed to Cragmire's side, his other hand fluttering circles in the air. The Deputy's grip went limp around his captive and Sarah took advantage of the freedom. Her first instinct was to run for the door—*why should I try to save Cragmire?*—but something in Uncle Frederic's distress sent her racing instead to the King's side to put pressure on the wound. The blood was bright, suggesting that, perhaps the shard had nicked an artery.

"Uncle Frederic," she said, urgency quickened in her voice, "Hurry...Uncle Frederic!...bring me some of those cobweb clumps." He stood rooted until Sarah yelled.

"Now!"

He jumped as if struck and Sarah felt a small twinge of guilt but pushed it aside as Frederic rushed to bring her the cobwebs.

"I'm going to need more and I also need some cloth strips. The gash is deep. We have to stop the bleeding and then bind it together." She looked back at the Deputy's scarred face and saw his eyes cracked to slits and a strange quirk to his lips. "Frederic, tell him to get the cloth for you and help us get the King sitting in his chair."

"No...I'll do it."

Cragmire still gripped the edge of the table. His Steward pushed the chair forward and turned him to sit just as the King's legs buckled under him and he collapsed backwards. Sarah's hand slipped off the wound and a small geyser splashed red over her hand. Oh my God! Would she be able to get this bleeding to stop?

She turned in time to see the Deputy back from the room, his eyes glued to his King's wound, his expression unreadable. What was wrong with this guy? This was his *King* in trouble. Why wouldn't Worl help? The blood just kept coming! Sarah pressed as hard as she could, and looked around for something that could create a tourniquet to slow the flow. Uncle Frederic hustled back to her side with more wads of cobweb. A slow burn of annoyance that the Deputy wouldn't step forward to offer his aid didn't alter the relief Sarah felt when the door closed behind him. He was much too volatile to trust.

The King sat with his eyes closed, his face a mask turned away from her. Sarah continued to keep pressure on the deep gash, while Frederic squeezed the arm above the wound. She changed the wads of cobweb as they soaked through, worry beginning to rise that the flow would never stop. She spared a quick glance first at Uncle Frederic and then Cragmire's pale profile. Why did he react before he even heard the translation of her question? What did the Steward leave out in his interpretation? Slowly, as the piles of reddened discard grew, the flow of blood diminished. Too busy to think more deeply about the King's response, Sarah added another mental note to her list to ask Uncle Frederic—*why would two such fierce warriors be scared of blood?*

Frederic was finally able to release his grip and fetch some strips of cloth for Sarah to use as binding around the king's wound. The steward's eyebrows wobbled in anxiety. After handing Sarah the bundle, he stepped back and stood with his hands folded together in front of him, his chin on his chest, his white hair had come loose and flowed forward now to hide his thoughts.

Sarah closed the edges of the four-inch gash together, pressed a fresh wad of cobweb over it and wrapped the whole with the strips of cloth. She stood up and stretched her back and looked down at

Cragmire. He did not look at her. With fierce, inscrutable eyes, he stared at the newly exposed wall: the books, the painting, the sculptures. Then his eyes fell on his Steward. Frederic cringed.

King Cragmire gestured to him with his good arm, spoke a few words to him, then waved the back of his hand at Sarah, still not making eye contact with her. Frederic bowed low, stepped back, and came to Sarah's side. His eyes were wide and his lips trembled.

"I am required to tell you," he said, "that you are the King's new healer."

CHAPTER TEN

Jonathon

The brush and deepening evening shadows hid the Grue guards on the fortress wall from Jonathon's view. If he couldn't see them, they couldn't see him. But that small comfort barely registered as Jonathon continued to blink in shock at the talisman he had clutched to his ear the second before.

That was Mom's voice! She's here!

He bolted upright then remembered where he was and slouched back down beneath the cover of the branches. He scanned the cliff-like sides of the fortress.

She's in there!

Jonathon had to get behind that wall and find her! His heart hammered against his ribs as he remembered the image of the fierce Grue Deputy in Memgarr's crystal. He filled his lungs and closed his eyes for a moment. Jonathon knew what he needed to do. He had to face his fear of that image to help his mom escape. His dad would have to wait.

Mom needs me.

He looked up to the edge of wall that met the sky. A blur of movement between the crenels told him that watchers still stood on duty. Visions of the storm of arrows that injured one of his Maorrr guides and took the other's life still shivered in his memory.

Nestled beneath the bushes, Jonathon palmed the talisman again, turned it over and over between his fingers and thought about Memgarr's lesson. His gift had special properties, only one of which was the ability to hear through walls and across distances. Memgarr called it a "blender" and said that the other power allowed him to blend in with his surroundings. He recalled being told to rub it over his hand. In the next instance all he could see at the end of his sleeve was the wooden table. When he wriggled his fingers, his hand reappeared. The Maorrr shaman had said he would acquire the knowledge to control the talisman's powers.

Instruction manual not included, so how am I supposed to learn how to control it?

He practiced rolling it over his right hand and then transferring it to the invisible hand to rub over the left one. His first hand reappeared as soon as he started to treat the second one. He tried blending his legs with the same result. As soon as he moved they shimmered back into sight. Jonathon groaned. This wasn't going to this work if he could only blend one part of himself at a time and make it last only while he was still. He thought some more about Memgarr's teachings. He remembered that, in order to hear voices, he whispered a command into the folds. What if he were to command the blending side?

Jonathon thought about what he should say and then held the talisman up to his lips.

"Let me stay blended with what is around me until I want to be seen again." Then he started to rub the talisman around his head and down his front. He stretched to reach his back, shoulders, arms and legs. Problem.

What was he going to do about his backpack? If he blended his backpack and put it down, how would he find it again? He experimented. Jonathon placed his blended hand over the strap. The strap showed through. That didn't work. There was only one thing to do, and that was to blend the whole backpack and not put it down. Ever.

He went through the pockets first to remove anything he wouldn't need, anything that might slow him down. He took out the container of drinking water, had a few gulps and then dropped it into the channel. He emptied out what remained of the food supplies. Those darn nut loaves were heavy! At the last moment he took a bite before he discarded the rest.

He was still chewing when his hand bumped against the slingshot. He hefted it and thought about the eagle. He needed to keep this weapon handy! He attached it to the weapon belt Pugg had given him to wear along with the pouch. He wished Pugg were here! The backpack was a manageable weight again. Jonathon blended it and slipped the straps over his shoulders.

Now he just needed a way in. Blended with the background, it should be easy-peasy—as his mom would say—to sneak around inside the fortress. He was determined to find her and get her out of there. From the vantage of the brush nearest the wall, Jonathon could see where the stream exited under the wall. A curved arch supported the tunnel through which the water flowed—a drainage system from the fortress.

A way in. This will be easy after all!

Wriggling on his belly, Jonathon wormed towards the wall, nervous of the fact that his weight flattened the grassy verge. When he reached his destination he manoeuvred into a crouch beside a pile of crumbled stone.

The water was too murky to tell its depth. When Jonathon lowered himself into the water, he couldn't touch bottom. He dog paddled against the gentle current into the stone tunnel. It smelled rank, like rotting food. The ceiling of the tunnel dripped with moisture.

A couple of metres in, he met his first obstacle.

Okay. Not so easy.

A steel trellis in a diamond-shaped lattice extended from the roof into the water. Little wavelets swirled around the grids. *Did the trellis go all the way to the bottom?* Jonathon gripped the V's of two of the lattices and stretched downwards with his feet. He couldn't feel the bottom of the channel but the lattice ended about two feet below the surface. He could get under that. *Easy!*

Taking a series of deep breaths to fill his body with oxygen, Jonathon pulled himself downwards against the current and kicked to keep from being swept back out the channel. He dragged himself to the spikes on the lower edge of the trellis. The eddies of the water made his manoeuvres trickier than he had expected. Just as he slid himself around the under edge of the trellis, the backpack caught. Jonathon kicked and struggled but remained hooked like a trout.

The swirls of the current blinded him. His air supply bubbled away as he wrestled to free the strap. With one last Houdini twist, he slipped out of the straps and kicked for the surface. He clung to the inside of the trellis, gasping and sputtering until he could once again draw an effortless breath.

Oh, sheep-dirt.

His backpack was gone. He patted his waist. Okay, the news wasn't all bad. He still had the slingshot and pouch and the magic talisman in his pocket.

When he recovered and got his bearings again, Jonathon followed the tunnel as it narrowed and angled upwards. The stream shallowed and became a waterfall, and he slipped and skidded on the climb upwards. The handholds were secure at first in the rugged rock but grew slippery and treacherous the higher he went.

The tunnel flattened a little, and the going became easier for a short while, but the light from the tunnel opening did not follow him around the bend. The sudden darkness made his progress trickier, and the increasing reek threatened to smother him. Unexpectedly, Jonathon crawled out of the water onto dry, smooth rock and patted all around to find out what had happened to the stream. The water that fed the flow drained from a smaller conduit in the side wall of the tunnel. His clothes stuck to him, but he ignored the discomfort and continued to inch forward feeling his way.

Jonathon's fingers scraped against solid wall. He felt all around. The tunnel came to an abrupt halt. His heart raced.

What happened to easy? His breath came in short panicky gasps. *What am I going to do?*

David

The tiny holes for air were hardly sufficient for one let alone two.

The ornately carved box David created as their Trojan offering had been intended to hold just himself. Memgarr had said that the Grue had once loved beauty and art. Perhaps his artwork carved into the rectangular surface would be just the ticket to entice them, tickle their curiosity. David stifled a sneeze when a bit of fur tickled his nose.

When will it be safe to come out?

He badly needed to stretch his legs while the crick in his back and the kinks in his legs screamed for release. Here he was, pretzeled in with the lanky Pugg.

Snugg had endorsed David's plan when he saw how Memgarr's present worked. The story of the Trojan Horse made sense to him, and he was pleased. The only thing that worried him was sending David in alone. Pugg immediately volunteered. He insisted.

"I lost your son, sir. It bein' my duty to bring him to you safe, and I failed. I must come with you to find him."

Tugg and Snuggla each put in their request to go, the youth with typical insistence. Snugg to his credit listened to both of their arguments and only then responded to his heir in a voice of firm authority.

"I need Tugg's strength and experience to cover my back when it comes time to fight and you, my young warrior, be needed to guard our defences here." David smiled to himself when he saw the mutinous look turn to pride.

David reluctantly agreed to take Pugg with him. He could not visualize how he and this rangy San would twist themselves into the box he had created with Memgarr's gift and the largest piece of parchment. But they managed. Snugg's concern had been how they would know when to launch the attack. David gave him a small corner of his remaining square of parchment.

"Keep this with you," David instructed Snugg, "I will send you a message and this parchment is the key for you to receive it. You will know it when the time comes." Snugg examined the blank piece of parchment and then placed it in his pouch.

When David and Pugg sealed themselves into the blackness of the box, the Maorrr lifted them up out of the ravine. The smaller of the San warriors hid behind and positioned the box out in the open where the Grue would see it when the moon rose and hit its carved sides like a spotlight. Another group recovered the fallen Maorrr warrior.

David lost all sense of time. Minutes or hours could have passed when he became aware of a horrible stench permeating through the walls of their box. He tried breathing through his mouth to stifle the urge to heave. Rumbling sounds followed the stench, and then he felt the box sway as they were carried into the Grue fortress.

When the swaying stopped, David heard a tap-tap on the shell of the box. He heard deep rumbling and the higher pitch of two other voices. He sensed the ornate mouldings he had drawn on the sides being pushed and prodded in the effort to find the opening but his design looked solid from the outside and could only be opened from the interior. He had used a simple hook and eye device to secure the door—not sophisticated perhaps but effective. He hoped that whoever was out there would not decide to use a sledgehammer.

All sounds faded away. David thought he heard a distant thunk like the closing of a door, but the sounds were more muffled by the box than he expected. They needed to wait until they were sure the inhabitants of the fortress had settled in for the night, leaving only the guards to worry about.

Time dragged until David could stand it no more. He had not heard a peep from Pugg, just felt the occasional wriggle that let him know the San was still conscious. Slowly, delicately, David wiggled the hook loose from the eye of the fastener and then pushed the door of the box ajar. Fresh air washed over them. He wrinkled his nose. At least it was fresher than the staleness inside their prison. He could still smell the distinctive Grue musk. He stopped his movement and tried to still his heart to listen for any sounds of motion outside of their confinement. The silence was intense.

With the slow deliberation of a snail, David eased himself out of the door of the ornate box he had created. He breathed out heavily, only just stopping himself from exclaiming out loud. He wiped something wet off his hand and onto his shirt. As his feet touched the ground, he turned to help Pugg ease himself out.

They stood together and allowed their eyes to adjust. It was a large room, but sparsely furnished with a long table and enormous carved chair. Half of the back wall was draped while the other half contained floor to ceiling bookshelves.

Eyes. Watching us.

David stepped back into Pugg and clutched his companion's arm as the warrior staggered under the impact. When the silence stretched out unbroken, they looked more closely and realized the eyes were part of an enormous portrait in the middle of the bookshelves. David walked up to it and gazed at the beautiful woman and man who looked regally down on him. Even in the gloom, he was still able to appreciate the intricacy and detail of the artist's skill. A nudge from Pugg brought him back to the moment.

They followed the periphery of the walls and found a draped entrance set in the far corner opposite the door. Together, they slipped behind the curtain and traced their way in the thick darkness of a tunnel-like hallway. Several paces brought them to an opening onto a gallery that overlooked what appeared to be a dining-hall. The large room was empty, so they continued unobstructed to the end of the gallery. A door—small by Grue standards—opened into another narrow hallway, lit at widely spaced intervals by smoky torches. David felt his heart sink in his chest.

Now where do we go? This fortress could be a maze of rooms and hallways. How are we going to find our way to the right corner of the outer wall?

Sarah

The last three days had been a whirl for Sarah as she tended to Cragmire's wound and to the many bumps and bruises incurred by the Grue warriors as they practiced their battle moves. The clanging of metal and the grunts and moans of their training sessions seemed unending. Sarah, exhausted, trudged back to her room to splash some water on her face. She mused that no blood ever seemed to be drawn during these sessions and realized, as she worked among them, that the King's wound was not common knowledge. Only she and Uncle Frederic and the King's Deputy knew. She wondered why it was kept secret. The Deputy had not struck her as someone in the King's trust. But she barely had time to sleep let alone ask Uncle Frederic anything from her long list of questions. And besides, he seemed to be avoiding her.

On her own, Sarah had still managed to find out some details of the castle workings. Like the King's reign was only three years old and it seemed he had yet to firmly establish his authority. His Deputy appeared to have a lot of control behind the scenes. In the battle practices, she noticed that two groups of warriors held themselves apart. One group wore red and gold badges on their shoulders. *Why were they different?* The warrior who saved her bacon on the first night when she delivered the meat stew wore a red and gold badge and would often give her a little salute in the hall. For some reason she felt safer when he was at the practices. His name, she discovered, was Aengus.

The constant call in her new duties as healer to salve bruises and massage knotted muscles, while not taxing on her skills, kept her busy—yet not so busy she forgot her San friend imprisoned in the dank cell below the fortress. Visions of home filled her dreams, and each morning she would wake with her heart aching to sit on the back porch with her husband and her son, listening to the cicadas. She longed to hear David tease the cardinal by imitating his call. Instead, during her waking hours, schemes and worries rolled around in her head. Sarah stressed about the captive's condition and the full moon and its dreadful ceremony marching upon them. She had to find an escape for her friend and for herself. She didn't want to spend the next forty years of her life keeping Uncle Frederic company and staying out of the Deputy's way. But so far, her strategies had been hampered by the close watch upon her by the Deputy's men.

She attended to the King in his war room each day to monitor his wound and change the dressing. Not even the Deputy, thank God, was allowed in this room anymore. Cragmire still wouldn't look at her directly. Sometimes she caught him throwing glances up at the wall that stood exposed. She hummed to herself and pretended that she noticed nothing, but all the time wondered what thoughts could be going through the King's mind as he looked at the delicate art and beauty of his ancestors.

Maybe he's asking himself what happened to his people, and wondering where their culture went?

All of a sudden the absence of her own culture hit her like a slap. She missed them, David, Jonathon and Matthew, with a pain that knifed through her until she could barely breathe. She missed Jonathon rolling his eyes when she gave him a hug and David's smile as he handed her her morning tea. She missed Matthew's quiet sense of humour and homey words of wisdom. She missed her home and long walks down the lane and the farmer's market. The portal had a strange hypnotic power that had drawn her to it. Why did she ever go into the Home Wood? Why did she cross the stream? Her quarrel with David, despite its seriousness, didn't seem reason enough anymore. She'd only intended to walk long enough to cool off. What a mistake! No matter how mad she was, she should have just stayed home and waited for the report. Finding out the truth would have ended the tension between them one way or another.

Sarah's ears rang with the King's sudden expression of wrath— or perhaps *frustration*—and looked up from the distraction of her thoughts and her wound dressing to see him glaring at her. It always made her heart thump when his face twisted like that, but she did not fear for her life like she did around the Deputy. *That* bully had no conscience or qualms. She had seen him strike down an underling for not moving fast enough. Worl did not seem to need a reason to unleash his violence. He enjoyed it. Sometimes she caught a look from him that made her shake down to her toes. The only thing that kept him in check was the King's authority.

Cragmire gestured to the bell pull by the fireplace that called Frederic. She went to it and gave a firm yank. Returning to the King's side, Sarah pretended to fuss with the dressing. She delayed the completion of her task so that she could see Frederic.

It seemed to take forever before a timid knock came at the door. Cragmire roared his command, and when the door opened a crack to admit the Steward, Sarah was relieved to see him. The last time they had a moment to speak was early the evening before, and he had not seemed himself. In fact, he had not seemed himself since the King was wounded by the ceramic shrapnel from his stein.

Sarah passed Uncle Frederic on her way to the door, but he would not look at her. When she reached the door, she stopped and turned and stood very still. He looked like a marionette whose wires were crossed and he could barely navigate his way. Neither Frederic nor the King seemed to notice that she had not left the room. The King spoke at length to his Steward. He gestured wildly, he pointed at the exposed wall then his shoulders slumped, he waved his wound-dressed arm around, his fist slapped the table. At times he seemed almost to plead although Frederic never moved and did not respond. Like two ears on a stick, Sarah thought to herself.

I wonder what is going on. Whatever—it has something to do with the royal injury and the painting.

She read much in the King's body language.

Sarah deduced the meaning of some words since the King magnified them with his gestures. As he motioned skywards, the tumblers fell into place and the thought cracked open in Sarah's mind. The sacrifice!

But is he worried about it? Does he want to stop it?

When the King's rant died away, Sarah was astonished to see Frederic lay a hand on Cragmire's forearm, as one would do to an old friend. He murmured in a low voice. The expression in his eyes and waggle of his eyebrows said volumes. Sarah's own eyebrows raised in dazed realization.

He's making a calm argument like a father to a son.

Frederic carried on until the King raised a hand in surrender, then he squeezed the King's arm in a gesture of comfort before he turned to go. His step hitched as he noticed Sarah standing by the door. Then he continued towards her, keeping between her and the King. Frederic opened the door the slightest crack and pushed her out ahead of him, a finger to his lips requested her to say nothing as he lead her down the hall. The evening torches hung from the walls and chased their shadows ahead of them along the hallways.

Without stopping, Frederic guided Sarah all the way back to her room and followed her in, closing the heavy door behind him. The fire had been lit by one of the lop-eared castle San, and by its glow, for the first time, Sarah noticed that Frederic looked exhausted. His eyes beseeched her. Sarah felt worry tug at her resolve. He needed her help, too.

"Uncle Frederic, please tell me what is happening!"

He shook his head—a brief reminder of how her son Jonathon, as a two-year-old, would deny her when she asked him a question. She pushed that memory deeper into her heart and asked again.

"Please, Uncle, I *must* know." Sarah hesitated for a moment. "What does the King plan to do? Has his injury changed something?"

Startled, Frederic looked at her with panic ringing his eyes. Again he shook his head, his long hair flying about, his face pinched closed. Sarah felt a sudden rush of tenderness and was moved to comfort the old man. She put her arms around him. A sobbing breath heaved his whole frame.

"What am I going to do?" His whisper rasped in her ear. All his resistance drained away as his frail body sagged to the cold stone floor and Sarah followed him down, her arms still cradling him.

"Tell me, Uncle Frederic. Tell me what's wrong."

Another ragged breath shook his chest. He spoke again without looking up.

"I just don't know what to do."

"Can I help you with this, Uncle Frederic?" Sarah's soft tones soothed the old man. He peeked at her through his straggly white hair.

"Tell me what is troubling you, Uncle."

Frederic sighed and sat up straighter.

"I have served the last three Grue kings to the best of my ability. When Cragmire the second died, I took over raising the present King because his stepmother became consumed with revenge against the San. She died, too, practicing to become a warrior in her husband's stead but not before she had filled her son with poison."

"Her son?" Sarah asked.

"Worl—the Deputy—he's the King's half-brother."

"His brother?" Sarah's brain swirled with this twist.

"It's Worl's push," Frederic continued as if she hadn't spoken, "to defeat the San once and for all and revenge his father's death. If he can gain power over his half-brother, the King, along the way, so much the better." Frederic sighed again so long and deeply, Sarah thought he would deflate like a balloon. She wondered whether to ask the question that blazed like a bonfire in her mind and then decided there was no time to lose.

"How does his wound affect the ceremony tomorrow night?" Sarah prompted.

"I loved that little boy."

"What little boy?"

Frederic did not seem to hear Sarah. It was as if the memories were creating old movies in his mind's eye and he was unable to tear his attention away.

"He was a rascal, but I loved him like my own."

The rough edge of frustration rubbed against Sarah's nerve-endings, but words halted in her throat as Frederic spoke again.

"I don't want Cragmire to die!"

CHAPTER ELEVEN

Jonathon

Trapped in the dark at the end of the tunnel under the Grue fortress, Jonathon's breath came fast and furious. His hands patted at the walls on three sides of him. The only way out was straight back down again. It was so dark! He began to feel light-headed and dizzy.

His father's voice echoed in his head. Jonathon then remembered a trick his dad did with Aunt Flo that time he went with his dad when she called all panicky to come quick, someone was trying to break into her house in the village. Turned out, it was just a raccoon hunting scraps through an open kitchen window. The coon had her trapped in a corner when they arrived.

Jon remembered the advice his dad gave his aunt, and he cupped his hands over his nose and mouth and took deep breaths. The heavy staccato of his heartbeat began to slow with his breathing. Now that he could hear beyond his own heart, Jonathon became aware that the blackness had lifted to a flickering grey through a small square above his head. He heard a shuffling sound that had a hesitation to its rhythm as though someone were taking a few steps at a time and stopping to listen in between.

The light and shuffling faded away, but Jonathon's mind's eye could still place the location of the upward chute. He felt the edges of it with his hands and rose to his knees, then to his feet. He squeezed up inside the chute and stretched up to feel for the topside opening. The channel from outside the fortress walls had turned into a shaft beneath a floor that led to this chute. He could get out of here! The walls felt slimy. His fingertips touched the upper rim of the shaft when he stood on his tiptoes. He pushed his back into the wall of the chute and bent his legs to press his knees into the opposite wall. He inched up his knees first, then wriggled up with his backside. The rough edges of stone dug into his back as he eased his way up.

It felt like forever even though it couldn't have been more than a few minutes before Jonathon reached the opening of the chute and pulled himself up and onto a stone floor. Compared to the chute, the room felt vast. Dark but not as pitch black as the tunnel, he could make out some long tables and a huge stone fireplace that housed a bed of glowing coals. A flicker of light through the open slit of a door drew his attention.

Jonathon tiptoed to the opening, mindful to pick up his feet and set them down carefully. He put the talisman to his lips and whispered a command into the ear-like folds then held it up to his ear. He heard snores and snorts. Clumping footsteps. His eyes widened when he heard a squeak similar to the one his runners made on the tile floor at school.

What does that mean?

Then he remembered: His father wore sneakers the morning he went into the Home Wood. Could it be his dad? Then soft shuffling steps, the rhythm of which reminded him of his mother shuffling in her slippers in the morning. The same shuffle-step had traced across the kitchen floor just moments before and led him up and out of the dead-end tunnel. They were now off to his left and getting fainter. It could be his mom. Jonathon decided to follow them. *What did he have to lose?*

The long stone hallways were striped with shadow and torchlight. He came to the foot of a broad staircase under an archway carved out of solid rock and paused to listen. Nothing. But just as he raised himself onto the first step, he heard a heavy tread at the top. He jumped back to the bottom and scurried along the wall until he reached the entrance to a smaller, darker stairway heading down-wards. His talisman may have blended him with the background, but there was no point in taking silly chances! The thumping foot-steps came closer. The smell buffeted the air ahead of the large body heading straight down the hall towards Jonathon.

No choice. Jonathon took the stairs.

David

David and Pugg pushed themselves against the stone wall of the cor-ridor while they took stock of their next move. Torches spluttered at intervals, leaving long stretches of deep shadow for cover. Pugg signed his suggestion for the direction they needed to go in order to reach the outer perimeter of the fortress. Unfortunately, the pas-sageway pointed in a different direction.

With more ear-semaphore, Pugg indicated that he heard no signs of Grue presence from the way ahead and that it was safe to proceed. Staying close to the wall, they threaded their way down the hall from one pool of shadow to the next. Once in a while, David's sneaker squeaked against the stone floor. Each time, he flinched and shrugged an apology to Pugg's fierce but silent reproach.

How did Jonathon get along with this San, he wondered. *He's so prickly.*

David's nose wrinkled. He remembered this smell, this sour Grue smell, from the night of the battle when Cragmire the Second was skewered on the spear held by his younger self. He learned that night that the Grue were a treacherous, cruel people. The mission he and Pugg were charged with—to breach the wall and let in the San and Maorrr troops—would save Meeri's life and halt the latest Grue assault.

Ages passed until they reached the end of the hall, to find that it dead-ended in the direction they needed to go.

Who designed this fortress? It makes no sense! It's like additions have been made to the castle at random.

They seemed to be no nearer their goal. David struggled to keep the rising tide of desperate urgency under control. They had to be at the corner of the outer wall well before dawn to let in the waiting troops. If they were not, the whole mission would fail, Meeri would be sacrificed and many San, Maorrr and Grue would die in the ensuing battle. David's memories of the long ago battle merged with the looming threat. The roars, the thunks and clanks of weapons on bodies and metal, the smell of fear and blood.

How can I keep that from happening again and find Sarah and Jonathon and get them home?

Hand braced against the wall, Pugg pointed his ear down the next hall. A ray of torchlight beamed off the whites of his eyes giving him a fierce, crazed look. Then, with a lightning reflex, the San shoved David back into the shadows.

Sarah

"But, Uncle Frederic, why would Cragmire die?"

The glow from the fireplace cast shadows around them. The last rays of sun from the evening sky gold-etched the window's mullions in Sarah's room away from home. Her arms circled Frederic's shoulders in an effort to comfort him. Still huddled against her on the cold floor of her room, the old man's eyes focused on Sarah. The lines in his face were set in sorrow.

"Have you seen the Deputy lately?" he asked.

"Not much. I have been so busy all day long tending to the bruises and bumps from the practice sessions and changing the dressing on the King's wound—*and* bringing him some of my best dishes—I haven't had time to worry about the Deputy." Sarah crossed her fingers at her fib. Of the list of things on her mind these days, staying safely out of Worl's reach was near the top.

"If the King goes forward with the ceremony on the night of the full moon, he will die."

Sarah's mouth went dry.

"I don't get it, Uncle," she said. "Tell me. Tell me about the ceremony. Why will it kill the King?"

Frederic resettled himself against Sarah's shoulder. It seemed he found it easier to talk to her if he did not have to look her in the eye.

"This is a very ancient ceremony. It hasn't been used since several generations before Good King Cragmire's time. Remember the page in the book on the war room table? Worl blames the defeat that took his father's life on not holding the sacrifice." He paused for breath. "What I found out when I read the book after we found it open...the days leading up to the ceremony must be blood-free so that, on the night of the full moon, the first blood drawn belongs to the sacrifice. This ensures victory for the Grue." Frederic drew in a deep breath.

"This means the King's blood cancels out the sacrifice and puts his own life in danger. He thinks...no, I'm trying to convince...well, maybe if he keeps his injury secret..." He sighed. Frederic wriggled as though his next words were stuck in his throat.

"He thinks...I think...that when...if...his people find out...well, that *he'll* become the sacrifice and his young son will be made King with the Deputy—Cragmire's half-brother—as Regent."

Sarah's breath came out in a disbelieving gasp.

"They would do that?"

"The Deputy would. In a heartbeat, my dear. He and his hand-picked men are cruel and blood-thirsty. Cragmire's son would probably not live the year, and Worl would rise to the throne." Frederic drew in a breath that trembled with emotion. "Worl has never thought Cragmire was tough enough to take his father's place." Frederic twisted to look at Sarah. "But I love Cragmire like a son. I *know* him. He could be great like his grandfather...but... "

"But what has that to do with the Deputy, Uncle Frederic?"

"I have no proof except experience, my dear, but I'm positive the Deputy is plotting against the King."

The expression on the Deputy's face made sense now. That strange almost-smile as he backed out of the King's war room on the day of his injury. Sarah's head felt like it would split with Frederic's information. She knew that the sacrifice of her San friend was meant to bring victory—as crazy it seemed—but now she was about to be caught in the middle of a coup? Home seemed even farther away now. What if the Deputy succeeded? Would she ever see her husband and son again? She had been so hurt by what she saw as David's lack of support when she went to the doctor. Why hadn't she just hung on until the test results had come in? All this would never have happened! Her wounded feelings didn't matter now. All she ached to do was put her arms around him and never let go.

The sudden ring of the bell hanging from the ceiling by the door to summon her, startled them both. They grabbed each other's hands for a steadying moment, and then Frederic accompanied her to the King's side. Sarah did not know whether to be frustrated or relieved that she had no time to think further about the brewing coup and what it meant.

They opened the heavy door to the King's war room. He stood by his chair in deep contemplation. A huge box dominated one end of the King's table. Ornate carvings covered every side of the box. Frederic hurried to Cragmire's side. The King gestured to Sarah to open the box. The sight of the carvings opened up a flood of words from Frederic while the King sat watching intently. The Grue guards who had seen the box were loyal to the King and brought it to his war room with deference. Uncle Frederic said it was known to a few of his most devoted men that he enjoyed artistry and regretted the loss of his grandfather's collection. His trusted guard had brought him the gift.

She poked and prodded and twisted any obtrusion that looked promising. As she moved to the side farthest from the King and Frederic, her eyes jerked to a halt on a delicate, caricature portrait amidst the carvings. She knew that she was being closely watched and dared not react.

"Ohhh...a splinter...I'm okay. Nothing yet."

Sarah ran her fingers over the portrait and then carried on with the search. Her hands found nothing new, but her heart beat fiercely. She did her best to keep a quaver from her voice as she made her report.

"I think that it is just a beautiful piece of art...I can't see any way to open it without destroying it."

Sarah watched Frederic whisper into the King's ear. His eyes narrowed as he stared at her, but then he nodded and gestured them both out again.

Frederic walked her back to her room again, but this time said goodnight and proceeded to his own quarters. Sarah paced her floor. She had to revisit that box in the King's war room. She had to see that portrait again.

Her portrait.

CHAPTER TWELVE

Jonathon

The maze of long stone hallways was staggering. Jonathon had no idea of the time, only that it had been several hours since sundown. He had followed the soft shuffling steps he felt sure belonged to his mom but lost track of them when the approach of a heavier tread of the Grue guard forced him down a staircase and along the lower hall. The narrow stairwell he had ducked into paused on a small square landing in front of a studded door. A waft of air came through the slight opening. He stood still and let his senses stretch out. The air coming through the door was uninviting and dank with moisture but sounds drew him.

Voices.

One voice had the squeak of a San. The other rumbled in a bass that held a taunting cadence. Jonathan squeezed through the opening made by the door and tiptoed down more stairs, confident in his invisibility.

He had also been confident in his silent approach, yet the owners of both voices turned to face the stairs as he reached the bottom.

Jonathan froze and held his breath. A few rapid heartbeats later, they turned to face each other again. *That was close!*

He had been right about the first voice. It belonged to a San female imprisoned behind thick metal bars. Was *she* the mate of the San leader? The one Memgarr said his father would help rescue? She stood with her hands on her hips and ears pointing forwards like sharp daggers. A carved bowl of something meant to be food rested at her feet. Jonathan thought it bore a faint resemblance to meat stew. On its greasy surface floated greenish chunks that were definitely not vegetable. The San kicked the bowl with her toe and toppled it into the dirt. The stains in the dirt of the floor showed this was not the first time.

Her antagonist was a Grue guard. The pock-marked, dirt-streaked skin of his face hung in folds and drool foamed in the corners of his mouth. His pig-like eyes glinted with nasty glee as he poked a long staff through the bars at his captive. Then with a deep rumble of laughter, he knifed his hand across his throat and bent forward to repeat the gesture over and over, letting his tongue loll out and his eyes roll back. Spittle flew as he cackled at his prisoner's distress. Her ears drooped to her shoulders and she turned away to block out the guard's pantomime.

A clattering bunch of keys hung from a thick leather belt around the guard's waist. He jabbed at her again to get her attention and each time he prodded with his staff, the keys clinked together like discordant wind-chimes and the low rumble of his laugh held a cruel mockery. Jonathon remembered that Memgarr had called the missing San Meeri.

How dare the guard treat her like that. It's bad enough she's behind bars like an animal in that horrible cell—but to feed her spoiled meat and taunt her about being sacrificed!

Jonathon felt rage boil up inside him. All the pent-up frustrations and fears of the last few days came roiling out like lava.

A pole with a hook on one end lay on the ground. The type of tool the Grue may have used to place the bowl of slop inside the cell. Silently, Jonathon picked up the pole and poked the Grue in the back and roared as loud as he could.

"How do you like it!"

With an angry growl the Grue whipped around—and saw a floating pole pointed at him. His eyes rolled back in his head. He pirouetted in a mock ballet and hit the floor with a ground-shaking thump. Jonathon saw the 'timber' moment in a slow-motion blur. He had a sick feeling that he would not have time to move out of the way as the huge Grue collapsed towards him.

Jonathon twisted and tried to zig to the side. He all but made it clear when a weight like a tree fell across him and knocked him down. He wriggled beneath the filthy, foul-smelling Grue but his right leg remained trapped. Meeri stood at the door of her cell and peered at the felled guard in wide-eyed astonishment. Jonathon flashed a look over the Grue again and saw the keys lying next to his hand. He gave them a tug. They were still attached to the Grue's belt. He pushed himself forward and wrestled the keys free. The guard never budged. He was out cold.

With the keys in hand, Jonathon took careful aim and flung them at the cell door. Meeri stared at the keys with alarm, her ears twitched wildly. Jonathon spoke to her in San.

"Do not fear," he said. "Leave quickly."

The San captive needed no further encouragement. She snatched the keys up and fumbled a little with their awkward size in her small hands. She found the right key on her second try. The door of the cell squealed as she pushed it open. She hesitated and looked around as she came out, as though searching for the owner of the voice who had freed her.

She can't see me, Jonathon thought.

He felt relief that his invisibility spell still protected him. He watched as Meeri leapt up the stairs, taking them two at a time.

This big lump is still out, Jonathon thought with disgust as he wiggled his trapped leg. The Grue moaned and began to shift. Jonathon grunted as the pressure on his leg increased and then he jerked free. Excruciating pain coursed like lightning as the blood rushed back down through his benumbed leg. He shook his leg like a dog and the pain diminished to tingling.

The guard regained his feet, but he weaved drunkenly and shook his head back and forth, a drool ribbon hung from his lip.

Sheep-dirt! The cell door is open.

To distract the guard so he didn't see the open cell door too soon, Jonathon picked up the pole again and waved it at the Grue, growling for good measure. The Grue's eyes once again rolled back. This time, Jonathon danced out of the way as the guard swayed like a crosscut tree and landed hard. The Grue's head struck the stone floor with the smashed sound of a ripe melon.

Jon's jaw dropped as he looked at the fallen guard. The smush of the Grue's skull striking the stone floor kept echoing through Jonathon's ears. A queasy, hot surge of bile rose up his throat. He only meant to deal back some of the guard's own medicine and delay discovery of Meeri's escape. He didn't mean to injure him. He tip-toed over to the guard's side. His chest still moved but in an irregular pattern and a stain spread from the back of his head along the rough stone flags. Tears burned Jonathon's eyes. He killed the guard! A new sound interrupted the downward spiral of his thoughts.

Footsteps on the stairs. He darted into the shadows behind the fallen Grue. He didn't want to be caught between the new arrival and the dying guard. After all, he was invisible, not disembodied!

The steps came closer. They had a peculiar step-drag quality. His body tensed again as his imagination conjured an image of an enormous Grue with feet like canoes. What was he going to do? He had no way out!

When the source of the sound stepped into the light, Jonathon's brain had trouble processing what his eyes saw.

Sarah

No question.

Sarah *knew* she was right. The picture on the side of the carved box contained a message meant just for her. She paced the small bedroom and found herself before the mullioned window staring down into the overgrown garden. For a moment, the continuous stress of five days' worth of uncertainty and malicious individuals threatened to overwhelm her. She blocked the rise of tears until they stuck in her throat and tightened into a lump. She had to keep in control. Just a while longer. Only *he* could have drawn that little portrait placed inside an anatomically shaped heart. David was here! She didn't have to face this place all alone, anymore.

First off, to prove her theory, she had to see the box again and examine it for any other cryptic messages besides the picture drawn into the intricate design. Sarah had only seen it briefly, but she recognized it. Years ago David had drawn a caricature of her riding a hobbyhorse and put it on a hand-made anniversary card.

...our fourth anniversary of when we first met in university and we were both broke students.

The caricature was sweetly drawn, but it had been a joke between them—he kidded her that she liked to take on lost causes and win. Anyone in the fortress would have difficulty recognizing her in the little drawing. But she knew. David was here. It was more than that, though. She paced another circle around the room before ending up in front of the window again.

Sarah felt a deeper meaning in the subject of the portrait. The drawing came from a time in their lives when she knew he always had her back. When she could count on him. This portrait and the heart that surrounded it told her that her husband's old reliable self had returned and that she could count on him again. He had come to rescue her because that's what happens when you're trapped in a castle. You get rescued. She put her hand on her chest, her heart beat with a thrum like hummingbird's wings. For the first time in days, the slightest smile trembled around her mouth as a tear sparkled on her cheek.

She decided to take the narrow servant stairs down to the kitchen and then wind her way back up to the King's war room. There was less chance of being caught by a roving guard. Once in the pitch-black of the kitchen, Sarah lit a torch from the peat banked fire. She crossed the room with unsure steps. Would the light give her away? She had to take the chance—unless the sconces in the hall were still lit. Then she would blow out her torch, keep to the shadows and only relight it when she got to Cragmire's war room.

As quickly as she could, Sarah traversed the long hall and then down another corridor, past the entrance to the warriors' dining hall to reach the stairway that would take her up to the passageway leading to the King's war room. First she had to cross the dark well of a downward stairway whose long hall below, she remembered, led towards the dungeons and the cavernous cell where the San captive was kept. She hoped to come back this way soon and free her friend. She had tried to send the San food that she could tolerate, but she found out through Uncle Frederic that her efforts had been prevented by the cell guard.

When Sarah reached the war room, the box rested on the table, just as she had left it.

No, not *quite* as she had left it.

The symmetry of the box seemed off. Sarah lit her torch from the banked fire in the grate and braced it where she would be able to examine the edges more closely—and the portrait tucked into the intricate design on the end of the box away from the King's chair. Her insides fluttered. *David.* He had definitely been here. However, did he know how to find her?

Sarah continued her examination. She moved around to the long side that met the edge of the table and could see why the symmetry of the box was disturbed. The whole surface was a door, slightly ajar, and it swung open on a hinge. Sarah pulled the door all the way open and looked inside. Just an empty box. She shone the torch into the box and reached down to touch a dark stain on the floor of the container. Immediately, she pulled her hand back in shock.

Blood.

Sarah wiped her sticky fingers against the inside of the container door, then carefully pushed it almost-but-not-quite-shut again so that it looked more as it had when first carried to the King's war room. Anticipation and alarm fizzed in equal proportion down every nerve. David had been inside this box.

Was he alone? Is this his blood?

She had to find him.

With her rush torch lighting the way, Sarah discovered drops of blood on the floor leading from the box to the smaller door that overlooked the warriors' dining hall. She followed. She smudged the droplets so they would be less noticeable to a patrolling Grue guard. Towards the end of the hall Sarah paused, then drew in a sharp breath of alarm.

Oh, dear God!

A red handprint on the wall. It looked a little oddly shaped, but she didn't have time to think as she wiped all traces of it into the stone. She had to find him *fast*.

At the corner, she paused and listened. Uncle Frederic had told her that, most of the night, guards patrolled the outer walls, but at least one prowled the hallways. She did not want to run into him. If the hall watch that night was one of the Deputy's men, the meeting would not go well for her. They had continued to treat her roughly with Worl's blessing when she attended the practices to salve injuries. The King's warriors provided protection in the daylight hours. In her rush to reach the King's war room, she hadn't considered the consequences if a Deputy's man discovered her alone.

Sarah followed the red trail downstairs and along a long hallway to another stairway entrance, but lost track of the drops of blood. With her rush torch searching the floor, Sarah continued on down the hall. She paused frequently to examine the floors and walls and to listen for footsteps that would betray the guard's approach. Not a single red molecule betrayed David's direction. Her heart beat so hard her breath caught. Every moment she traversed the halls increased her danger, but she had to find David. He didn't know this place at all, he couldn't possibly know the danger that he, too, was in.

Which way did he go?

Sarah paused to calm herself.

She must have missed the turn. The drumbeat in her chest ratcheted up again. Perhaps her husband went down the stairs after all.

As she turned to retrace her steps, a 'hssss' from behind froze her feet to the ground. Her overworked heart leap-frogged into her throat and Sarah saw black when a hand grabbed her arm.

David

David's inner antenna had become attuned to his companion's signals. They stood together in one of the stripes of dark shadow between the hall torches. Another long hall that didn't lead where they needed to go. They had to find the way to a ground level door that would take them out to the courtyard of the Grue fortress and work their way to the corner of the outer walls that way. The shiver of Pugg's sensitive ears said he picked up something. David trusted the San's ears more than his own. The silence was thick enough to chew. The hall, banded with torchlight, was empty. David's skin prickled with tension.

Will these darn halls ever head in the right direction?

When he thought of his wife trapped within these walls, he would volunteer to be in that box all over again just to find her. David recalled the effort it took to scrunch himself in beside Pugg in the box created as a gift to the Grue with Memgarr's charcoal pencil and parchment. Would Sarah be able to see the message he had sketched into the end of the box? Or was she a prisoner somewhere in this enormous fortress? In the swirling mists of Memgarr's crystal, Sarah had seemed to be standing against one of these walls, but she also looked afraid. David pushed down his fear for her. And where was his son? Pugg had last seen him outside the fortress walls. Had Jonathon found himself a safe hidey-hole? He hoped so. His son knew how to take care of himself outdoors. But in this world? The farm and boy scouts had few skills to offer to prepare him for this.

Damn! It's my fault he's here. Why didn't he stay home with Gramp?

David caught Pugg as he stumbled and the San rewarded him with a grimace. What happened between Pugg and Jonathan that had created such loyalty in so short a time? He could read in the San's actions a devotion that went beyond duty.

An inky black hole in the wall revealed a staircase down. Down they went. Surely, David reasoned, there had to be a hallway to take them towards the outer wall soon. At the foot of the stairs, Pugg stumbled again and David caught his arm. He dared not speak but signed with his hands to ask if the San was okay. Pugg nodded and straightened to lead the way again. He stopped and swivelled his ears to face back up the stairs. David heard it, too. A faint shuffle. They pulled back into the shadows and waited.

A figure appeared at the head of the stairs. A slim figure, curly auburn hair, highlighted by a wall torch. David gasped and lurched forward. Sarah! Pugg gripped him and held him back, a firm palm across David's mouth.

Sarah passed across the stair opening and continued down the hall, leaving darkness behind her.

David turned to Pugg, his eyes burning with emotion. The San refused to remove his hand until David promised not to give away their position by speaking. Then Pugg signed with emphatic pulses of his ears and hands that their first mission was to find the outer wall and let the allied warriors in. Anguish squeezed David's core.

To be so close...

He nodded his head despite the resistance in his heart. They needed to complete their mission. Sarah was here and she appeared to be well and unharmed.

Oh, to hell with the mission!

David started up the stairs, but Pugg put a vise on his arm and dragged him back to the bottom. He gestured for silence and then

David heard it. Light footsteps following behind Sarah. He couldn't risk exposing their position to a castle dweller.

Damn! So freaking close...

The halls seemed endless stretching away in irregular stripes into infinity. David shook his head to clear it. The air was Grue sour. He focused on the shape of the area between the stripes in the wall and saw that they had reached another opening to a downward stairwell. Pugg led the way down the first half dozen stairs and paused to listen by an open studded door. He motioned for David to go back up the stairs but staggered to a stop in the deep shadow. David caught him, back-stepped down a step and bumped into something soft that squealed.

Sarah!

The soft body attempted to flee, but David grabbed her and pulled her to him, lifting her face to the light.

Not Sarah.

David looked down into the frightened violet eyes of a San female. Filthy, she was about the same height as Sarah and her ears, tethered downwards by a swathe like a kerchief of fine brown-red leather the colour of Sarah's curls contributed to his mistake. Meeri. She continued to struggle in David's arms until she saw Pugg and she went still. Speaking through sign-language with his hands and ears, Pugg told Meeri that they were here to find a way to let the army in to save her.

Meeri waved off his explanation and signed back.

"What is wrong with you?"

Pugg straightened slightly, but his back still bowed. He in turn pushed aside her question, but she would have no defiance. Pugg shifted, then, into the light and showed her the hole in his tunic on his flank. Blood congealed like thick jelly around the rent in the fabric and fresh blood still oozed. David bit his lip to keep from exclaiming.

How had this stubborn San warrior stayed on his feet? Even as he thought it, he saw Pugg's knees give out and he sagged to the stone step. Meeri knelt down to hold him and put pressure on his wound. With great effort, Pugg pushed her away so that he could sign to her.

"You must take my place."

Meeri shook her head.

"You *must!*" Pugg's lips were drawn back over his teeth in a grimace. "We will change clothing. Take me back to where they kept you."

David added his silent protest to Meeri's, but the fierceness in Pugg's eyes gave him pause.

"I cannot go any further. I cannot help you find your son. I am dying." Pugg's eyes closed for a moment but then gathered himself to finish.

"Meeri is a warrior, too. She will guide you in my stead."

CHAPTER THIRTEEN

Sarah

"Wake up, my dear. Wake up."

She opened her eyes to Uncle Frederic's worried basset hound gaze. The long hallway stretched away from both sides of them and the cold flagstone floor chilled all the parts of her it touched. Her head rested on Uncle Frederic's outstretched legs. The flickering torches made her feel dizzy as she returned to full consciousness.

"Come my dear. We can't stay here." Sarah felt foolish for letting fright overcome her. She couldn't remember ever fainting before. She nodded, gripping Uncle Frederic's arm to steady herself as she stood and regained her feet. He started to lead her back in the direction of her room. Sarah resisted and put her mouth to his ear.

"David is here, Uncle Frederic." She leaned back again to look him in the face. "Help me find him." Her eyes implored.

"What?" Confusion flickered across Frederic's face. "My nephew! But if Worl finds him first..."

She watched the struggle of emotions cross his pale features punctuated by the waggle of his eyebrows. He shook his head.

"I have to go back to watch over the King." He placed his hand on Sarah's arm. "I only came out to check on you because I had a feeling something was wrong when you saw the box. I have to go back."

From their long conversations, Sarah understood his first loyalty lay with the King—he had grown up and grown old protecting Cragmire—and he feared any action that might cause his King harm. But she needed him too. Right now.

"But David can help us save the King, Uncle Frederic. I know he can."

The indecision in the old man's face firmed into resolve. He bobbed his head.

"Let's find him."

Sarah led the way back to the stairwell where she had last seen the trail of blood. Holding the rush torch lower, she saw what she had missed. Drying blotches stained the stairs going downwards.

Even the air seemed to tingle with the anticipation Sarah felt at the possibility of seeing her husband again. More than a week had passed since she had flung herself out of the back door of the farm-house. All the fury she had carried with her into the Home Wood had long since evaporated. He had come for her like her shining knight. Angry? After all the dangers of the last week, the quarrel from home, founded on apparent indifference on David's part and hurt on hers, seemed not important enough anymore to keep them apart.

The droplets of blood drew them along the maze of hallways until another small stairwell was reached. A smudge of red, like an arrow, smeared the edge of the stairs and then disappeared. Sarah recognized the direction of these stairs. She crushed Uncle Frederic's hand. He gave her a look mixed of compassion and pain and she eased her grip. Together they followed the treads downwards to the heavy studded door at the base.

The door was ajar. Silence weighted the sour air that wafted through the narrow space. A small red dab on the jamb of the door pointed their way anew. Sarah and Frederic eased the door back on its hinges and then pulled it closed once more behind them.

More stairs.

A coiled boa of fear slithered up Sarah's body and squeezed the breath out of her lungs. Was David really down here? Was he mortally wounded? The red trail they had been following bespoke a heavy loss of blood. Her heel caught on the edge of a riser, and she stumbled and cursed her clumsiness. Uncle Frederic caught her by the elbow and steadied her, squeezing her arm to still her. Sarah tried to mute the thud of her heart to hear whatever had stopped him. She looked at the old man, her mentor, and then followed the direction of his gaze.

Poking out of the shadows were the feet of a supine Grue.

Sarah and Uncle Frederic went down the last few steps and approached the sprawled guard. He lay very still. A slight gurgle expelled from his throat. Then silence. A dark pool spread out from the back of his head. There was no more hope for him.

Where's David?

Sarah backed away and looked towards the cell.

Beyond the open barred door another figure lay prostrate on the stone floor stained with the ruins of stew.

Oh dear God! What's happened to her?

Sarah handed the torch to Uncle Frederic to hold. Panic fuelled her feet. Sarah flew into the cell and lifted the San's head onto her lap. The eyes fluttered a bit and opened slightly. Blue eyes.

Sarah gasped.

"Uncle Frederic! This isn't her. Where could she be?"

David

A suffocating balloon of sadness expanded in David's chest as he cradled Pugg in his arms and carried him down the stairs and past the fallen Grue guard. In the hours of their joint mission to breach the wall of the Grue fortress, David had grown to admire the San's determination and toughness. He could see now how Jonathon and Pugg grew close in such a short period of time. Pugg moaned as David set him down on the floor of the cell. Meeri supported his head and looked at him with huge sad eyes. The pain in that moment felt familiar to David. A black tinged memory. With a deep breath downwards, he forced the thought beneath the surface. David gave Meeri a gentle nudge and signed to her. "You must change with him."

"What do you mean 'change'?"

The words, spoken out loud, made both Meeri and David jump.

Where did that voice come from?

It was a voice he knew like his own. David saw nothing at first. Then the air seemed to shimmer and the outline of a body became visible and started to fill in like a line-drawing in a colouring book. Stunned for less than a heartbeat, David lunged forward and wrapped his son in a bear hug. He bit his tongue to keep from spilling out all he was feeling.

How the heck did he get here?

Instead he poured his love into the hug he folded around his son and held him like the moment would never end. But then he felt Jonathon push back.

"Dad, what's wrong with Pugg?" He said aloud in a voice that seemed to echo off the walls.

Jerked back to the business at hand, David signed in response.

"We must be quiet. We don't want to be discovered."

Jonathon nodded. An array of emotions played with his expressions as he searched his father's face. Devotion and tenderness gazed back. Jon rested his forehead against his dad's chest.

David signed again. "I will explain. Pugg had been wounded by Grue archers." David glanced over at the fallen warrior. "But he didn't tell us. He wanted to help me find you."

He watched his son kneel, then, beside his the fallen San. Jon took Pugg's hand and whispered into one long, drooping ear.

"Pugg, it's me. Jon. Please look at me. Don't die, Pugg."

The wounded warrior moaned and struggled to open his eyes.

"I see you, lad...You will make a fine warrior one day..." The San's hoarse whisper trailed off, and his eyes closed again. Tears blurred Jonathon's vision.

David felt a familiar blackness edge his thoughts, but he pushed it away and allowed himself instead to feel his heart squeeze for his son's loss of a good friend. Time, however, would not wait for them. He risked the consequences of sound and whispered into Jonathon's ear.

"Meeri must change clothes with Pugg. He volunteered to take her place so that her rescue won't be detected too soon." David pressed his son's shoulder. "This is Pugg's plan."

Jonathon nodded. Together they removed the warrior's weapon belt and tunic and handed them to Meeri who awaited them in the shadows. Then they dressed Pugg in Meeri's clothes.

Out of the corner of his eye, David saw Meeri attempt to clean off the congealed blood and disguise the rent in the tunic. She placed the weapons through the clasps around the belt. Soon she bristled with weaponry like the fiercest San warrior.

David suggested that they move Pugg to the stone bench that had been Meeri's bed and arrange him to appear asleep.

At the moment the three of them circled Pugg to lift him up, a noise, faint but unmistakable, tumbled down from the stairwell.

David signalled to Meeri and Jonathon, and they faded back into the darkest corner of the cell. He saw two figures, shadowed behind a rush torch, enter the vestibule of the cell and approach the fallen Grue. Then they turned towards the cell. The torch changed hands as one of the figures ran ahead to the supine San. The companion came forward with the torch. Light fell on the first figure's face.

Sarah's lovely face.

His feet grew roots and his voice strangled in his throat. A sharp poke in the side woke him from his daze and he stepped forward.

"Sarah!"

His voice was constricted by emotion and her name came out in straggled a croak.

She turned and saw him come out of the shadows into the light cast by the torch. Her sherry eyes shimmered with tears in the torchlight. Her lips moved, but no sound came out. She threw her arms around his neck and strangled him with her embrace. The mission forgotten for the moment, nothing felt sweeter than this.

Jonathon

As Jonathon watched the shadowy figure kneel over his San friend's body, he was startled to see Pugg's eyes flutter open again for a moment. Pugg was tough. Could he survive? Then the torchlight shifted and illuminated the stranger's face.

Mom. She's here. I knew it!

With rising joy, he looked up at his father only to see David turned to stone.

What the heck? Is he still mad?

Anger and fear that his parents' scrap had followed them powered the sharp poke he gave his father. But then in the next moment, his mother's fierce hug and the tears on his dad's face relaxed Jonathon's worry for his parents. He stepped forward and put his arms around them both.

Sarah gasped when she saw Jonathon. Tears flowed down her face as she turned to put both arms around him.

"What are *you* doing here?"

The look on his mother's face was impossible to read entirely.

"Mom, can we save Pugg?"

He saw her turn to Pugg and kneel beside him. Pugg's eyes were shut. She placed her ear on his chest then looked up and, with saddened eyes, shook her head. That's when Meeri came forward into the light. Jon's mom jumped up to give her a quick hug.

She signed, "I am so happy to see you, my friend."

Meeri's ears dipped in acknowledgement, her large violet eyes shone in the torch's glow.

"We gotta go," David said.

The four of them lifted Pugg, set him to rest on the stone bench that had been Meeri's bed and arranged his limbs in the posture of sleep.

David stepped back and signed, "We will come back for him. Now we must go."

"What is with all this sign-language?" An aggrieved voice asked aloud.

Jonathon realized that none of them had paid any notice to the torch-bearing figure. Sarah stretched out a hand and placed it on the arm of a snowy haired old man and moved the torch so that it shone into his face. To Jonathan he looked a lot like his Gramp except with whiter hair and amazing shaggy eyebrows.

"Uncle Frederic," Sarah whispered, "can you take us somewhere where we'll be able to talk without being overheard?"

Uncle Frederic? The one Dad and Great Aunt Louise talked about?

CHAPTER FOURTEEN

Sorrow dragged Jonathon and David's movements as they closed the barred cell door and left Pugg's body behind. Meeri and the reunited family followed Frederic, single file, down a narrow stone corridor away from the prison cavern along uneven flagged floors through a rough arched doorway. The room within smelled sour and stale—a safe place to discuss the mission. David swung the torch around the walls and wished that he could block out the vision forever. Instruments of torture lined the walls and filled a rotting wooden table that rested in the centre of the room.

Frederic's gaze followed the torchlight around the walls and he gulped several times. David studied him for a moment and wondered. His uncle led them in here. Was his shock real? When the old man ripped his stare away from the walls, he fastened his eyes upon David's face and leaned forward as though to examine David more closely.

"You look like someone I went to school with," Frederic said, his voice thick with memory, "many, many years ago. I remember sea-green eyes and she had beautiful cheekbones...you have her eyes."

David was stunned. Uncle Frederic was talking about his mother, a woman whose beauty went beyond her face. Her gentle soul ruled the James house until the day she left. She left him—David shook his head to clear the familiar blackness that threatened to block his vision—except of course she *didn't* leave. "You have her eyes." Frederic's words repeated in David's head. He reeled and put his hand out to steady himself.

"David..." said Sarah. "Are you all right?"

Jon saw his father gasp and sink to his knees.

"Dad?"

"David?"

Sarah's eyes brimmed with tears as she watched her husband struggle with the memory that he had so long refused to acknowledge.

He was quiet for a moment, as though trying to catch his breath. "I can still see her, Sarah."

"Who?"

"My mother. She's lying in a coffin...in the parlour."

"But David, you—"

"When we were arranging poor Pugg on that stone slab, I could feel it surfacing—that memory—like a terrifying whale threatening to breach and crash down on me. And when you went to the doctor's, I just—"

David looked to Frederic, who seemed confused.

"You knew her in life," said David. "But my mother passed away a long time ago, when I was just a boy."

"That grieves me, David," said the old man. "Truly. She was a beautiful person. How did she die?"

Before David could answer, Sarah knew what he was going to say, and it broke her heart.

"Cancer."

Frederic walked over and put his hand, for the first time, on his nephew's shoulder.

"I am sorry. That must have been very difficult."

Then with the skill of a man used to deflecting issues and navigating difficult situations, Frederic turned to address the others.

"So how are we going to save the King?"

Jonathon looked at his uncle then back and forth between his father and his mother. He wasn't sure what had just happened, and now he was even more confused.

"Save the King? *Which* king?" Jonathan asked. He looked at Meeri who had taken a step back and was regarding them all warily. "The Grue king, who is trying to sacrifice Meeri and wage war on the San? *That* king?"

"Yes," said Frederic with waggling eyebrows and a voice that betrayed nothing at all. "That King. How are we going to protect him?"

David shot Sarah a questioning look.

"I promised Uncle Frederic that you would help us save the King. He's in great danger from his half-brother, Deputy Worl, who's plotting to take over." She paused to glance at Uncle Frederic. He nodded encouragement.

"The King's not the threat to the San," she said. "It's the Deputy. If we can protect the King, we can stop the war."

David looked at Meeri to see if she understood what was being said and then translated for her since Sarah was in too great a rush to sign her message. Meeri hesitated and looked from one to the other. Her eyes, their expression unreadable, seemed to rest longest on the old man with the white bushy brows.

Sarah grasped the tension between the two, remembering Uncle Frederic's seeming nonchalance about the captured San's fate. He had grown old steeped in two Grue generations of intense, irrational dislike of their neighbours. She pictured the first day when Uncle Frederic showed her the kitchen gardens and reluctantly helped her find vegetables for her now-famous meat stew. He confessed later that, with the King's blessing, he helped the castle San maintain in secret the purposely overgrown gardens, and Sarah came to realize that Frederic's apparent indifference to the San was all about survival. The Deputy had been known to beat an unlucky castle San half to death just for standing too close. Worl created a poisonous, deadly environment. Frederic did what he could to make the castle San happy and healthy, but he didn't dare let anyone allied with the Deputy catch him at it. The inhabitants of the fortress, Grue and San alike, were victims of the Deputy's brutal bullying. Sarah despised bullies. But at this moment there was still a tension between Frederic and Meeri to fix.

"Uncle," Sarah said, "Meeri and the San are the King's only hope. Without their help, we have no chance of defeating the Deputy. If we can—"

"Hang on, I only came here for you and Meeri," David said. "Now that I have both of you, why should I put everyone at risk again to save the son of the king who tried to kill me?" Even as he said the words aloud a memory of something Memgarr had said to him wavered. Something about the son carrying on the father's work. He couldn't quite put his finger on it and it slipped away.

Sarah drew in a quick breath and Uncle Frederic stiffened beside her, but David saw his son smile at him and nod proudly as though he knew a secret. A small glow grew in his core.

"You've encountered the Grue before?" Sarah asked, her eyes wide with astonishment.

"Yes," David said. "When I was Jonathon's age, I came through the portal and landed in the middle of a war between the San and the Grue." He rubbed the scar on his scalp. "I got this in the battle, and the San placed me back at the portal. Searchers found me in the Home Wood. That's why my father has always been so adamant that I—or anyone else in the family—stay out of the Home Wood. He worried someone *else* might go missing."

They both turned to look at Uncle Frederic whose face had closed in on itself as he seemed to contemplate something deep within himself. Sarah placed a hand on Frederic's arm to draw his attention. She noticed a tear leak from the corner of his eye and wrapped him in a hug.

"I always wondered," the old man whispered almost to himself. "who it was that killed the old brute because I thought he was too tough for the San to kill." His voice gained strength. "I tried to raise his son to be more like his grandfather, Good King Cragmire the First. I did my best, but my King's stepmother and then his half-brother, the Deputy, did everything in their power to destroy the beauty of the Grue—they saw it as weakness—and remake themselves as conquerors. This war with the San is the Deputy's push, I swear." He raised his eyes to his nephew's face and gazed at him with budding hope.

"Can you help me save my King?"

David looked down into his uncle's eyes, and it seemed for a moment as though his father gazed back at him. He missed his dad's gentle wisdom. He had a lot to share with him—and apologize for—when they returned. *If* they returned. He gave himself a mental shake. And what if they brought Uncle Frederic back with them?

"You will have to tell me more about Cragmire, Uncle, but right now our time is running short. We need to find our way to the outer wall before dawn...which can't be far off now."

Frederic's mouth firmed into a stubborn line.

"You must promise me, that you will help me to save King Cragmire."

Sarah could tell by the look on David's face that he was about to launch into Frederic for his blind devotion to Cragmire—after all he had nothing to go on but their too brief discussion—but she knew that nothing would be served by it.

"More than anything," she said, drawing her husband's attention, "I want to just go home with you and Jonathon and start over again, but David, we must help them. The Grue people are victims, too. Of Worl's bullying, treachery and war-mongering. If we just sneak away, it won't stop the war. We have a chance to make a change here. What if we can help restore the balance?"

"Restore the balance?" Jonathan sounded incredulous. "But Mom, that's crazy. If the current king is really such a good guy, and it's only this *deputy* of his that's the real problem, then what are we talking about? Why does he need *our* help? I mean is he king or not? Whose castle is this anyway? It sounds like he needs to sit his butt in the throne and act like a king for crying out loud."

Sarah didn't have an answer for that. She looked to Frederic.

"Jonathan," the old man said well aware that he now had four sets of eyes on him. "It's more complicated than that. Or...maybe it's not. Cragmire has grown up with nothing but the hate of his step-mother and half-brother around him. He has a good heart, I *know* he does. When your mother showed him the truth of the past greatness of the Grue he began to see a different path for his people. He knows he must be strong for them. And he can be. I'm sure of it. Maybe if he'd grown up with you to advise him instead of me..." Frederic looked genuinely pained. "I will tell you this though. Mark my words, if the Deputy manages to wrest the throne away for himself, the reign of

Worl the First will make the Reign of Cragmire the Third look like a sunny day at the beach."

"So wait!" David said. "You're really saying that it's not the King who is behind the sacrifice and the threat of war?" Frederic nodded again.

"It's his half-brother, the Deputy. He's forcing the issue and plotting behind the King's back."

In a blinding flash, David recalled the whole of Memgarr's speech atop the Maorrr stronghold. The evil son he spoke of was not the King but the brother! He told them about the prophecy.

David could sense his son chewing on a comeback.

"What do you think, son?" he said. "Do we help the Grue and the San back to peace?"

Jonathan thought of Pugg. He looked to Meeri and thought about the faces he'd seen at the San village.

"Yes, Dad. I think we need to help."

David turned to Frederic.

"Okay, deal."

"I can show you a short way to the wall." Uncle Frederic nodded his head so vigorously that his long unruly locks of white hair flew about his face as though caught in a high wind. David laid out the strategy. They already had the rescue plan in place, so it only needed a couple of tweaks to include the King.

With a quick sketch of words, David outlined the changes to the plan. He looked to Meeri to see if she understood and agreed. With a graceful dip of her ears, she indicated her accord. His wife caught his sleeve as he turned to lead them out of the torture chamber.

"Wait." Sarah stopped them. "We have to hide the guard's body first. It could spoil our plans before they're in motion if he's found too soon. And at the time of the ceremony, we will need someone to take

Pugg's place." Her eyes were sad. "We need a live body to be brought out to the altar. What can we do?"

"First let's get out of here," David squeezed her shoulder, "and get the plans moving. We still have a few hours to figure that one out."

"And Dad, I want to go with you."

David felt his pride glow as he regarded his son. He reached out and squeezed Jonathon's shoulder.

"More than anything...more than *anything*, I would love to have you come with me, but I need you to see Meeri safely back to the San encampment. I'm counting on you. I'll wait for the contingent on this side...if we have too many alien faces like ours hanging about we have more risk of being caught."

"But Dad, I can—"

"Sorry, Jonathon. We must get a move on. If we're not in position by dawn, our chance will be lost." Jonathon hung his head and agreed.

It took all of their combined strength to move the Grue guard. He had grown stiff and cold. Uncle Frederic searched out a long disused cell thick with moss and mold and then guided them as they carried their stinking burden. Sarah went back to the spot where the guard had fallen and kicked sand over the expanse of blood that had drained from the guard's broken skull. Jonathon, it seemed to her, had an ashamed air. She gave her son a thoughtful look.

Then Uncle Frederic took the lead and guided them down a narrow warren of little-used passageways until they ended at a cramped upward staircase that looked as though it had not seen use in decades. At the top of the stair, a short tapered door of petrified wood opened with a moan into an overgrown garden. At last, they were out in the open air. The small group huddled together under the black-green darkness of a willow's drooping bows. The spray of bright beams from the nearly full moon deepened the shadows.

Uncle Frederic raised his arm and pointed the way to the outside wall. Now they were outside that horrible room, they were again limited to signs and the briefest of whispers. David took only Jonathon and Meeri with him. A few moments later, he became aware that Sarah and Frederic trailed behind them. They followed the shadows and moved slowly so the eyes of a guard on the top of the wall would not be drawn to their movement. Fortunately the section of wall they needed was sheltered from above by an over-growth of ivy. The ivy created a little cave against the stone in which they could stand.

David unwrapped his magic charcoal from Memgarr and sketched a door and heavy-duty doorknob on to the solid rock. Then he drew a square about eye-level with hinges and a handle. He waited a couple of moments and then pulled on the handle and opened the peep hole. He stood frozen to the spot, dismay weighing his limbs.

Leading away from the fortress, the blaze of unobstructed moon-light lit the ground before them like a stage. How were Jonathon and Meeri going to get safely across now? They would be fully exposed to the guards on the ramparts.

CHAPTER FIFTEEN

"Damn!"

At David's exclamation, Jonathon squeezed in beside his dad. He saw dismay sketched across his father's face. As they gazed out onto the moonlit plain through the opening of the door created with Memgarr's magic charcoal, the stretch glowed like a stage between the outer wall of the fortress and the shadowed protection of the trees. The wide expanse of bare ground left Jonathon and Meeri's escape route bright and exposed to the arrows of the guards on the battlements above. David waved them back and started to close the door.

Jonathon stood firm, however, and pulled Memgarr's talisman out of his pocket and held the shell-like side to his ear. At first he heard only silence but then, in a few heartbeats, a faint rustle of movement from the direction of the battlements, feet trudging on stone. Moving away from them. He risked a whisper.

"Dad, I can get Meeri and me across the space safely."

David shook his head. It was impossible.

"Trust me, Dad."

A new timbre in Jonathon's voice made David take another look at his son. He could see a glimmer. Something different in his son, a heightened confidence present in the tilt of Jonathon's chin and the tone of his voice. The events of the last few days had matured his son years beyond his age. David felt both proud and sad. His son had strength and an edge to his intelligence tempered by recent experience. It seemed like he had grown six inches in the last three days. David nodded and gestured for Jonathon to share his proposal.

Jon's plan started with a demonstration. When he had stalked the halls following his mother's footsteps, he had noticed an interesting characteristic of his invisibility. In the same manner that Memgarr had taught him, Jonathon knew that showing how the talisman worked would pack the best wallop in the delivery of his idea. He reached for Meeri's arm and began to rub the smooth side of the talisman over her as though erasing her existence. With each stroke, Meeri disappeared a little more. At first her look of astonishment made Jonathon smile. Then understanding replaced her disbelief as she allowed Jon to pull her arm out of the shadows and the hand she could no longer see shed no shadow in the moonlight.

"See Dad? This stone will make us like glass. The moon will shine straight through us and we'll be safe."

Stunned for several moments, David absorbed this new Memgarr magic, and then he clapped Jonathon on the shoulder. "Way to go, Son!"

Another heartbeat passed and he couldn't stand it anymore. David gave in to impulse and clutched Jonathon in a bear hug. His son looked a little embarrassed. David smiled and whispered in his ear. "I know, I know...next time fist bump."

Jonathon looked past his dad to his mother's tense face.

"I'll be all right, Mom. This will be easy. They'll never see us."

Sarah rewarded her son with a half smile. She wasn't ready to feel happy about this situation yet. Not with her son here in the same dangerous place as that lunatic Deputy, his band of madmen and a coup brewing. She wouldn't be happy or breathe easy now until they were all out and on their way back to the portal. She slipped her hand into David's and crushed his fingers together.

"We will see you in the camp," David said. "Remember what to tell Snugg?"

Jonathon bobbed his head as he finished with Meeri and then proceeded to rub the talisman over himself. When he was done, he tucked the talisman into the pouch on his belt, reached out to where he knew Meeri had last been standing and felt for her hand. She grasped him tightly.

Together they stepped out onto the stage created by the moonlight. The ground was a little uneven and strewn with rocks but otherwise unobstructed for several hundred steps right to the tree-line. Just over half-way, Jonathon tripped over a loose stone and sent it rattling. He looked up at the battlement. Was that movement? A moment later the head and torso of a Grue guard stretched forward through the narrow gap of the crenel with a bow and arrow. He leaned further out to look at the ground closer to the wall, looked in all directions and then pulled himself back in behind the protective solid merlon. Whew! Jonathon thought. That was close. He took a step and was pulled up short by the tether of his companion's arm.

Meeri froze to the spot. Jonathon tugged at her hand then he noticed an odd shimmering in the moonlight. He'd been so anxious to prove he could get them safely across the exposed area between the fortress and the tree-line, he forgot to teach her how to hold on to her invisibility. Horror made jelly of his insides. Meeri was beginning to re-materialize.

No! Not yet!

—

David watched the open space. How far had Jonathon and Meeri travelled? The moonlight glimmered off the expanse of stones that surrounded the fortress. He felt so proud of his son, but bigger was his relief Jonathon headed to the safety of the allied camp. Snugg would protect Jonathon and keep him out of trouble. David tried to imagine where his son and the San, Meeri, were now. It seemed impossible they were out there, somewhere.

He pushed the door until it was almost closed and then, together, Sarah and David arranged the ivy so it was obscured. David remembered something when he saw Sarah shiver in the chill of the deep shadow. He dragged the backpack off his shoulder and rummaged in its depths. Sarah blinked back sudden moisture as she stroked the soft material her husband placed in her hands. Her sweater. She wrapped her arms around his neck and whispered in his ear.

"You found it!"

David rubbed his cheek against Sarah's auburn curls. His heart felt ready to burst with the emotions that filled it.

"It's how I knew you had gone through the portal. I knew you were in trouble."

Sarah put a hand up to his cheek and wiped away the dampness her touch discovered.

"You found me..." Her voice tight with emotion.

"Hold onto it for me," she whispered again after a pause. "If I wear it now, it might be noticed by the wrong group." David tucked it once more into his backpack.

With a touch of impatience, Uncle Frederic said, "Let's go over the next steps before we go inside. We won't be able to talk, and I don't do that sign language."

Sarah patted his arm, and they went over the strategy. Before Uncle Frederic led them through the maze of shadow and moonlight back into the fortress, David took out a small piece of parchment he had saved. He tore off a small corner and handed it to Sarah then took out his magic charcoal. The last piece of parchment and just a nub of charcoal left.

Once back inside the fortress walls, the need to move quickly became urgent. Dawn was not too far off now. Absolute silence was also imperative since they had to travel back up through the long hallways and stairwells to the King's room. To meet the patrolling Grue guard now would spell disaster, especially if he was one of Worl's men.

Fortune smiled.

They reached the door to the King's room without discovery. The door gave a muted squeak as Uncle Frederic pushed it open. The box remained undisturbed on the table. The old man gave the King's chair a long look. It had been turned and now faced the half bared wall of books and art.

David opened the box and pulled Sarah to him for a brief moment before he curled himself inside. The fact that the box was roomier without Pugg struck him hard as the door of the box closed without a sound and David flicked the catch that locked him in.

Sarah breathed out her tension and turned to the door. Uncle Frederic's hand halted her.

She turned to see what he wanted and stopped dead.

Fortune hiccupped.

Sarah's blood ran cold.

The King glared at them from behind his chair, but it wasn't his glare that froze her veins—she was used to that by now. Cragmire the Third, no more than a lunge away held a wicked-looking sword, and it was pointed at her heart.

—

For a breath, Jonathon stared at the shimmering light that hinted at Meeri's position. They were still several yards from the shelter of the trees, fully exposed on the rocky killing field below the ramparts of the fortress. Without further hesitation, he squeezed her hand hard and dragged her forward, caution tossed aside. The stones skittered away from their path. A whooshing sound startled them and the thump of an arrow on the ground behind them accelerated their feet. More arrows fell but they all struck the rocky scatter in their wake. With a last breathless effort, they heaved themselves into the deep shadows of brush and trees that surrounded the broad skirt of rocks around the fortress.

Meeri was fully visible once again. A ray of moonlight filtered by the branches glanced across her face, and Jonathon looked into her eyes, greyed with the shock of the close call. With one hand, she followed up his still invisible arm until she reached his face.

"My thanks, young warrior," she said. His broad unseen smile translated relief to her palm resting on his cheek. "Let's find camp."

Composure regained, Meeri lead the way. They scrambled over fallen trees and down and up again through deep ravines until Meeri paused, her nose raised in the air.

"We're close to the camp."

A chasm yawned open at their feet. Meeri grabbed some roots that dangled into the abyss and swung herself over the side with the grace of a gymnast. In less than a heartbeat she had disappeared into the gloom of the root-lined ravine. Jonathon flashed back to his near tumble over another cliff just days ago when Pugg saved him. A painful squeeze of his heart threatened to overwhelm him.

Jonathon climbed over the side of the ravine. As his feet touched the ground, and his eyes adjusted to the deeper shadows that nestled in the base of the ravine, he saw Meeri standing by a low fire under a constructed overhang. Several San and tall Maorrr warriors approached. They circled the new arrivals. Jonathon felt intimidated by their numbers and the clank of weapons until he noticed the San warriors jostle each other with good humoured pokes and ear jabs. The Maorrr stood serenely, tails curved around their feet. A broad-shouldered San with the air of a leader broke through the throng around Meeri and reached her side in strong strides. He stopped short of her. One hand extended and rested on her arm. Their heads came together until their foreheads touched and their ears entwined. Then they stood back and nodded their heads. Jonathon was touched by the brief tenderness between them.

It seemed he was not the only one. He saw a young San, a little shorter than himself, draw near to Meeri. The San looked at her with the adoration and relief of a child who thought he had lost his mother. Jonathon related to that look.

"Jonnn."

He saw Meeri look around her. He allowed himself to shimmer into visibility again. The astonished expressions never failed to cheer him up, and he grinned as he appeared before the crowd of warriors.

CHAPTER SIXTEEN

Jonathon

Meeri approached him and looked him in the eyes, and he felt like an adult. Then she signed, "So what do we do now?"

Jonathon stared at Meeri, dumbstruck.

Why is she asking me? I thought the plan was set.

The faint light of the fire flickered across the tense faces of the San and Maorrr gathered around him. He realized she had given him an opening to tell the broad-shouldered San warrior, Snugg, the plans. Not exactly battle plans. More like support plans—how to *save an enemy* plans.

Looking around at the assembled warriors, Jonathon realized something for the first time. Convincing them might be tough. The San had already completed their mission: Meeri was safe. Pugg, however, had been left behind as the sacrifice. Jonathon felt a stab of sadness when the San leader learned of Pugg's brave exchange with Meeri. The shadow of pain in his eyes served to remind Jonathon that the leader hadn't just lost one of his warriors—Snugg was Pugg's older brother.

The Maorrr seemed ready to break camp having fulfilled their mandate of support. Jonathon *had* to persuade them all that saving the Grue King was just as important. And besides, his parents were still inside the castle. They owed his father. He had killed the evil Grue king and saved Snugg's life—he was their Legend!

Jonathon looked to Meeri for support. A huge Maorrr warrior interrupted Jon's halting speech and shouldered his way into the circle. Several others followed, each twitching their long tails with furious whips. They didn't want to be convinced. They'd fulfilled their task. Meeri put her hand on Jonathon's arm to steady him. He drew himself to his full height—half of the Maorrr's. As he looked up into the first warrior's eyes, he heard his father's voice in his mind. He could do this. The tightness in his chest loosened, and the fear that blocked his throat shrank from a rock to a pebble.

"The King is not your enemy. The Deputy is plotting to take the throne. If we help the King, the war can be stopped..." Jonathon thought for a moment. "It will, uh, save lives." His hands dropped to his side. Did they believe him? He saw the determination in Meeri's eyes as she turned to her mate. Before she could speak, Snugg spoke up.

"What about a leader's pride?" he said. "How can he continue to lead if he can only be saved by outsiders? Would he not rather go to war to protect his throne?"

Meeri and Jonathon shook their heads in unison.

"The King's life is in danger," Meeri said. "Because the ancient Grue ritual has been broken. The Deputy knows and will use it tonight at the Rite of the Full Moon. If the King dies, there *will* be war, but if the Deputy is stopped, a chance for peace lives. Better a chance for peace than certain war."

Jonathon watched Snugg as the San leader lowered his ears, deep in thought. Snugg turned to his Maorrr counterpart, Maorla. They conferred in low voices. The tension twisted in Jonathon's stomach. Bile burned in the back of his throat. Did they believe him? His parents were both still back there. He had to convince them! His tension unwound slightly, and he realized the battle had been won when he saw the leaders nod together and then nod to them.

"We will help the King. It is always best to prevent a war," Snugg said, raising his arm in an orator's gesture. "A warrior does not fight or take another life lightly. A warrior sacrifices for the good of others, to protect the defenceless, the old and the young. We must go back now into our ancestral memories and recall the time when the Grue were our friends." He turned to include all the assembled warriors. "This young warrior," Snugg placed his hand on Jonathon's shoulder, "brings us the opportunity to heal the wound between our people: the Grue, the San and the Maorrr."

Jonathon pulled himself up straight. He warmed in the glow of Snugg's acknowledgment. At that moment, all ears turned toward the sound of fluttering through the trees. A blur of white floated out of the shadows and landed on the San leader's shoulder. A pigeon. The pigeon plucked at Snugg's tunic. An unspoken *ah-ha* lit the leader's eyes with understanding, and he dug out of his belt pouch the corner of parchment that David had left with him. The pigeon stopped plucking, then, and offered up a leg. Something had been wrapped around its ankle.

Snugg removed the parchment and unfolded it. A puzzled look flickered through his eyes and then he passed the parchment to Jonathon. It contained a message from his father. He read the instructions to himself and then aloud. Uncle Frederic would meet the contingent at the door in the wall—and he had disguises; David would remain in the decorated box in the King's war room; send messages by pigeon to Sarah; Jonathon was to stay with Snuggla.

Who's Snuggla? Jonathon thought and then looked again at the youngster who had greeted Meeri. Snuggla was Meeri and Snugg's child. Fierce, determined eyes stared back at him. He recognized that look. It reminded him of someone. *Who was it?*

Jonathon broke eye contact with Snuggla and returned his attention to the parchment.

"We need volunteers. The smallest are to go back into the Grue's fortress. They will be dressed in the uniform of the castle servants and blend in with the others. My Dad calls it 'hiding in plain sight'."

Snuggla stepped forward but was snatched back into line by Meeri.

The San sorted through their ranks and a group came forward.

"How will they cross through the moonlight to the fortress?" Snugg asked.

At last, action! Jonathon felt encouraged. The warriors going into the fortress to protect the King would defend his parents, too.

Jonathon demonstrated the talents of the talisman and explained how they could remain invisible until they reached their destination. To minimize the risk of exposing their position, they would cross the rocky scree between the tree line and the fortress one by one and re-materialize inside the walls where Uncle Frederic would meet and disguise them.

A stocky San warrior stepped away from the group of volunteers and approached his leader to rumble a request into his ear. Snugg nodded in answer.

"I'm Tugg, young sir," the warrior said to Jonathon. "Do you have any news of me young brother?"

Jonathon looked at him blankly. "Your brother?"

"Me brother, Pugg. He went with yer father to find yer."

Jonathon's eyes blistered with moisture, and he turned to Meeri. She put out a hand to the grizzled warrior and with a few tender words relayed Pugg's bravery. His long ears drooped with grief but his expression remained gruff. Jonathon swallowed hard and reached out to grasp the warrior's arm.

"He was my friend." Jonathon said through the tightness in his throat. "He saved my life." Jon had an inspiration. "Pugg was a brave warrior. I know he would want to help find a peaceful settlement with the Grue." Growing confidence made him feel taller and stronger. He turned to face the gathered allies. "In Pugg's honour, let's defeat the Deputy and protect the King!"

A hum of approval rose from the crowd around him. Tails and ears twitched in mute support. Jonathon held himself back from a victory dance. He did it. This was proof he had won them over.

"A fine tribute for our brother, lad. My thanks." Snugg said. "We must move now or Pugg's efforts will be wasted with the sunrise."

Snuggla accompanied Jonathon and the contingent to the top of the ravine. Jonathon noted the piercing attention with which the young San watched him as he erased each of the volunteers from sight. Jonathon felt a strange, almost electrical, connection with Snuggla.

When the last volunteer eased his invisible self across the scree, Snugg poked the two adolescents and pointed back to the camp. They each gave a dutiful nod to the leader and a sideways look to the other.

Sarah

The silence was tense in the King's war room. Cragmire's laser gaze seared across both Sarah and the trembling Frederic.

Sarah became aware that she had been holding her breath. Even with the war sword pointed at her heart, she stared hard at the King, so she would not be tempted to glance at the box concealing her husband. Had he seen David? Would it matter if he did? She and Uncle Frederic had agreed to keep David's presence from the King, something about sparing his feelings or protecting his leadership. Her memory was fuzzy with a mix of fatigue and stress. Better stick to the plan. Not a good time to improvise now!

She spared a look at Uncle Frederic, wide-eyed under bushy brows as he nibbled his lip. Two heartbeats—or perhaps two hundred—passed before the tip of the King's sword dipped and then waved Frederic to the door. Sarah heard a sigh escape from Uncle Frederic—relief?—and then felt the absence of his support as the door closed with a faint squeak behind him. Sarah was alone with the King. Despite the ferocity of his glare and the sword pointed at her, she sensed his anger wasn't directed at her. He had not expected them. Who had he expected?

Cragmire held up his arm. He let fall his long, embroidered sleeve to show the bandage on his forearm. It was bloody again. While he came out from behind his turned chair and went to the table, she took a deep breath and fetched her medicine kit that she kept in the corner by the exposed wall of book and art. Sarah felt relieved to have a task. The room held a middle-of-the-night chill despite the faint glow from the embers in the fireplace. She lit a torch from the fire.

"What happened here?" she muttered to herself as she stripped down the bandage and examined the wound. The pink of healing flesh extended down the King's arm, but at the central point of the gash a small split had opened and oozed dark red drops. Sarah sniffed. No smell or sign of infection.

She looked up at the King, who shrugged his shoulders, and if she did not know better, she would swear he looked embarrassed.

"Calyb...my son..."

Sarah sat back on her heels and stared.

What? He just spoke English!

Then she remembered that Uncle Frederic said he had been taught the Grue language when he arrived. It seemed he had shared his own language with the King. She could imagine the two of them talking together as though in code, a secret language no other Grue understood. It made sense now why the King responded before Uncle Frederic could translate her words in front of Worl—the day he'd sliced open his arm. Cragmire stepped back toward his chair again and beckoned her forward. His re-bandaged arm pointed down at the seat. Sarah stifled a gasp.

A sleeping Grue child lay curled on the cushion.

He had short, wavy brown hair and wore a snuggly one piece outfit of pale yellow lambswool. His thumb slid in and out of his mouth with each suck of his tongue. Thickets of lashes rested on his cheeks and hid sleeping eyes.

Sarah looked up again. The King watched her closely. *What is he thinking behind those black eyes?* Just then, the light from the fire flickered off a gleam on the King's cheek. *Was that a tear?* An intuitive question leaped from her lips before she could stop it.

"Where is his mother?"

The King started to turn from her and then faced Sarah again. His eyes squeezed closed for a long moment.

"She is missing. I thought to send her to safety, but her carriage was attacked. Her escort was found slain. My men search for her." His hand stroked his son's cheek. "I brought my son here to protect him."

Protect his son from what? Or whom?

And the Queen, Sarah hadn't even realized the King had a wife. The presence of the King's son here and his missing wife added a new layer to the unfolding crisis.

Sarah knew all too well the strategy they had agreed upon, but she had a decision to make. She chose her words carefully.

"Do you trust Frederic?"

"With my life," Cragmire's voice rumbled. His eyes softened. *He keeps surprising me*, Sarah thought.

"Do you trust me?" she asked.

His hard gaze searched her face and then he nodded once.

"I can help you. I know where we can hide your son." Sarah paused as a possible wrinkle struck her. "Does he speak my language?"

Again the King nodded.

Sarah rounded the table to the carved box and gave a quick double tap and returned to the side of the sleeping child. When she picked him up, he whimpered, then snuggled into her arms with a sigh. His weight was solid and warm against her. He smelled like fresh grass. As she carried him back to the box, the carved door swung open and David opened his arms to receive Sarah's bundle. The door closed again, but she noticed it stayed ajar by the slightest margin. *The better to listen?* She could trust David to do his best to keep the boy calm and later she would sneak some food and water to them.

"No one will look here," she said. The King stood still, tension radiating from him. *What must it be like to have his own half-brother plotting his death?* If Worl grabbed control over the throne it would mean disaster not just for the Grue people, but for the neighbouring lands as well. Cragmire came to her side and stared down at the box hiding its secret so well. His hand caressed the carvings.

"What does the—"

Cragmire's question was interrupted by a sound at the door. They both turned as the knob rattled and then rotated. Instinctively, Sarah ducked behind the King who stood in battle stance, one arm on his hip and the other extended with his sword. Peeking under his arm, she saw the Deputy Worl in the open doorway, pig-like eyes narrowed suspiciously, not a hint of deference in his attitude. To Sarah's astonishment, the King lowered the tip of his sword. *He doesn't trust him does he?* But the stiffness of Cragmire's posture gave her the answer. An image flashed across her mind's screen like a movie trailer: the King and Deputy standing together before the gathered Grue court to perform the ritual; the Deputy revealing to the masses the King's wound, the Grue turning against the King. The Deputy had no need to act against the King before the ceremony. The ceremony would seal the King's fate for him and give the Deputy's coup legitimacy. Worl seemed to have trouble reining in his attitude, though. It oozed out of his eyes and painted his every move.

A realization blazed in her mind. To solidify his position after the King was killed, the Deputy needed Cragmire's wife out of the way so that he could gain uncontested custody of the prince. The gloating in his eyes said it all. He didn't intend to wait for the ceremony for this part of his strategy. Worl's evil plan was in motion. That's what was he doing here now.

He was hunting for the child!

David

David grimaced as he eased his cramped knees where he knelt in his wooden sarcophagus in the King's war room. He strained to hear through the door of the box. After a few heartbeats, he heard the deep rumble of the King's voice. Fear for Sarah gripped his insides. He eased off the lock and opened the door a crack. He heard enough of Sarah's reply to realize that she was safe and had a plan in mind. He was not surprised when he heard her knock on the door of the box. He was surprised, however, to receive the warm, soft weight of the King's sleeping son. He folded the shrimp-like curl of the child's body into his arms and held him against his chest. He flashed to a tender memory of holding Jonathon and rocking him to sleep. Soon this would all be over and he could take his family home.

The interruption of his reverie returned him to the present when he heard Sarah's frightened gasp. David felt the movement of the box's door as Sarah pushed it shut. He almost flung it open again to leap to her rescue, but the realization hit him that such an action could spell instant death to both of them. He had no choice but to trust her. David felt the expansion of a renewed concept in his heart. He had trusted her with his life until the last few months when events unfolded that caused him to retreat into himself. She would never leave him. He knew now he trusted her on a whole new level. The last few hours had made him realize that he could trust her to handle whatever situation to the best of her ability.

The child shifted and moaned. David held his breath. Could the sound be heard outside the box? This hiding spot was not going to last for too long. They needed to find something better for the King's son.

CHAPTER SEVENTEEN

Jonathan

With the invisible contingent safely away to the fortress, the remainder of the San and Maorrr returned to the make-shift camp in the ravine. Jonathon noticed a thoughtful look on the San leader's face as he gazed around at the mix of warriors.

"A distraction, that's what they'll need—to split the Grue forces!" Snugg's eyes searched until he saw his wife and Maorla. "We must create a distraction and time it for the ceremony." Meeri nodded. Snugg said, "The Grue will have to split in order to answer us, and our hidden contingent will have a better chance to protect the King."

Jonathon turned to his young San companion.

"That's brilliant!" his voice broke into a squeak in his enthusiasm. "Let's send the pigeon back to my mom with the message."

As Snugg handed the scrap of parchment to Jonathon, the pigeon fluttered into the open and perched on a nearby branch. Using a pointed stick and a charcoal paste from the fire, Jon printed out the message with great concentration, his tongue peeking from the side of his mouth. The note complete, he wrapped it around the bird's ankle and then tucked the creature inside his tunic. With a little help from one of the Maorrr warriors, he climbed to the top of the ravine, accompanied by Snuggla. Jonathon felt a great need to watch the pigeon's flight. He couldn't put it into words, but he visualized a wire along the path the bird would take and it connected him to his mother and father.

They crouched beneath the bushes that encircled the wide rock-strewn space around the fortress. Jonathon lifted the bird out of his tunic and caressed its feathers before he pushed it up into the air.

The pigeon's wings stroked the early morning breeze and circled higher and higher. Jonathon gripped his hands together. The pigeon gave them a way to communicate. Their plans were all coming together! By the end of the day, he would be back with his mom and dad for good. They would go back to the farm and Gramp would be glad to see them.

A panicked tug on his arm broke Jonathon's hopeful train of thought. His eyes followed the direction of the young San's point-ing finger.

A haze of white feathers floated downwards, a gentle counter-point to the arrow-pierced body that plummeted to the ground, elegant flight brought to an abrupt end.

Jonathon and Snuggla shared a horrified glance for a few heart-beats before a sly look gleamed through the San's eyes. Jonathon read that look like his first grade primer.

Sarah

Alone in her room, Sarah splashed cold water over her face and around her neck. Damp tendrils of auburn hair clung to her cheeks. Her heart rate had returned to normal after the King's confrontation with Worl. The Deputy had backed out of the room, no attempt made to hide his searching eyes.

The cheek of the man!

The stillness and deepening of shadows told her sunrise advanced and her to-do list was already long. Besides overseeing the celebration feast to keep up the appearance that the Grue plans were still on track, she had to check on the San contingent and make sure they knew what to do to blend in. Most importantly, Sarah had to find something that would keep the King's son asleep long enough to find a safe place to hide him. She could hear David's voice in the back of her brain saying, "Delegate!" But that was never something she did easily. After all, if you wanted something done right, most times you had to do it yourself. First off, she had to find Uncle Frederic. He was the linchpin in the wheel of her day's plans.

As she plotted out what needed to be done in the next few hours, the kitchen hit the top of the list, and Sarah headed there first. Her chances of finding Uncle Frederic were greatest in the warren of the kitchen. The wee San serfs were scurrying around the great tables as Sarah came through the door. She could smell loaves of bread rising, vegetables steaming and savoury meat roasting. The kitchen San waved to her and trilled happily about their work. Uncle Frederic said they were joyful since Sarah had arrived and made changes. They were still cautious about the presentation of the vegetables, but one little San told her, through Uncle Frederic, that they were hopeful to bring back their full repertoire of menus.

Uncle Frederic popped his head around the door of a side room when he heard Sarah's voice. He gestured her into the room. Sarah slipped through the opening and saw the new contingent of San. They were taller than the fortress San and they bristled with knives and short swords. The first worry that bloomed in her mind was whether the tunics of the fortress San would cover them convincingly. They would just have to hope that the Grue warriors—and the Deputy in particular—would be too preoccupied with their conspiracy to kill the King to notice the sudden growth of the San workers.

A pile of clothing rested on the floor. A couple of the San warriors rummaged through the pile and passed out tunics to the others. They helped each other cover the weaponry under aprons and disguised their military bearing by mimicking the posture of the fortress San. Sarah gave them brooms and instructions to clean and help decorate the amphitheatre at the ceremony site. Then Uncle Frederic would show them where to stand ready to protect the King when the ceremony began and remain undetected. As the Steward led his contingent out, Sarah laid a hand on his arm.

"Please find me when you're done with them, Uncle Frederic. I have something to ask you."

From under his wild fringe of white hair, he looked at her for a heartbeat and then nodded and disappeared through the door.

Sarah went out into the kitchen garden next with the aim of finding an herb to make a tea for the King's son to keep him calm. She had no idea when Calyb last ate, so she planned to take him something to eat as well. It would not be good for him to be found in David's custody. It would not be good for him to be found *at all* until the King was safe from Worl's machinations. As she picked her way through the overgrown garden, identifying herbs and root vegetables and raspberry bushes, Sarah almost brushed over a fern-like plant with multiple leaves on each stem. Sweet smelling pink flowers bloomed amongst the leaves.

Valerian.

From her studies of herbs, she understood that valerian root had sedative properties and decreased anxiety. She could use some of that herself! She scrabbled around the base of the plant pulling away layers of dead leaves and then loosened the soil with her hands until the root came free.

It seemed like both ages and mere moments had passed, when Sarah edged her way up to the King's study. The halls were empty. Whenever she heard the heavy footfalls of the occasional Grue warrior, she cringed and tried to will herself to blend with the walls. The last thing she needed now was to be stopped and questioned with the mug of valerian tea in her hands.

Almost to the King's war room, Sarah paused. She threw a hasty glance over each shoulder. Did she hear shoes on stone? No one was there. She frowned and then carried on to the King's door. It was heavy to open with two hands and impossible with only one. She set the mug of tea on the stone floor and heaved the door open. The room was empty. Sarah sighed with relief and entered, put down the tea and again two-handed the door closed.

David's ornately decorated box still sat on the end of the King's table. Sarah double knocked softly on the door of the box and listened. She thought she heard some squeaks and thumps before the click of the latch released. The door swung open to reveal David struggling with the King's now wide-awake son.

"David, I have some Valerian tea for him to drink. It will calm him down."

David looked out at his wife with relief crisscrossing his face.

"He has been awake for a while and getting more restless all the time. It's hard to entertain him in the dark." David unfurled himself from the box, the struggling child held against his chest until his feet touched the ground. Then David sat cross-legged on the floor with the King's son secured in the nest created by his limbs. Sarah knelt down beside them, her face close to the child and she smiled.

"I have something for you to drink. Are you thirsty? Are you hungry?"

A deep frown punctuated with a pouting lip answered her. He nibbled at the honey bread but frowned again at the mug. Sarah widened her smile and made goofy eyes and was rewarded by a giggle. She was about to congratulate herself for not losing her touch when she realized that the child was not looking at her but gazing past her shoulder. She followed his gaze and barely choked off the scream that rose in her throat.

Behind her floated the disembodied face of her son, tongue lolling, eyes crossed.

CHAPTER EIGHTEEN

David

"Jonathon!"

Dang that boy! David thought, his relief once again short-lived as he gazed in disbelief at the disembodied face of his son floating behind his wife's shoulder. *Now what?*

Just moments before, his sense of relief had been profound. It swirled his insides at the sight of Sarah's beautiful, anxious face through the door of his carved box. Help had arrived. The King's son, Prince Calyb, had grown more restless in the dark despite David's best efforts to keep him entertained. Chubby arms reached out for Sarah. A smile dimpled his cheeks and replaced the threatening pout.

There was no getting around the fact most games played easier in the light. David had tried word games and 'this little pig' and sang nonsense songs in a whispery voice. He wracked his brain to remember all the sweet silly games that made Jonathon laugh and gurgle at that age. In the mid-ground of his thoughts, David felt a vast sense of comfort that his son was safe in the allied camp. He trusted Snugg especially and now Maorla, too, to keep an eye on him. David had walked his fingers up Calyb's arm in imitation of different animals (the names didn't matter to him but the action bought giggles - the elephant tip-toed, the snake hopped, the pony hop-scotched) and then tickled him under the chin. The child—about Jonathon's size at the age of five—was easy to make laugh, but his attention span paralleled that of a two-year-old. To add to David's concerns, he had worried a conspiring Grue might enter, unauthorized, into the King's war room and be suspicious of the squeals and giggles coming from the decorated box. But what else could he do? The child had been awake and demanding attention.

Dust motes sparkled in the air as the midday light streamed through a high window of stained glass and cast dancing rainbows across the exposed wall. The benevolent faces of Good King Cragmire the First and his Queen smiled down on them. However did they beget a cruel monster like Cragmire the Second? He was like a cuckoo in an unsuspecting nest of doves.

Sarah had dragged a heavy chair and placed it in front of the door to protect them from sudden intrusion. As David climbed out of the box and sat on the floor with the child, he absorbed the sight of his wife's smile. His heart expanded as he took in every nuance of her mobile expressions while she first fed the little prince pieces of bread and honey then coaxed him to take a drink from the mug she offered. How had he lost sight of the miracle that she was in his life?

Ever since university, she had brought light and laughter into his life. The tableau was as clear in his mind as if it had just happened. Under a tree on campus, she sang a song made up on the spot at the top of her lungs surrounded by eager, mostly male volunteers taking her flyers for donations of money and time for St. Andrews' Shelter. Her first hobbyhorse. Until the magical moment he first beheld her, he felt he had not smiled in years. He found himself joining in with her song, humming and beating the rhythm on his chest. Her smile was all the reward he needed. They gave away every last flyer together. Under Sarah's gentle guidance, he found the self he lost at twelve when his mother left. David's thoughts stuttered with the new memory of his mom but his heart was firm.

David glanced down at the precious Grue heir. She had little success with the mug, so Sarah entertained the hungry Prince Calyb by feeding him more bits of honeyed bread as if they were planes coming in for a landing into the bird-like opening of his mouth just she had when Jonathon was a persnickety toddler. David allowed his thoughts to continue.

No. Not left. Mom didn't leave. He could think it freely now. *She died.*

All the strange yet familiar events of the last two days had had a deep affect on the barriers in David's mind, barriers that had helped him cope with the loss all these years since he first came through the portal the day of his mother's funeral. He had returned home through the portal with a head injury, thanks to Cragmire the Second. Like a bomb exploded and burst apart the walls around his memories in one go, they all came rushing back in the prison cavern with Uncle Frederic's simple words, "You have your mother's eyes."

His mother had received her diagnosis just before he was sent off to summer camp. In less than two weeks, David came back only in time to see her lying in her coffin. When Sarah had come home with the preliminary report from the doctor of the changes on her mammogram, his world closed in on him. Desperation and clouds of fear guided him. Misguided him. To cope, he turned away from his wife. He couldn't name what drove him to do that. He could now. He could face it all now and he would never take Sarah's love and support for granted again. Much more than that—he would never again deny his love and support when she most needed it. She said the final doctor's report was still to come. He would be there. Every step. Wherever it took them.

The biggest miracle of all was that he had his wife's forgiveness.

Or am I assuming too much? First chance, I will make sure. No more lost chances between us.

Over the last three days, the fear of losing Sarah forever had paled every other problem at home to insignificance. In his mind, David reached out a hand to touch his wife's cheek but his motion arrested when a gurgle of laughter interrupted his reflections.

David's attention refocused on Calyb's pointing chubby fingers and Sarah's head turned to follow their direction. He felt a wobbly sense of disorientation as the floating face of his son bobbed in the air behind Sarah's shoulder.

Sarah's exclamation burst in an overheated hiss of tension and surprise. "Why didn't you stay in the camp?"

Jon's hand materialized and stretched towards the Grue Prince's hand and wiggled just out of reach. He winked at his mom and dad as though he hadn't heard her question and then shimmered into full view. David and Sarah both jumped when Calyb shrieked with laughter and they shared a panicked look. Their son put his fingers to his lips and brought his face up close to the child.

"We must be quiet," he whispered, "let's play a game!" He held the mug to his lips and pretended to slurp and then held it to the little Prince. "Your turn!" His effort was rewarded by a hearty gulp and then the child pushed the mug towards him again. Jonathon again pretended to slurp and passed it back. Before long the mug was empty and Calyb's eyes lowered to half-mast. It was a relief for the little group to see the prince relax into sleep. His safety—his life— and now theirs as well, depended on him remaining undetected by Worl or his men.

Jonathon glanced up through his lashes at his parents. A tinge of red coloured his ears.

"I can see *how* you got here," David said. "But does Snugg know where you are?"

With the immediate danger snoring in his arms, David gave his son a stern look. Jonathon shook his head and had, at least, the grace to look abashed.

"He wouldn't've let us come. But we *had* to. The Grue guard shot the pigeon mid-flight after I put the new message on its leg. I had no choice. I had to bring you the message myself."

David sighed and caught Sarah's eye.

Just like home. Always the quick defence.

He and Sarah often joked they were lucky Jonathon only used his intelligence for forces of good because that kid could talk his way out of any tight spot. Like the time he was ten, skipped class and hitchhiked into town when he found out his best friend had been admitted to hospital with a broken leg. Sarah and David had found him playing cards with his buddy and telling jokes to distract him from the pending surgery. Two strikes. Base hit. How could they stay mad when his intentions were good?

"Okay. What's the new message?" David asked. Jonathon relayed Snugg and Maorla's scheme to provide a distraction outside the walls at the time of the ceremony.

"They'll need a signal, won't they?" Sarah asked.

A kitten-like moan from the King's son diverted their attention. They all watched him anxiously for a moment. Then the child sucked on his lip and snuggled deeper into David's arms. It was okay. For now.

"Hmmm. We need a new plan for this little guy," David said, his eyes thoughtful as they rested on Jonathon.

"We can take him to me Maam." A new voice said.

David started as Snuggla materialized at his side.

"I should have known *you* wouldn't be far away," David said with a half smile.

Sarah

"Who's this?" Sarah asked. The young San, grey-brown pelt and wearing a too-long tunic, gazed at her with frank, fearless blue eyes and slight smile curved around an overbite.

"This is Meeri's child, Snuggla." David ruffled the fur between the young San's graceful ears. "Snuggla's bravery helped me find the warriors—and you." His warm glance caressed his wife's face.

"Mom, Dad, we have something to tell you before we go." Jonathon shuffled his feet and then looked from parent to parent. David nodded encouragement.

"Snuggla and I explored the fortress a little before we saw Mom and followed her in here. We followed some of the San servants and found a spot that looks like the ceremonial place. It's on the roof. There are lanterns and a ginormous stained block." Jonathon paused to shake his head as though trying to clear it of the memory. "We saw two Grue warriors alone, one with a huge scar down the side of his face, and he was doing all the talking. So we snuck up next to them." Jon grinned and then stopped when he saw his mother's face. "They never knew we were there. Snuggla understood most of what the big ugly one was saying."

"That sounds like the Deputy," Sarah inserted. She forced down her worries of the danger her son had been in and concentrated on the moment. Here and now. After all, he was standing safe in front of her. A bubble of realization burst on the surface of her mind: not only did Jonathon seem inches taller in the last few days, but he seemed as comfortable navigating his way around this mad world as he did around the farm. Her train of thought rounded the bend and opened on a greater vista.

Why hadn't she seen it before? It was so obvious. The success of their mission to save the Grue and their King from Worl was going to command the resources of each of them. And whatever her fears for him, Jonathon's actions were a clear demonstration that, no matter what they said, he had no intention of staying out of the way while his parents remained in the fortress.

No one was safe until they were all safe.

Not just them as a family, but the San and their allies. Sarah's vision crystallized. The King's life was tied inextricably to theirs. If the King died, all were in danger and that threatened their chances of making it back to the portal and home. Even if the three of them had slipped away last night when they reunited in the prison cavern, how far would they have gotten before Worl and his men led the army after them, San, Maorrr and the James family? They would have been slaughtered mercilessly. Tonight, they had a chance to change that scenario.

Oh, dear Lord! What I wouldn't give to be home right this moment!

Sarah linked her arm with Jonathon's and gave a squeeze to comfort herself with his solid presence.

"You're right, he *is* ugly inside and out." She pushed herself to respond. "What did he say?"

"He gave orders that, at the ceremony, the Deputy's men are to mix with the King's and take them out on Worl's signal. Then just before the sacrifice," Jonathon winced as he said the word, "the lanterns are to be covered so that the only light'll be from the full moon." He paused, his eyes shadowed as he stroked the dozing child's hair.

"Then Deputy Ugly got very angry when the other warrior didn't know where the King's son was. Mom, he's one scary guy! He grabbed the other guy and nearly strangled him. Then he just dropped him and left."

David could tell by the expression on Sarah's face that she agreed. Scary barely covered it.

"Jonathon, we need your help," Sarah said to her son. Surprise flashed across his face but brightened into pride.

"I know what we can do, Mom. We'll take the Prince with us to Meeri, now, while he's asleep. It'll be easy 'cause we'll be invisible."

Sarah turned to face David and her eyes questioned him. Could their son handle it? Jonathon intercepted the look.

"I can do it, Mom. Trust me."

He knelt down beside the prince with Memgarr's talisman poised between his fingers.

"Oh, wait!" Jonathon's eyes popped wide as a thought returned. "The signal for Snugg and Maorla to begin their distraction!"

"Perhaps, Uncle Frederic would be the best one to give the signal," David suggested. He still cradled the sleeping child in the nest of his body. Although Sarah nodded, her gaze trailed away into the distance.

"What do you think the best signal should be, David?"

He looked at his wife for a moment. Jonathon cut in.

"Some kind of a flashing light..."

David nodded in agreement.

"Right! Good idea!" David said. "If Uncle Frederic were to take a covered lantern to the wall, swing it twice and then drop it to the ground—"

"They'll know the time is right," said Jonathon, "create their distraction and then send in a team through the new door."

Sarah frowned. "But why Uncle Frederic? I can do it!" She paused. "Wait...you're trying to keep me out of the way, aren't you! It's going to take all of us to make this work, you know, David."

"Please, Sarah. I'm going to be in that dam—dang box. I need to know that you're out of danger when I can't do anything to protect you." He could see the objection building in the pink of her cheeks. Jonathon came to his rescue.

"Dad's right, Mom. Why *can't* Uncle Frederic do it? Besides, Cragmire is his King more than ours."

"All right, all right," she said. "If you're both going to gang up. I'll go find Uncle Frederic and let him know the plan."

"Wait!" David added. "Be sure to give him Jonathon's news, too."

For a moment, Sarah looked down on the tableau of her family and the two additions. The ache in her heart made her reluctant to leave them. She whispered into her son's ear a steely request to take no more risks then gave him a tight hug, touched Snuggla's cheek and left them.

—

David watched her straight back until it disappeared through the doorway knowing the effort it cost her to go, and then he looked up at his offspring.

"Son," David said and gestured for Jonathon to kneel down to him. "I have something I want you to do for me before you go..."

Jonathon's grin grew as he listened to his father's request.

—

As she hurried through the halls to the kitchens, Sarah marvelled at her son. Confidence was never in short supply in Jonathon's makeup, but he seemed taller and more mature in the last few days. How did he handle the strangeness of this world as easily as breathing? He made friends with the San warriors like they were long-time neighbours and not long-eared, furry and sword-wielding. She still pinched herself every morning, hoping that she would wake up from this nightmare and see her lovely airy bedroom at home. Even though she worried about their safety, it felt comforting to know that her husband and son were close. She was no longer alone amongst these harsh people with only Uncle Frederic as a buffer. He was a dear old man, but he could hide better than a snowman in a blizzard.

And come to think of it, where is he now?

Sarah's crew of San servants buzzed around the kitchen like a hive of bees. She searched through the maze of storage rooms off the kitchen to no avail. *Where's that man? Time's getting short!* Her anxiety increased as she spread her search to the gardens and then back into the halls of the castle. She sensed the tension in the Grue warriors she passed in the hallways. Most of them barely noticed her now, but there were a few whose eyes followed her. The skin crawled on her neck and she wondered if they were the Deputy's men. The Deputy demonstrated a special animosity towards her from the first moment his cruel eyes watched her enter the dining hall like fresh prey into the open. Her chest tightened when she remembered his scarred, snarling face looming, his foul breath on her cheek and black stare declaring her imminent death, before, Aengus, one of the King's warriors drew his attention away from her. Sarah let out her breath slowly. Even now the memory of that moment scared her.

She headed for the staircase that led to the upper chambers. Perhaps Uncle Frederic still attended the King. The upper halls were nearly deserted compared to those below. The door to the King's chamber, ornately carved in the same motif as his massive chair, offered a slight crack for Sarah's ear. Only silence greeted her at first and then she heard the King's rumbling bass followed by Uncle Frederic's higher pitched response. How was she going to talk to him in there? She needed an excuse. Sarah retrieved her first aid box and brought it back to the King's door. She knocked and waited.

The King's Steward opened the door and peeked through. His eyes looked wary but not surprised when he saw Sarah on the other side. Sarah was puzzled that Uncle Frederic seemed almost reluctant to let her in. Did he have a change of heart?

"I've come to re-dress the King's arm," she said in a low voice, holding up the first aid box as proof of her intention. "Then I've got to talk to you! We need your help."

"Come to my room when you're done," he said with cool dignity as he swept out of the door.

Sarah turned to face the King. He remained seated in the padded recess of a mullioned window. Light through the east facing window was subdued and reminded her that the day was marching onwards. The walls were covered with dark tapestries, designs of warriors and ladies, trees and strange animals, faded with age. One whole wall was taken up with a fireplace surrounded in massive carved stonework, detailed with flowers and birds. An enormous canopied bed occupied a recessed portion of a wall angled away from the windows. As she approached Cragmire, Sarah could see that the King looked weary, to the point of exhaustion. Despite his bearded visage, he looked young and vulnerable. An air of defeat surrounded him. The bandage had tangled under his sleeve. She struggled to release it to see how the wound fared. The edges were a healthy pink and the scab was beginning to dry and lift away. Its appearance had already shrunk since she had last seen it. The quick progress of the King's healing amazed her. If only it could be completely disguised somehow, Sarah thought. She reflected on David's talents and an idea began to take form.

"I'll be back," Sarah said as she gathered up her tools. She smothered a gasp when the King's hand thrust out and grabbed her as she turned away.

"My son..."

Sarah flushed with shame. *C'mon Sarah, you're a parent. Why didn't you think to reassure him?*

"He's safe." She crossed her fingers. Her heart thumped heavily. She hoped that was true and her intrepid Jonathon had been able to smuggle him out undetected. Jonathon got in safely—even eavesdropped on the Deputy without incident, dang his buttons—he could find his way out safely.

"Be strong, Sire! All is not lost yet." Despite her own tension, Sarah forced a bright smile to lend confidence to her words. She could almost have smiled for real when she observed the return of a glimmer of the King's former ferocity to his eyes. He nodded and released her.

Sarah found the King's Steward pacing a rut into the stone floor of his room. His room was larger than hers, with a door that led to a balcony, a four-poster bed, a dresser and an arched stone fireplace. Braided rugs were scattered around the stone floor. He had changed into a plum red tunic with flowers and bees embroidered along the seams.

"You're wearing a path, Uncle Frederic!" He turned to face her with panic and distrust mixed in equal measure.

"You're going to get him killed anyway!"

Sarah stopped short and gazed at him in dismay. He'd lost his confidence in the last few hours. What happened?

"I promise, we're not!"

"You can't promise such a thing. What do you know of the Grue warriors!" He turned away.

Defeat, so similar to what she had seen in the King, molded Frederic's shoulders.

"Uncle Frederic, what happened? Why are you afraid?"

"I don't know...just bits of plans I've overheard when they don't know I'm there...the King seems so down, and I don't know how to reassure him without giving away your plan. I'm not even sure your plan will work." Frederic dragged his hands through his hair making it stand on end in wild spikes. "And when I see Worl...I'm not sure anything will work against him. Worl is so determined. He's always gotten his way."

"What do you mean?" Sarah asked. "Got his way over the King?" She grabbed his fluttering hands. "Why would you say that? Tell me about Worl!"

Frederic released himself and paced another lap then dropped in an exhausted heap onto a chair beside the small table in the corner. He gestured to the other chair. His chest heaved up and down as he stared at the marble swirls in the table-top.

"My King's mother, Sofi, was a wonderful young lady. Beautiful and gentle, everything her husband, Cragmire the Second, was not. The match was made by Good King Cragmire and his Queen. Sofi died when my Cragmire was just a toddler. Did she die naturally, you wonder? I don't think she did. The manner of her death was too similar to how the Good King died, and the whispers were his son was behind it. And then Cragmire the Second remarried within a month. Worl, I didn't tell you before, is my King's *older* half-brother from...well, a liaison...oh, it was messy. Messy, but forgotten the instant the Good King died and Cragmire the Second banished his own mother to the Outlands." He shook his head over the past.

"Worl's mother had sent him away to keep him a secret from the good King and Queen." Frederic continued. It had taken so long for Sarah to get him to talk and now the flood gates had burst open. "But then Cragmire the Second married her and she became the new Queen and step-mother to the prince. She brought Worl back to train with my young Cragmire. They were well matched on the practice field, but Worl always had a mean streak he concealed behind his cunning." Frederic sketched a line on his flank.

"My King has a four inch scar across his ribs as a result of Worl's treachery. I saw him spook Cragmire's ride and cause him to fall from a bridge onto a jagged log. Worl threatened to kill the prince's falcon if he told. In the Queen's eyes, Worl could do no wrong. If she could have put her son above her husband's legitimate son, she would have." Uncle Frederic shook his head.

"My King was fierce and proud, but he was never mean. He was better at his lessons than Worl. I taught him my language so we could talk together unheard. Having something just his own, even if it was a secret language gave him confidence to hold out against Worl. But the stepmother was different; she all but buried him under her anger and lust for revenge for her husband's death." Frederic leaped up and took a quick spin around the room before dropping into his chair again.

"The King takes responsibility now for allowing himself to be carried along." He stared at Sarah's chin. "His heart was never in the revenge business. Only I knew that. As his step-mother lay dying, she made him swear an oath in front of Worl, that one day he would go through with the ceremony and at last take final revenge on the San. He thought he had no choice." Uncle Frederic raised his chin and looked into Sarah's eyes.

"But you changed all that when you exposed the wall in his war room, the wall his father had covered up, and revealed to him the glorious, honourable past of the Grue. Cragmire knew then taking revenge was *not* his inevitable fate; the Grue had been different before and could be again."

Frederic's voice began to tremble. "The King knew his Deputy hated him, but I couldn't convince him Worl was dangerous and out for the throne until his Queen disappeared..." He broke down and sobbed. "He is afraid for his son's life now, too. If Worl's plans work tonight, Prince Calyb will be dead shortly after his father." Frederic's head wobbled on his neck. "You don't really know Worl's warriors! The King doesn't have a chance!"

Sarah drew in a deep breath to steady herself under the onslaught of Uncle Frederic's anxiety. Instinctively, she wanted to pat the Steward's hand to comfort him. She held back and used her words instead to persuade him.

"But Uncle Frederic, they don't know us either! And they don't know we're here in the castle." Sarah's tone pleaded with him. "You have to believe we will do everything we can to keep the King safe."

"Ahhh, but will it be enough!" His ears drooped to his shoulders; even his eyebrows drooped.

"Snap out of it!" Sarah grabbed him by both sagging shoulders and gave him a shake. "There are other lives on the line here not just Cragmire's. My life for one. The lives of my husband and son. Not to mention countless San who are entirely blameless for what's about to be unleashed upon them."

Frederic looked startled—Sarah did, too, she hadn't meant to get physical with him. He backed out of her grasp and straightened, pulling his shaky dignity around him. He tidied the wild strands of his hair and nodded.

"I'm sorry, my dear. You're right. This won't help the King."

"Okay then," she said in a calmer tone. "We have a job for you. It's very important for the King's safety." She willed him to look at her as she outlined the new information and the signal. "Will you do it?"

Jonathon

Jonathon's hands laced with Snuggla's under the burden of the sleeping child. The terrain across the treacherous, stony space between the fortress walls and the protection of the tree-sided ravines was now familiar. This trip, the midday sun warmed their backs instead of the moon. The King's son became heavier with each step. They stepped carefully so as not to dislodge any rocks.

Not far now.

He could hear Snuggla let out a deep breath when at last they reached the edge of the ravine. It mirrored his own relief.

"Let's show ourselves before we go down," Jonathon suggested. They both shimmered into view and called down to the San warriors keeping watch below. The invisible weight of the child still burdened their arms. They dared not set him down because they might not find him again. Meeri appeared from inside the shelter. She looked grateful to see them and then puzzled by their posture.

"Where have you been?" She asked as rising suspicion coloured her tone. "And what do you hold?"

Snuggla answered, voice hushed to avoid waking the sleeping child. "We have the King's son. The Deputy's men look for him to kill him."

Meeri's eyes narrowed at the news her offspring had gone back into the fortress against her wishes. Nevertheless, she reached up to them.

"Poor child. Can you let me see him?"

"Not until he wakes up." Jonathon responded.

"Place him in my hands, then," Meeri said. "And I will mind him until he wakes."

Jonathon and Snuggla knelt down at the edge of the ravine. They reached downwards as far as they could but there was still a gap between them and Meeri's up-stretched hands. She looked behind her and gestured to a broad shouldered, towering Maorrr warrior. He lifted her straight up until her arms were level with Jonathon. With Snuggla's help, Jonathon eased their burden into Meeri's hands. Her violet eyes widened as she hugged the unseen weight of the child to her chest. The Maorrr lowered her to the ground. Meeri stroked the child's invisible head. Jonathon felt surprised as tears filled her eyes.

"His name is Calyb." Jonathon said.

As he and Snuggla clambered down the ravine wall, Jonathon thought he heard Meeri whisper.

"Poor child. You're the hope of your people and ours."

Snugg, the San leader, appeared behind Meeri's shoulder.

"Do you have news from Daavid?" Snugg asked. His broad shoulders were rigid with tension.

Meeri's head snapped up at her mate's question. Her eyes narrowed again and her ears flicked in agitation. Snugg held up his hands in self defence. His expression melted in the heat of his mate's gaze.

"I guessed," he said. "I didn't know for sure...I didn't *send* them." He added as Meeri pointed an accusatory ear at his chest.

"Yes, I saw my father," Jonathon said. "The signal will be a lantern swung twice and then dropped to the ground when it's time to start the distraction."

Snuggla stood up straight and proudly added details of what they had seen and heard around the fortress. Weaponry tinkled around the double-cinched belt.

Meeri squatted on a padding of leaves and hugged her armload tighter to her, rocking side-to-side. She flipped her ears at her mate, not quite ready to forgive.

"These two need something to eat."

Snugg passed along his mate's message, with more ear semaphore, to a San warrior tending the fire behind them. He waited for the morsels of berry and nut loaf and mugs of water to arrive and be eaten. Jonathon and Snuggla ate with enthusiasm. Jonathon watched several dark-pelted Maorrr warriors playing a game with stones in the shadows. The low fire gleamed off the eyes of one who turned his head and met Jon's gaze.

As he wiped away the last crumbs, Jonathon looked up at Snugg.

"I have an idea."

Snugg crooked his ear in question.

"Can I take some Maorrr warriors into the ceremony to add more protection for the King?"

"We!" Snuggla nudged Jonathon with a sharp elbow.

"Can *we?*" Jonathon said.

"And how...?" Snugg leaned in to listen. A sign of a good leader, Jon remembered hearing from somewhere. His Dad?

A hiss stopped Snugg's question short.

"No!" Meeri spoke emphatically. Her violet eyes were wide with an expression that blended fear and anger.

"But why not?!" Snugg and Snuggla spoke together.

Meeri's ears twitched several times in agitation. Her shoulders seemed to expand. Jon thought she looked about to explode and stepped back. The volcanic eruption that followed made his jaw drop and he looked from one to the other of the San family.

"Because Snuggla is not your son!"

CHAPTER NINETEEN

Jonathon

What?

Jonathon shook his head to clear his hearing.

"Snuggla is not your son," said Meeri. "You know how I feel! She is my *last* child and she is our daughter! Our only daughter! *Not* your apprentice."

Meeri's exclamation caught Jonathon by surprise.

Snuggla's a girl. That's it! Marly.

That's who she had reminded him of the first time he saw Snuggla's determined stare. Marly Dunston. His best friend. *It makes sense now.*

Marly lived on the next farm and played a tough and competitive game when neighbourhood friends gathered to play baseball and soccer. Then she turned back into a girl when the school bell rang. He smiled to himself as he noticed the scarlet flare of colour inside Snuggla's ears.

If her face wasn't covered in fur, I could probably see her blush, he thought.

Then he felt bad for her. He gave her a poke in the arm to show his support.

Snugg spoke then, in a calm but determined voice. "This is not our argument anymore, Meeri. Ask Snuggla." Snugg turned to face his daughter.

Her spine straightened as she looked back at her parents. Her ears, too, stood straight up like masts, adding to her height. But when she spoke, her voice was hushed, and Jonathon had to strain to catch her words.

"Maam, I want to be—I *am*—a warrior!"

The fierceness in Meeri's eyes softened.

"I know, my sweet blossom, your father wants the same thing, but I want to protect you. Can you—"

"Wait. *Father* wants me to be a warrior? I thought you fought because it was he who did not want it!" Her confusion was plain in the twitch of her ear, then she thrust both ears forward for emphasis. "But Maam, *you* were a warrior. It's not fair! Can't you see I can do it?"

A battle of wills flickered through the air between Meeri and her strong-minded daughter. Jonathon suspected that, if he squinted, he might be able to see the sparks. Stoic, Snugg stood at his daughter's shoulder and allowed the heat to die down.

Meeri's gaze dropped to her cradled arms where the King's son still slept on, invisible to all but palpable to her. Did she accept Snuggla's assertion?

Jonathon thought this might be the moment to ask his question of Snugg again.

"The San warriors are already in the castle, but if I—"

"WE!" Snuggla inserted with vehemence.

"Okay if *we* take some Maorrr warriors to the ceremony site and hide them in plain sight, like my dad says, in the shadows around the altar—"

"No."

The intensity had returned to Meeri's eyes. "It is too unsafe. What if the warriors cannot hold on to their cloak of invisibility? I could not, and it almost killed us!"

"There *is* that," Snugg said. "If the warriors become visible at the wrong moment it could put the King in more danger."

"Perhaps I have a suggestion that might help." They turned to see Maorla, the Maorrr leader, standing a few paces away. She stood alone, her golden fur highlighted against a wall of shadows. Jonathon shook his head and looked more closely. It was like Maorla had read his mind. An uneven string of glowing, black-centred green orbs floated in the shadows behind the Maorrr leader. As she made a sweeping forward gesture with her tail, the shadows took solid shape and the floating orbs revealed themselves as Maorrr eyes set in the faces of black and dark brown-furred warriors.

"These are my Shadow Warriors. If Daavid's son can place my warriors in shadowed spots around the King's altar, they may stay concealed even if their special cloak is lifted."

Jonathon felt a surge of hope as he turned back towards Snugg. *Shadow Warriors! Like a secret weapon.* They already had the San warriors in place pretending to be fortress workers. The Shadow Warriors would be insurance. This was what he had tried to tell Snugg.

"It can work, don't you think?" He kicked himself for allowing his voice to sound pleading. "I mean, we can *make* it work, sir."

"I fear still that, if we are seen to help the King win," Snugg said, "he may yet lose the confidence of his people, perhaps even confidence in himself. He is young and still inexperienced. It could work against our aim. He may be seen as not strong enough a leader if he needs outside help to hold his throne." His left ear crooked downwards to rub against the worry lines that grooved his brow.

Snuggla placed her hand on her father's arm.

"Baba...we have been inside the fortress already. Jon—*we*—learned the way around. We'll be careful. But what we saw, Baba... if the King doesn't have enough support against the Deputy tonight, we're all in danger, even out here."

"Your daughter speaks with the wisdom of a seasoned warrior," Maorla said. "We must use the advantage their knowledge gives us of the fortress interior." The Maorrr leader turned to Meeri. "You were one of the bravest San warriors once, my friend. Your daughter reminds me of both you and her father. She will do well!"

"With or without my approval, it seems." Meeri's ears stood stiffly, and her violet eyes glistened with moisture. "Come here, child."

Jonathon felt Snuggla's tension as she left his side and approached her mother.

"Maam?"

"I am not trading *this* child" –Meeri's ear dipped towards the unseen bundle in her arms– "for you. Do you understand me?"

The agitated twitch of Snuggla's left ear telegraphed her indecision. *She doesn't know whether to nod or shake her head*, Jonathon thought. He wouldn't either. Meeri scared him, but she sort of reminded him of his mom. He felt his lip quiver and forced himself to smile instead.

Meeri looked over her daughter's shoulder and summoned Jonathon to her side. His forced smile remained glued in place. He bowed low, but a sharp rap on his forehead made him straighten up with a jerk.

"None of your cheek, young lad!" Meeri's eyes burned through Jonathon's bravado. "I expect you to have my daughter's back at *every* moment." Her voice vibrated like tempered steel. "Deliver the Maorrr Shadow Warriors to their strategic positions, and *then* the two of you return here right smartly."

Jonathon glanced over to where Snugg stood listening and their eyes caught. He saw a warning flash in the intensity of Snugg's gaze. He turned back to Meeri. He thrust his hand into his pocket and crossed his fingers.

"I will, ma'am. We will."

Sarah

"Will you do it, Uncle Frederic?" Sarah asked again. "We have a chance to foil Worl's plans." Her voice softened as she squeezed the old man's forearm. "This can work, if we all do our parts." She watched the tug of emotions cross the face of the King's Steward once more, his confidence fragile. Hope and determination then won out, and he turned to face Sarah.

"Okay. We *will* do it!" The bold strength of his words reflected in his eyes. She breathed out relief and stroked Uncle Frederic's cheek. At her husband's request, Sarah asked the Steward to arrange for David's container to be taken up to the ceremonial site and placed near the King's throne and then ended with her idea to bolster Cragmire's confidence.

"I have some ideas of my own," Uncle Frederic said, "to cause confusion to the enemy."

"Excellent! What have you got in mind?"

"There still exist ceremonial robes that belonged to Good King Cragmire—and something else." He rubbed his hands together.

Sarah looked at him, her curiosity piqued, but the Steward turned and hurried ahead.

Moments later, the Steward led her into Cragmire's war room and together they pushed back the edge of the heavy cobweb curtain until the entire wall was exposed. A grand doorway emerged from the corner. It was finely carved with symbols of the kingdom. In the centre of the door was an emblazoned crest, which featured a creature that looked like a cross between a gryphon and a snake. Sarah rubbed away decades of dust to get a closer look and then smiled to herself. With a few quick words she outlined her own idea.

They opened the door, each holding their breath lest the unused hinges scream and give them away. The door opened only a foot before it became stuck. They were afraid to force it further. Frederic brought over a torch and they squeezed into the darkness beyond the opening. He peeled back a heavy wrapping. The torchlight sparkled off a magnificent robe of fur and jewels. Sarah wanted to squeal with excitement, but then she sobered immediately.

"How do we get this back to the King's room?" Sarah's voice dropped to a whisper. The discovery had put them at greater risk than they were already in.

"Leave it to me." Uncle Frederic's tone modelled his newfound assertiveness. "You go now and get your other plans in motion. I will meet you back in the King's chambers."

Before she left, Sarah went over to the carved box on the table and stroked the sculpted forms that decorated it. She whispered into the seam of the hidden door.

"I'll be back soon."

As she wandered through the kitchen garden, Sarah tried to remember Uncle Frederic's directions. He said that the courtyard was beyond the kitchen garden. Sarah fought her way through the overgrowth and ducked under the low branches of fruit trees. She smelled the freshness of apples and looked up to see some still clinging to their boughs. David would love some of these, she thought, and tucked a couple into the pocket of her apron.

On the far side of the small orchard, Sarah came to the stone wall. She followed it as instructed and looked for a subtle archway with an inset door. Just when she thought she had missed it and needed to turn around, Sarah saw a slight bulge in the stone. The arch. She pushed her way through the gate, stiff on its hinges. There was a great deal of vegetation, shrubs, tall grasses, but the centre was still unmistakable.

An arena.

Uncle Frederic had called it the "Mudiation Arena". In Cragmire the First's time, it had been used to settle disputes and for entertainment on special occasions.

"I see what it is! It's a mud wrestling ring." Sarah mused aloud. The arena was made up of two different colours of clay: one a rich umber and the other a red that reminded her of the farm. A hint of design remained in the confusion of dried clods of churned up clay. Two folded halves that curved into each other. *Like the symbol for yin and yang*, Sarah thought. *It must represent the position of the opponents at the beginning of their conflict, but by the end of their match, they would both look alike. How clever the Grue once were and how sad they have lost this part of themselves.*

She gave herself a mental shake.

So much to do! Can't moon around here all day.

Sarah unfolded an oiled cloth and gathered up two clumps of red and umber clay and took them back to the kitchen. She set up on a counter, away from the eyes of the small, bustling San kitchen workers, and gathered some oil, a bowl and searched through the cupboards for something that she could use as a muller to grind the clay and oil together into a pigment paste.

The grinding was slow work, and Sarah had to stop several times and rub feeling back into her arm. At last she had enough pigment to work with. If only she could ask David to do this next task, she thought. In the end, Sarah realized, it would not require David's finesse. The execution of her idea just needed to be a close enough replication to convince the Grue audience by the light of the moon. David could help her prepare, though. She looked for a scrap of parchment paper and some charcoal, added them to her bundle and made her way back to the King's war room.

The room was empty save for David's carved container. Fortunately, the San recruits had not moved it to the ceremonial site yet. Sarah would have to hurry lest the movers arrive and interrupt them. Sarah scratched on the door of the box and whispered to David. The door opened, and she saw him nestled into the shadows of the interior. David extended his arm and gave her hand a squeeze. Sarah passed him the apples she had gathered and a bit of fresh baked bread as well as a small flask of water and then got down to business.

"David you can't come out in case someone arrives, but could you do me a favour?"

"Whatever you need!"

Embers of warm feeling heated up the edges of her heart, but Sarah tamped down those fires for later—when they got home. *Home. Concentrate!* She thrust the parchment and charcoal at him.

"Do you see the crest on the door in the corner?" she asked. "Can you sketch it simply enough for me to copy?"

Sarah watched in fascination as David's fingers flew over the parchment and within seconds she had her sketch.

She was about to lean into the box to give David a grateful kiss when the squeak and shush from the hinges of the hall doorway announced a new arrival. Sarah straightened and in one fluid motion pushed the box door shut, shoved the sketch into her pocket and turned to face the intruder.

David

David took in a deep breath and held it, hoping that the pounding of his heart would not give him away. *Should be getting used to this by now*, he thought, *but just a little tired of all the adrenalin! Oh, for a peaceful Sunday morning breakfast of ham and eggs, sitting across the table from Sarah and Jonathon and Dad.* He tried to listen to what was going on outside of his prison. Except for a brief murmur from Sarah, he heard nothing.

The sudden tilt of the box sent him off balance, and he slid into the back wall of the box. He hoped that the slight thud of his body had not been noticeable to the movers of his container. He braced himself for the next shift. By the gentle sway, David realized that the carved box was being carried. The final arrangements for the evening's ceremony were taking shape.

When the movement stopped, David put his ear to the wall and listened. The only sounds were indistinguishable. He took out the stub of Memgarr's charcoal and drew a small eye-hole into the wall of the box.

He peered through. He saw long shadows and moving bodies carrying dark blobs around what appeared to be a throne and an altar. He shivered. Across its flat top, the altar had reddish brown stains that had dripped down the sides. It did not need much imagination to figure out what had caused them. David felt an ice cube skitter down his spine. He shifted his gaze through his spy hole.

The direction of the fading rays of sunlight made the view clearer from this side of the box. San carried branches of evergreen and draped them around the escutcheons that hung at intervals around the walls of the ceremonial site. The dome of the sky roofed the entire area. Wispy cirrus clouds traced patterns against the fading blue of the late afternoon. The reminder of the hour triggered a low rumble from David's stomach, and he realized that it had been nearly twenty-four hours since he had last eaten. He nibbled at the loaf and hefted one of the apples in his hand. He wasn't much good with a weapon, but baseball was another story. He tucked the apple away, finished the loaf and washed it down with a swig from the water flask Sarah had provided him.

An odour that was quintessential Grue permeated David's enclosed space and made him want to gag. He peered out of his spy-hole and saw an enormous Grue warrior. Even by Grue standards. He stood with his back towards David, hands on hips, and radiated attitude as he turned to watch the San decorate. David nearly choked on the water when he saw the scar that curled and warped one side of the warrior's face. *The Deputy. What is he doing here? Surely not to supervise!* David would recognize the evil dude anywhere from the description and terror inspired in his wife and son. The sun glanced off the deputy's face and turned his misshapen eye a fiendish red.

The huge warrior grabbed one of the San workers, unfortunate enough to be too close, and lifted him off the ground to shake him like a rag doll. His voice rumbled a question that David could not hear, but that thought and all others left his mind when he saw a San behind the Deputy draw a sword hidden beneath his grubby apron and take a stand to strike.

CHAPTER TWENTY

Sarah

With relief, Sarah saw that the new arrivals into the King's war room were friendlies: San warriors disguised as the Grue's petite fortress San. Several generations ago, when the Good King held sway, the fortress San had been hired to run the kitchens and gardens. Under his cruel son's reign, the fortress Sans' lives had changed, and they became slaves. The warriors were taller and sturdier with muscles that strained against the dingy fabric of the fortress Sans' tunics. The length of the tunics came to their thighs instead of mid-calf. To strengthen their disguise and to distract from the deficiency of their clothing, the warriors held themselves humbly, drooping ears brushed rounded shoulders, eyes on the floor.

They hefted the weight of the carved box easily onto their shoulders and barely disguised their disciplined march with a shuffle. Sarah followed them to the site of the full moon's sacrificial ceremony. It was just past noon. Scant hours to go until moonrise. And still so much to do!

A shiver vibrated down her spine when she spied the red-stained altar where the sacrifice was to take place at moonrise. She closed her eyes, turned away and placed her hand on the box that concealed her husband. As her sprinting heart slowed to normal, Sarah examined the area. The sun's shadows had stretched out long legs in the hours since she had last had a chance to notice. The ceremonial site curved in a broad circle and seats made of stone followed half of its arc. An amphitheatre.

Sarah imagined plays like the ancient Greek comedies and tragedies being presented in this space. *And now here's a Grue tragedy*, she thought. Her heart clenched into a fist in her chest. It made her so angry. Her friend, Meeri, was meant to have been sacrificed on this altar. A sacrifice to the Grue—no, to *Worl's*—success in the war against Meeri's people. A war that would keep her and her family from going home.

The San helpers had decorated the walls with boughs of cedar and floral knots. In between the embellishments, displays of lances crossed with swords and spears with crossbows declared the intention of the evening's gathering. As Sarah turned back towards the altar, she saw the Deputy enter, rip down one of the florals and stalk towards a San decorating the front of the altar. He grabbed him by the shoulders and shook him.

In the same instant, Sarah gasped to see another San—a warrior by the shortcoming of his tunic—draw a sword from beneath his apron and assume a battle stance behind the Deputy. It took two tries to swallow her fear of the ugly Grue warrior before she stepped forward to get his attention. Knowing they had no language in common, Sarah pantomimed a trumped up concern about the setting sun and the torches, with her best damsel-in-distress look. Worl stopped mid-shake and glared at her, then with a look of loathing and disgust, he dropped his captive back to the ground and strode back into the castle. *Just flexing his authoritative muscle*, she thought. *But he can't afford to give away all of his cruel self too early.*

She turned to the disguised San warrior in time to see him tuck the sword away. She signed a warning.

"Careful!"

The San warrior bowed his head in respect, but the cool look in his eyes said that he would do the same again.

Satisfied with the set-up and the placement of David's container and of the San warriors, Sarah returned to the King's quarters with the paint she had created from the red and umber clays. The King still sat in the curtained window seat. Was he thinking about his son and missing wife?

Knowing the trap set for him during the ceremony must make the wait excruciating. My nerves are stretched tighter than a bowstring, his certainly must be.

Yet his face was a mask beneath his trimmed beard, his eyes hooded in a stare as he watched something out the window.

Uncle Frederic fussed over a garment he had stretched on the bed. Sarah came up behind him to look over his shoulder at the magnificent robe and jumped back a foot when the Steward turned and squealed in fright. He threw his hands up to his heart.

"You near scared me to death, girl!"

"I'm sorry, Uncle Frederic, I was focused on what you were doing and didn't think you might not hear me." Sarah felt contrite. Her heart skittered a little against her ribs. She allowed herself a brief reprieve from the stress. Her hand brushed the fur sleeve.

"It's so beautiful!"

"I hid these robes when the Good King died," the Steward said in a whisper. "I knew one day the time would be right for my King to wear them!"

The sound of a throat being cleared drew the attention of both Sarah and the old man. The King watched them through narrowed eyes and raised his arm to flick his fingers at Sarah in summons. Despite her changed perspective of Cragmire's personality, Sarah still felt residual nervousness around him. She approached the window in which he sat, at the same time digging out of her pocket the sketch David had made for her and the umber and red pigments.

"I am going to hide your wound," she said.

A puzzled look furrowed Cragmire's brow. She showed him the paints and the picture. Using her finger for a brush, Sarah dabbed and rubbed the pigment into the King's forearm, glancing often at the parchment sketch on the bench seat beside her royal canvas. The tip of her tongue peeked from the side of her mouth, and her intense concentration scored a vertical line between her eyes. She drew a bit for her classes, but her talent was far below David's. The dour expression on the King's face lightened as Sarah continued to dab away the healing wound.

Little by little the picture took shape. At last Sarah stepped back and gestured for the King's Steward to give his opinion.

"Come see this, Uncle Frederic. Do you think this will work?" For the first time since they had met, Sarah saw the old man's eyes light up in delight. He turned to her and gave her a hug that huffed the air out of her lungs. Frederic grinned up at Cragmire. Sarah caught the look—of love? gratitude?—that the King gave his oldest friend and turned away to give them their private moment. A tug on her arm brought her attention back.

"It's beautiful! I can't see the scar, and it goes perfectly with the robes." Frederic's words ran together in his excitement. "Come see." Sarah glanced at the King and saw what could almost be interpreted as a smile. The corner of his mouth curved upwards a hair's breadth. She sighed with relief. They walked over to the bed where Frederic turned the stretched-out royal robes so Sarah could see a jewel-encrusted version of her drawing on the back. He swept away some invisible lint from the sleeve. *Magnificent.* Any further description failed her.

"Uncle Frederic," Sarah said. "I need to leave you now, but will you tell the King about the signal?"

He threw a quick look at his lord and waggled his eyebrows in concern, then leaned in to whisper.

"Do you think so?"

The King's narrowed eyes tracked between them.

"He knows we're up to something, Uncle Frederic," Sarah said. "Perhaps the time is right to let him know that he has allies. Has the King hand picked some warriors that he knows he can trust to stay at his side? After the signal for the distraction, they must stay with the King. Can you suggest that he order the Deputy to check it out? We both know Worl won't go, but if he is forced to send some of his men it will lessen the number the King must face at one time."

The Steward nodded his head with new confidence.

"Consider it done."

Jonathon

Jonathon could tell that Snuggla was as anxious as he to erase the Shadow Warriors' visibility and get out of there before Meeri changed her mind. Snuggla explained to the Maorrr how to maintain their cloak of invisibility and the importance of staying physically in touch with each other while Jonathon erased each of them. The trip across the open space up to the fortress was uneventful. Even entering the door David had drawn presented no problems. Though as they crossed the threshold into the ceremonial area, they both began to feel anxious. Jonathon could feel the tension in Snuggla's nerves through the strength of her grip on his arm.

In the lead, Jonathon paused, just inside the archway entrance to the site, in time to see his mother gesturing to Big Ugly. The Grue Deputy had a grip on a San worker, but as Sarah talked and waved her hands the Grue dropped the San like a rag doll. Jonathon barely had a heartbeat's warning to whip his invisible line of warriors out of the way as the ugly Grue Deputy stormed past them. As Jonathon caught his breath, his mother signed to a disguised San warrior and then she swept past his little troupe.

Jonathon studied the ceremonial site in the amphitheatre. Behind the altar and throne, the wall stretched upwards and bulged out in a shelf about the height of an average Maorrr warrior—twice that of a San and two-thirds of a Grue. Jonathon led his team into the shadows under the shelf. They knew what to do now. The wait drew out before them like the lengthening shadows.

Jonathon became impatient. He whispered to Snuggla.

"Let's see what my mother is doing!" He felt his companion shake his hand up and down in agreement.

The stone halls of the castle had filled with Grue warriors and ordinary folk since their first trip that seemed like days before but was only hours. Nerves fuelled Jon's speed. Where could his mother have gone? To the kitchens? The King's war room? Snuggla's grip on his arm tightened, and Jonathon saw what had attracted her attention. Big Ugly. The King's Deputy had come around the corner and stopped in front of a door just paces from them. He looked both ways and then entered the door.

As the Deputy pushed the door shut, Jonathon and Snuggla slipped through behind him, confident in their invisibility. The meeting room was small and made smaller by the crush of Grue bodies that surrounded a wooden table in the centre. The smell threatened to overwhelm Jonathon's senses. He found it hard to concentrate on the unfolding scene. The Deputy glowered at the group and then began to speak in a bass rumble. A short but stirring speech judging by the reaction of both the Grue and Snuggla. Her grip was fit to break Jonathon's arm.

The warriors quieted and then began to slip out of the room, one by one. The silence was so deep that Jonathon thought they were alone and was about to complain about his companion's vise like grasp when he saw the Deputy come around the table. He walked slowly and sniffed at the air like a dog on the hunt.

Jonathon held his breath and hoped that the pounding of his heart didn't give away their position. The Deputy stopped just inches from them and looked around the room. He shook his head and followed his men out the door. He closed it firmly behind him.

Snuggla waited several hundred heartbeats before whispering into the general vicinity of Jonathon's ear.

"Worl gave his warriors their instructions for the attack tonight." Snuggla pulled Jonathon closer. "The prisoner will be brought up— they don't know it's Pugg!—and then as the Ahman begins the ritual, the King will stand to join him. Before the sacrifice, when the crowd is fevered, Worl will expose the King's lie, he said." She paused for breath. "That will be the signal for Worl's men to start a riot. And as the blades clash, Worl will kill the King."

"We must tell my Mom," Jonathon said, excitement hiked his voice to a squeak. "No, hang on, we're not supposed to be here. Let's go back up to the ceremony place and tell the Maorrr about the Deputy's signal."

Together they tiptoed to the door and eased it open a crack to look down the hall. Jonathon closed it again double-time, pushing Snuggla back into the corner of the room.

"What's the matter?"

"Worl left a guard on the door!"

David

His hand twitched on the latch of his prison, and he screamed inside his head and his heart pounded as he watched his wife speak to the hideous Deputy to distract him from the San warrior poised to attack. Every fibre wound tighter and tighter, and then released when he saw the Deputy turn on his heel and stomp off. *Bless Sarah's nerve*, he thought, feeling wrung out with relief.

David squirmed around to find a more comfortable position as he continued to peer out of his tiny spy-hole. The busy San workers rushed in and out of his view. Gradually, the bustle slowed until the space was emptied of visible bodies. The outdoor venue made quick work of vile Grue smell. As it dissipated, David breathed deeply. There was a different, familiar scent in the air, but he couldn't quite place it.

The quality of the light changed almost imperceptibly, heartbeat by heartbeat. Even as he became aware that the world outside his box had grown dimmer, torches were lit in the sconces around the walls, and the air glowed and flickered in soft yellow hues. The air thickened again with the smell of Grue and the sound of chatter grew like a theatre crowd excited for the play's opening. The difference lay in the harsh gutturals and the cackling hoots that he interpreted as laughter. He took a chance and with the stub of Memgarr's charcoal, drew several other spy-holes around the walls of his box so that he could enlarge his field of vision.

The tiers of seats were filling with all manner of Grue. David wasn't sure what he had expected, but to see Grue women in their finery had not formed part of the picture. Some wore gowns, embellished with feathers and furs; others wore aprons over tunics and what had the appearance of old-fashioned mob-caps trimmed with lace, but as one passed close by, David saw the lace was just tatters that distance gave a decorative illusion. Even the gowns, on closer inspection, looked to have been dragged wrinkled out of mothballs. He was surprised to note not all the male Grue were dressed as warriors. They were the minority, however. Warriors ringed the audience seating area and were scattered amongst the Grue people.

The question is how many are still loyal to the King and who's defected to the Deputy?

He saw the attention of the audience focus on the stage area. He swivelled in his container to peer out of the hole that faced the altar and throne. The white-haired old man who looked like a rumpled version of his father guided the removal of the throne and its replacement with a huge shrouded object that, once set down, resembled the shape of the other throne but on a larger scale. The King's Steward made some adjustments to the cloth but left it in place. Then the Steward bowed to the shroud as though to the King himself and backed away, head lowered in obeisance.

He is reminding them who is King, David thought. *Hope it's not too subtle for this crowd.*

David pivoted again to eye the audience. The older members of the crowd nodded and whispered to the younger ones around them. *Telling them about the good old days?* David wondered.

In the few minutes his attention had been distracted by the growing crowds, the sun had settled behind the parapets. It was that peculiar time of the day when the sky still glowed while the ground level was dim. He noticed, as the last of the torches were lit, that the San helpers who lit them stayed in position surrounding the crowd. The Grue audience appeared oblivious to the San. Hiding in plain sight. *Works every time.* Just like his own ploy, hidden in his version of the Trojan Horse.

Bang!

David's hands flew to his ears as the thud against the side of his box repeated. He twisted to peer through one of his peep holes...

...and straight into the expanding pupil of a Grue eye.

CHAPTER TWENTY-ONE

Jonathon

Jonathon, his throat tight with fear, hissed into Snuggla's ear. "What are we going to do?"

They shrank together into the corner of the room in which Worl had held his brief pre-sacrifice conspiracy meeting. When the Deputy sniffed around the table like a hunting dog, he had seemed suspicious. But he couldn't have suspected that two unseen intruders were in the room—could he?

Who would ever think that?

Yet Worl's guard stood in front of the door. No sneaking around him.

Snuggla squeezed his arm and travelled her hand upwards until she could run it across Jon's eyes. A gentle reminder they were still invisible. The Deputy could suspect all he wanted. Until he could see them, he couldn't do anything about them or *to* them. Jonathon felt his heart rate slow. He acknowledged with a single nod against his companion's hand, which still rested on his face. They may be invisible, but the fact remained they were trapped in the small meeting room with a Grue guard on the other side of the door.

Snuggla's hands pressed down on Jon's chest, her message clear. *Stay here.* In the next heartbeat, Jonathon heard her release a soft grunt as one of the heavy chairs rose up and flew through the air hitting the wall opposite them behind where the door would open. Her muscular body hit Jonathon like falling timber just as the door crashed open and the Grue entered the room. Fear and bewilderment sketched the guard's face as he stared at the broken chair behind the door. Apparently—lucky for them—he hadn't been informed of the Deputy's suspicions.

Jonathon and Snuggla didn't need an invitation to exit. Hands linked, they slithered through the opening and shot down the hall like arrows. Their feet barely touched the ground. As they turned the corner, Jonathon looked back and saw the Grue guard outside the door, swivelling his head both ways, bafflement rearranging the droopy wax of his face. Then the guard raised his arm as though to signal someone out of sight down another hall.

Snuggla yanked him around the corner, and they flew down the now-empty hall back towards the ceremonial site. Was that the clank of armour behind them? Or was it an overworked imagination? His mom often said he had one of those. Breathlessness forced them to stop for air. Even though they were still invisible, they no longer felt invincible.

What if the guards corner us and begin to stab and sweep at the air with their swords? We won't be able to escape. What if—

They could hear deep murmurs up ahead. *Guards at the door to the amphitheatre?* Jon snuck a peek back down the hall as the phalanx of Worl's warriors turned the corner and started down towards them, shoulder to shoulder, wall to wall.

Dang it! Where can we go? We're going to be crushed like walnuts between the advancing and the standing guards.

"Oh, sheep-dirt! Deputy Ugly's onto us! They're trying to flush us out!" Jonathon wheezed into Snuggla's ear. "Not good!"

The solid support of the stone-wall Jon leaned against calmed him enough to notice something he hadn't before: an opening to a narrow upward-spiralling stairwell, just feet away from the entry to the ceremonial site. Protection.

They turned as one and skipped up to the first turn in the spiral of the stairs. They paused to listen. The clink of armour drew closer and then halted at the foot of the stairs.

With hearts pounding, Jonathon and Snuggla winged up the remaining flights to find themselves at the top of a small tower. They clasped each other's hands in mutual support and terror and tried to listen over the roar of their own heartbeats. Had the search turned into pursuit? Had Worl figured out they were invisible? No escape from this dead-end tower. In this confined space, Worl's men wouldn't need to see them to slice them to pieces with their longswords.

They were trapped like rats.

Sarah

Sarah left the King's chambers and sprinted to the kitchens to do a quick check of the preparations. The San kitchen workers acknowledged her presence with winks and ear-waves and showed off their dishes. Would the masses of food ever be eaten after the ceremony? It didn't matter. The feast kept up the appearance that the Deputy's plans were still in play. From the kitchens, Sarah dashed back to her room to tidy up and compose herself. So much rode on Uncle Frederic's ability to carry out his task. Maybe it asked too much of him to attend the King and create the signal for the distraction. *Will this work? Will Uncle Frederic have the courage to go through with it?*

Sarah sighed as she looked at her reflection in the glass of the window and noted the wildness of her hair and the wide-eyed expression that dominated her face.

I've lost weight, she thought, unable to remember the last time she had eaten. *Never mind. I'll eat when this is over.*

The thought broke the surface of her control for the umpteenth time—*is there a message waiting at home from the doctor?*—and she pushed it down again. It didn't matter right now. Surviving this day mattered. Protecting her family by saving the King mattered. The presence, absence or contents of the message was beyond her control right now. She tried to draw in a deep breath, but it seemed to bump against an obstacle in her chest.

Sarah looked past her reflection to see the round, orange moon peeking like an intruder through the trees in the garden. She had been keeping track of the relentless minutes, but the sight of the moon struck like a hammer. Her heart pounded with a surge of adrenalin. It's almost time!

She patted herself down, straightening the pinafore she had added over her denim dress. The second they got home, she promised herself, she would throw this dress on the bonfire.

Sarah rubbed the goosebumps nerves had raised on her skin. If only she could hide them with the pink sweater David found a million years ago in the Home Wood. Hide. Cover up... she was good at covering up. Her random thoughts ruptured into a sudden awareness that nearly blinded her. She had been sublimating her fears into efficiency—first at home and now here. *Can't let go now!* Could she just hold onto it for a while longer? *It's going to be okay*, Sarah told herself firmly against the rising tide. *It's all going to be okay.* But her hands persisted in kneading her arms.

Is it? Can you be so sure of that?

The helium balloon of emotions and denial Sarah had forced below the surface of awareness emerged like a rocket and exploded as it hit the atmosphere of her conscious thought.

No, it's not! Oh, God! It's not! There's going to be a battle! What am I going to do in a battle? What can David possibly do in a battle? He didn't know anything about sword fighting!

Those swords scared her spit-less! During the practice sessions, she had seen the damage they did to the straw and wood dummies.

Oh, no, oh, no, no! Deep breath! Deep breath. Calm down, calm down, calm down! Thank goodness, Jonathon's in the allies' camp...but did he stay there this time? Oh please, Lord, let him be safely away from here tonight!

Sarah splashed water on her face to get under control again. Her emotions had been so tightly reined over the last six days, it caught her by surprise when her grip grew slippery. She raked her fingers through her hair as though sweeping the fear out of her head. She'd come too far to waste any more time in worry. One clear thought came rushing to her head: *I can do this.* Getting her family back together and back home for good depended on the success of the next couple of hours. Success measured by saving the King's life and his throne. There was one thing she knew with absolute certainty: the King's survival meant their own survival. If Worl won, she and her family and the allies would either be dead or enslaved.

The King's chambers had filled with attendants during Sarah's absence. Each attendant wore their dusted off finery proudly, adjusting shoulders and touching badges of red and gold sewn to their sleeves. Sarah hadn't realized the full significance of the badges before until she saw a room brimming with them.

She slipped into a corner and watched as Uncle Frederic stood on a step ladder to hold up the heavy robes for Cragmire. The King shrugged the robe over his big shoulders and then turned for his Steward to make the minute adjustments and close the golden clasp at his throat. His beard had been trimmed and long hair waved back from his broad forehead. Sarah felt a jolt of surprise at how young the King looked, and realized, when she put together the timeline of David's last visit, that Cragmire must only be in his mid-twenties. He was an infant when his father was killed in the battle. His step-mother, the Queen, had been dead three years. Could this be the first time that he flexed his own power? From hints that Uncle Frederic had dropped, Worl had maintained the tight control of his mother. The glint in Cragmire's eye, as his Steward placed the crown on his royal head, said he was ready to take the reins in his own hands and not be just a figurehead.

The warrior attendants closed ranks around the King. Sarah recognized the massive warrior who had saved her from the Deputy's wrath the first day she delivered the new menu to the warriors' dining hall. Aengus. His manner was always respectful when they met on occasion around the castle. He turned now and saw her in the corner. She could have sworn he winked at her. Her spirits felt buoyed by Aengus' optimism.

The contingent marched out of the room. Sarah followed a few paces behind.

David

The Grue eye peering through David's spy hole in the wall of his carved box blinked and then disappeared. Reflexively, David had pulled back against the rear wall of the box—or was it now his cage?—and strangled the gasp that threatened to give him away. When he could catch his breath again he looked out the spy hole in time to see a young Grue man join an older couple, his parents perhaps, on the bench seats. Just a bit of curiosity, David told himself, that's all. He felt foolish for overreacting. But had he made his spy holes too obvious? Would his concealment be exposed before the right time? No one could get in and it was pitch-black inside his box.

Impossible to see inside. Right?

The hammering in his chest proved logic a lie. In the presence of the Grue masses, the safety he had felt inside his Trojan gift melted into illusion. His thoughts twisted down a darker path. Was their whole enterprise to save the young Grue King from the Machiavellian plots of his half-brother and restore peace between the kingdoms an illusion—a grand fantasy? Were he and his family doomed to be trapped here forever like his Uncle Frederic? He needed to distract himself from this fruitless line of thought. He shifted to peer through the spy hole closest to the throne and altar.

David heard a murmur of Grue voices right outside his box. He strained to hear them. They moved into his sightline and their words carried to him.

"Sacrifice or not, this battle won't be no gift." A muttered response was lost as they shifted positions and then another snippet floated in to David.

"...tough little debbils. Hamstring you quick as look at you and then finish you when you're down..." The voices moved away again as a whirl of activity entered at the end of the stage. *Ah!* David thought. *They do have a healthy respect for the San.*

An elder had appeared, dressed in garb that set him apart from the Grue crowd and warriors. With minute care, he examined the altar and swept away invisible specks before spreading a gold and red cloth over the centre. He pressed his hands together before his chest and bowed his head before raising his hands to the sky. Next he moved to the head, the foot and opposite side of the altar and repeated his performance. When done, he returned to stand beside the throne.

David then had a chance to study the elder's attire. His bowed head, draped in long feathers, resembled the headdress of a golden eagle. When he raised his face to the sky, David felt astonished to see that the elder's skin did not have the melted waxen appearance of many of the Grue, especially the Deputy's men. His eyes were dark holes in a smooth, pale complexion. His mouth cut a thin line between the sharp beak of his nose and a pointed bare chin. An intricately patterned cloak hung from his shoulders, fastened at the shoulders by circlets of golden metal. Beneath the shroud of his cloak was a simple woven tunic, but the colour of the tunic blazed in sunset red glory.

For several hundred heartbeats, the silence stretched out as the presence of the elder hushed the Grue audience waiting in the tiered seats. David first heard the indrawn breath from the crowd and swung his eyes to the arched door in time to see heralds enter, stand on either side and raise their trumpets to the sky. He expected to hear something thrilling and majestic announce the entrance of the King, but the notes fell flat and sour as though the instruments had not been played in eons. The heralds, with sheepish looks, shook out their errant trumpets and fiddled with the mouth pieces then hoisted them once again and blew. The sound *approached* melody this time.

The Deputy and four of his men entered and turned to the left, then split to stand on either end of the altar. Next through the door came a troop of Grue warriors, heads up proudly, eyes shifting from side to side in watchfulness. *But are they loyal to Worl or their king?* When they had entered and taken position behind the throne, the heralds raised their instruments once again. The sound rose sweetly and built to a heart thumping climax just as the King appeared, alone, on the threshold. The irony in the different musical announcements was not lost on David.

The crowd cheered wildly. Their young King presented a thrilling sight in the regal splendour of royal robes not seen for many years. The bejewelled crown on his head threw rainbow sparks in the flickering torchlight. The King seemed taller and more magnificent than David had imagined. He recalled Uncle Frederic saying that this was the first ceremony of Cragmire's reign since his coronation three years before. Worl had tried to keep the King isolated from his people.

Slipping out from behind the King, the Steward slid over to the shrouded object behind the altar. As King Cragmire the Third approached with a dignified pace, Frederic theatrically removed the shroud to reveal the glorious throne of Cragmire the Good, the King's legendary grandfather. *How did Uncle Frederic manage to preserve it?* Beneath his nervous exterior, he hid more than just survival talents. *He's a wily one.* The cheers of the audience rang off the walls and rose higher and higher into the deepening night.

David peered out at the audience. A sprinkle of older individuals—old enough to remember the Good King—stood and pointed to the throne. One old man in an elaborately embroidered tunic and a raspy bass voice that carried several rows, explained the significance of the throne. Heads nodded and the murmurs grew as his message spread through the audience. The throne had not been seen since the time of Cragmire the Good. David glanced over at the Deputy to see his reaction. The ugly twist of his features into a fierce scowl revealed what David had expected, but an icy fear still ran down his spine. *This man*, he thought, *does not take a dare lightly*. And the pomp that Uncle Frederic and Sarah had engineered represented a serious dare to his plans.

The thought of Sarah made David look frantically around and beyond all the warriors, hoping she had been sensible and stayed away from the ceremony. The relief that began to trickle into him reversed and flooded out when he caught sight of his wife's sherry-coloured hair behind one of the heralds. *What am I going to do with that woman?* David thought, half in desperation, half in admiration.

Movement from the altar split David's attention.

Sarah

The halls echoed with the marching feet of the King's cohort. Uncle Frederic skipped along in Cragmire's wake, his hands fluttered in the air around the train of the King's robes, as though willing them to flow in orderly folds.

At the entrance to the ceremonial amphitheatre, the heralds waited. Also standing to the side, Sarah saw Worl and his squad bristling with armament. The heralds entered first to announce them. Sarah gritted her teeth as the trumpets squealed through the opening notes. When the Deputy and his men went through the door, the King paused and looked around at his attendants. Uncle Frederic whispered a translation of the King's speech into Sarah's ears.

"Tonight, we call upon the Moon and her bounty to bless our enterprise with success. May she uphold us with her justice and guide us once more to peace and prosperity."

Sarah saw the determination in the King's eyes answered by trust in the gaze of his handpicked warriors. The high, sweet melody of the heralds' trumpets suspended the spell. The King turned and with full majesty entered the stage of the amphitheatre. Uncle Frederic beetled through the crowd of warriors and whisked the cloth off the King's throne. Sarah peeked around the heralds and felt relief when she saw David's carved box untouched on the far side of the stage.

Now, where did Uncle Frederic hide the signal lamp? *There is no way he is going to be able attend the King and create the distraction, too. What was I thinking?* Sarah berated herself.

I'll have to do it.

CHAPTER TWENTY-TWO

David

Through the peep-hole closest to the altar, David watched as the Ahman shook his feathered headdress and pulled an object from under his robe. A rattle, round and bumpy like a defensive armadillo. By its long carved handle, he flourished the rattle at the sky then pointed it left and right with a shake in each direction. In a shuffle-dance he circled the altar, twitching the rattle to both sides and skyward. The jiggle of the rattle became faster and faster until it sounded like the attack warning of a snake. With a final frenzied shake of the rattle across the front of his body, the Ahman froze, then stretched his arms upward. His body weaved backwards and forwards as though to conjure a vision. With an emphatic thrust of the rattle, he aimed at the edge of the wall surrounding the amphitheatre. At the precise apex of the Ahman's aim, the moon's orange rim glowed like a candle flame.

David listened to the deep silence of the Grue audience. As the moon rose, it reminded him of a reluctant performer peeking around the stage curtain, and the Ahman became the maestro who twirled his rattle-baton and beckoned the shy moon's appearance. Once over the brim of the wall, the light of the moon shone down like a beacon on the floor of the amphitheatre. Its beam inched towards the altar.

The Ahman motioned to someone outside of David's view. He strained to see through his spy-hole. A pair of the Ahman's acolytes entered the stage. They struggled to carry something heavy between them. As they approached the altar they turned and David could see their burden. The sacrifice.

Pugg.

In all their planning, they had forgotten to find a stand-in for Pugg. *Would they notice that their sacrifice no longer lived?* Still dressed in Meeri's clothes, the San warrior's head lolled as limp as a rag-doll, and his feet dragged parallel lines across the dust of the stone floor. With exaggerated gentleness, the aides stretched the disguised warrior down the length of the altar and arranged a plain robe across his body. *Maybe they thought the San had fainted.* Once again, the Ahman repeated his dance around the altar as the beam of the moon continued its advance.

When the sacrifice was placed upon the altar, David thought he heard a sound much like a collective groan from the audience. What did they think they had come to see?

Closer and closer the moon's beam crept to the centre of the stage.

Heartbeats before the lunar spotlight struck the altar, the Ahman gestured to the King and Deputy to join him beside the sacrifice. David felt his heart begin a drum crescendo. His chest was tight with tension, so tight it was fit to explode. His trembling fingers reached up to the latch and practiced finding and opening it until his movements were smooth and automatic so that when the time came, he would be able to burst into the open without sluggish thought.

With a suppressed grunt, David turned to another peep-hole inside his box in time to see looks and signed messages pass between Sarah and Uncle Frederic.

Wait! What was that? The lantern? That wasn't her task!

Then his blood ran cold. The Deputy, with a questioning frown, stared down at the Steward and David could see him try to follow Uncle Frederic's gaze. Sarah was no longer in sight.

Jonathon

Jonathon stuck his head over the parapet of the small tower in which they had trapped themselves.

How will we get out of here if they come up the stairs after us?

Snuggla signed a message into his palm. She could not hear any pursuit up to the tower. The phalanx of Worl's warriors had not followed them. Jonathon took stock of their surroundings. His panic slowed as his eyes took in the scene below. He could see the entire Grue-filled amphitheater and the stage below them. All the seats were filled and the faces of the audience turned towards a doorway directly beneath the tower in which they hid.

His ears still rang with the screech of the heralds' trumpets from courtyard. The sound had pierced into his brain like sharp needles. He had a good idea of the agony Snuggla experienced—she nearly ripped off his arm. He desperately felt for her hands and pried away her vise-like grip, retaining one hand in his own. He almost regretted that move a moment later when the trumpets sounded again. But the squeal factor was much less with the second announcement. This time Snuggla only cut off the circulation to his fingers. The two of them strained up on their toes to look over the parapet.

The King, preceded by his men, came out and paused before the crowds to receive due adulation. Then he moved to stand with another strange looking man in feathers who seemed to be leading the ceremony. Big Ugly had positioned himself on the far side of the altar.

If only I had something I could toss with my slingshot, Jonathon thought. *Ugly is standing at a good angle from me.*

Jonathon pulled back inside the tower and searched around the floor. He found chunks of stone and mortar swept to the back wall.

"Help me pile up these stones," he whispered to Snuggla. Together, they massed a foot-high pyramid of projectiles. He tried to work out the difference between Worl's and the King's men. He had near perfect angles from up here. Jonathon grinned to himself.

Look out, Big Ugly!

Sarah

Sarah peeked around the herald's elbow and tried to catch Frederic's attention without drawing anyone else's. The ceremony was well underway, and all the key actors in place except for Pugg, the sacrifice. Her mind hiccupped on that thought. They forgot to change that part of the plan. *Too late now!* A rising tide of desperation energized her. Uncle Frederic couldn't leave the King's side. It was up to her now! She had to do it. She had to get out to the battlements with the lantern before they brought Pugg out. If the distraction didn't occur on time, Worl might succeed in killing the King before help could move in. It seemed like forever, until Uncle Frederic glanced over and Sarah caught his eye. With a couple of flicks of her wrist and hand, she asked about the lantern. His eyes widened in remembrance and his mouth formed an 'O'.

He forgot! Why did I let David and Jonathon talk me out of doing this task in the first place?

She interpreted Uncle Frederic's eyebrow signals and nervous jerks of his fingers. The lantern had been hidden nearby.

Sarah ducked back into the dimness of the doorway and scanned the recesses of the walls on either side.

There!

She grabbed the handle. The lantern was unlit. She'd light it from a hall torch when she reached the outer walls. She hurried down the empty hallways and around corners, angling her progress towards the battlements and parapet that fronted the fortress and overlooked the direction in which the San and Maorrr hid.

A narrow door exited onto the parapet walkway. Sarah set down the unlit lantern and peeked around the corner. The battlement stretched to either side. In the deepening gloom, bartizans— turret towers—overlooked the corners of the battlements. The guards were probably in the bartizans, Sarah reasoned. Before her, the merlons were tall, tall enough for the Grue warriors to hide behind, and each one slit with arrow loops through which marksmen could take aim on an approaching enemy. Sarah noted quivers of arrows stored by each merlon.

Ah ha! Another way to put a spoke in the wheel of their defence.

On mouse-feet and keeping to the shadows, she collected as many quivers as she could without approaching too closely to the bartizans. She hid them in an enclosure off the hall and then lit the lantern.

As Sarah returned to the doorway, she froze. The unmistakable odour of approaching Grue guards glued her feet to the stone floor. She glanced down at the glow of the lantern in her hand.

She was exposed.

CHAPTER TWENTY-THREE

Sarah

She stared down at the yellow glow of the lantern that dangled from her fear-loosened fingers; the reek of approaching battlement guards punctuated the sound of heavy steps.

With a fortifying breath to clear her thoughts, she came to the conclusion her only course of action was to be bold. She stepped out into their path and stopped. Widening her eyes in mock surprise, she smiled and gave each guard a brief curtsey. She recognized both of them from the weapons practice sessions where she bound up strains and salved bruises in her capacity as healer. One she knew for sure as Deputy Worl's man, but the other she thought might be loyal to the King. The Deputy's minion presented more danger for her. From their first meeting, the Deputy had intimidated and terrorized her, and his men followed suit.

Their narrow-eyed suspicion followed her. She smiled and waved her hand around and moved almost by accident towards the closest crenel. She could almost smell freedom through the space between the merlons.

"Hail, fellows well met!" Sarah sang in a trilling voice, grateful for the language barrier, intent to distract them from her purpose. *So far, so good.* They had not budged a whisker since she entered the parapet. Worl's man watched her, though, like his next meal. She shivered inwardly. With shoulders straightened and head tall, she wiggled the lantern a couple of times and then set it on the ledge of the crenel. A side glance warned her that the eyes of the Deputy's man had narrowed to mere slits and the twitch of his hand on his sword hilt twanged against her nerves like untuned guitar strings.

Her best move—perhaps her only move—was to foil his reaction.

"I thought I'd see what the moon looked like from out here! Isn't it beautiful? What a view!"

With arms outstretched, Sarah twirled around and *accidentally* knocked the lantern out through the crenel. It crashed to the stony ground several beats later. She leaned over the wall and stared down, breathing consciously for one, then two, and spun to face the guards with her hands clasped at her throat, her eyes wide in mock dismay.

The Deputy's man grabbed her by the arm and shook her. *He didn't buy it. It was worth a shot.* He marched her towards the door, growling at the other guard over his shoulder. She let her breath out and with it released her fear in the guise of bravado.

"It doesn't matter!" Sarah blustered. "It's done now. You can't change it!"

The guard yanked her arm higher, until one foot barely touched the ground and he forced her forward in an awkward tippy-toe hop. Even if he could not understand her words, he got her tone. Her bravado drained away. Now she wished he could understand her.

"Where're you taking me?"

David

David's heartbeat slowed to a more normal pace when he realized the Deputy could not act on his concern about the communication between the Steward and Sarah. Worl stood at the Ahman's right hand, his scarred cheek towards David, his eyes on the King. Cragmire faced his people. He appeared serene and calm except for his hands fisted at his side.

The light of the moon's beam drew to within an arm's length of the altar. The Ahman held up a long knife with a wickedly curvy blade. He repeated the ritual moves that he had made with the rattle. This time he drew out his pace allowing the tension to grow in his audience. The Deputy's jaw muscles bulged and slackened, his eye a mere slit.

The moon's beam crept closer.

David shifted again to look out at the audience. As one, they sat forward on their stone benches, anticipation—no—horror captured in their posture and rapt expressions. He reversed his position again to monitor the ceremony.

The moon's ray had reached the edge of the altar.

The drum beat in his chest grew more forceful until each whoosh of his heart sounded in his ears and drowned the activity outside of his box. The Ahman's lips were moving, but David could not hear his words. *Get a grip*, he ordered himself.

"Get a grip!" he said again just loud enough to reach his own ears. "Easy does it!"

The moon's spotlight climbed the altar and touched the sacrificial cloth draped over Pugg. The moment was upon them all. The Ahman circled his arms in front of his torso, then up and above his head.

Like a snake's lightning strike, Worl grabbed the sacrificial knife as the Ahman's right arm passed near him. The Deputy shoved the elder out of the way to clear his path to the King. His scarred face contorted in a grotesque mask as he roared out to his men while he faced the King. David could tell by the rigid carriage of Cragmire's head and shoulders that he was ready for Worl's move against him. The King allowed it.

David clenched his teeth with tense anticipation as the Deputy pulled back the King's sleeve in one move and turned the captive arm towards the Grue people.

"See the mark of the deceiver!" The Deputy roared.

As Worl turned his gaze down to the King's arm, a look of stunned confusion stretched across the Deputy's face. In place of the wound, the King's family crest circled his arm. In the flickering torchlight and reflected moonlight, the clay painting Sarah had created looked detailed and magnificent and complemented the effect of the gorgeous traditional robe and magnificent throne the Steward had placed just before the ceremony. Cragmire pumped his painted arm in the air and bared his teeth in triumph at his traitorous Deputy. David read the interaction between the half-brothers—royal and usurper. A dare. The King's fierce glare dared Worl to take his throne.

The audience murmured in uncertainty. Sounds of growing bewilderment swelled. David swivelled from spy hole to spy hole studying the temperature of the crowd. How would they react? Would they support Cragmire if the Deputy attacked him? Some on the benches were murmuring to each other and pointing towards the King and the Deputy.

Worl's men, who had spread out at the signal and flanked the King's loyal men, now seemed as confused as their leader. *Worl's losing his advantage*, David thought. A wild look twisted the Deputy's gnarled face into a crazed snarl like a crouching tiger. A tiger about to take back his advantage.

Before the Deputy could react to his half-brother's dare, a Grue warrior crashed past the heralds in the entryway and onto the stage. He dragged with him a struggling Sarah.

"She were on the par'pet with a lantern," David heard the Grue report. The Deputy turned his head to listen, still holding on to the King's sleeve. Cragmire jerked his arm away and placed his hand on his sword hilt. With his other hand, he reached out to move Sarah behind him. Whatever the reporting warrior had to add was drowned out by the screech of a trumpet call followed by a muted but clear warning,

"Enemy attack!"

A mass inhale of breath from the audience—like the retreat of the sea before a tsunami—exploded the murmurs of bewilderment into wails of fear. The Grue ladies and gentlemen began to scream and howl as they fought their way to the door, tripping and trampling each other in their haste to escape to safety. Some of the San warriors disguised as castle workers soothed and helped the panicked where they could.

The King called out commands in a booming voice of authority and ordered warriors to the battlements, choosing an equal mix from his own loyal troops and the Deputy's faction.

The King has received the information, David thought. Under his orders, his men matched the Deputy's crew and prevented Worl's henchmen from gaining control in any area of the fortress. *Cragmire has some wily strategies of his own.*

To David, the next few heartbeats of action stretched to a lifetime. The clang of Worl's sword as he withdrew it and charged the King; the King's men and Deputy's henchmen turned to fight each other; the deafening clash of metal on metal, grunts and shouts.

A disguised San warrior passed close to David's box and turned to face him. Tugg! David felt as if the gruff San looked him straight in the eye through the spy hole. Tugg put out a hand, palm down—a message to David to stay put—and took up station in front. David strained to look past the San. *Where is Sarah?* He'd lost sight of her when the trumpet announced the attack and Cragmire pushed her behind him. He opened the door a crack and hissed for Tugg's attention.

"Find Sarah."

"Ordered to stay here and protect you," Tugg said from the side of his mouth.

"Tugg. I'm okay. Sarah's out in the open and in danger. Please find her. Protect her."

The San warrior bent the tip of his ear in capitulation and headed towards the fray around Cragmire.

The King held his own well against the Deputy, with each parry and thrust pushing his vicious half-brother further back. Worl's rear touched the altar and he whirled to the side and lunged at the King with a snarl to press him backwards. Cragmire continued to answer him blow for blow, determination blazing from his eyes and sparking from his gritted teeth as he cut with his sword to meet the Deputy's blade. Then Worl lunged forward again.

David yelled a warning from inside his box.

One of the Deputy's minions crouched behind the King's knees as Worl switched his sword for the sacrificial knife and rushed at him.

Jonathon

Snuggla nudged closer to Jonathon as they watched the melee below them. Big Ugly lunged out of position from his missile range and he could not get a clear shot.

"Do ya see the two fighting at the end of the altar?" Snuggla asked.

"Yes." Jonathon gripped his slingshot tighter and twisted the chunk of rock to better sit in the pocket. He had a second tucked in his sleeve within quick reach.

"See the one with the red'n'gold badge on his shoulder?"

"Yes!" He hissed and launched the projectile hitting his target in the forehead knocking him cold. The Grue opponent lowered his sword and looked around in surprise.

"No! Ya bammy nidjit! The one *without* the badge!"

Jonathon let loose his second shot and struck the badge-less Deputy's man between the eyes and laid him out beside the other.

"Sorry." His cheeks burned. He was grateful for the cover of invisibility to hide his embarrassment.

"No damage." Snuggla mollified her friend. She picked up more rocks and fed them into Jonathon's hand as he let fly with his projectiles. He kept an eye on Big Ugly, but it was almost like the Deputy sensed the danger and managed to keep the King between him and Jonathon's slingshot.

"The Shadow Warriors are helpin'. Did ya see that Grue trip and fall and not get up again?"

It seemed to him that Snuggla's brogue thickened and thinned with her excitement.

He released another rock, missed the forehead target but struck a shoulder, which caused the henchman to lose the grip on his sword.

"And do ya see our San? They're teaming with the King's men." Jonathon took her word for it. He was too busy looking for his next target and trying to get a bead on the Deputy.

"Whhssst! Do you see your maam?!" Snuggla asked and put her hands on Jonathon's ears to make sure that his eyes faced the right way. He saw Sarah peek up from behind the throne, cheek to cheek with the old man he had heard her call Uncle Frederic. *What is she doing?* It looked like she was going to make a run for it. *No! Don't do it!*

From atop their tower, Jonathon could see all the players like they were chess pieces. His mother and Uncle Frederic crouched beside the throne; the King two lengths away faced Deputy Big Ugly; a badge-less Grue knelt behind Cragmire's knees; the Deputy's body angled away from the King, the ceremonial knife pointed at the King's heart, but Ugly faced Jon's mom; creeping up behind the Deputy, a San warrior...*is that Pugg's brother?* All around them in blurs of circling movement the Grue warriors fought each other.

Flames spurted from a torch knocked sideways in the melee and pine decorations caught fire. As the blaze spread along the walls, some warriors ripped down the fiery decor and stomped out the impending inferno.

In the flickering gloom, Jonathon could just make out the form of his mother as she straightened and moved out from the throne in a crouch to head towards the door. At the same moment, the King lost his balance and wheeled his arms. Even as Big Ugly lunged with the ceremonial knife at the King, Cragmire somehow regained his balance. Jonathon saw the moment the Deputy spotted Sarah's move. In the next instant, the huge Grue switched his battle sword for a wicked looking short sword and sprang towards her, still pointing the ceremonial blade at the King.

Oh, no. Sheep-dirt. Crap!

"Hey!" Jonathon yelled. Knowing his mother was in danger, he buzzed with fear for her as he watched the strategic dance below. "Ugly's in my sights."

He took shaky aim with the slingshot.

David

Shock washed over David like a bucket of ice water. The scene on the far end of the altar unfolded almost faster than his brain could process. As the Deputy lunged forward, the King lost his balance and pedalled his arms in a fight to stay upright. The warrior who had knelt behind Cragmire's legs flattened and disappeared into the shadows like a fish on a line while the King straightened as if by invisible helping hand. When the King turned to face his Deputy again, David saw what had been blocked to his view before.

The huge, scarred Deputy had Sarah and he held the sacrificial knife to her throat.

Sarah

Sarah felt a scream hit the back of her teeth and turn into a squeal as the keen edge of the knife touched her throat just below her jaw. The smell of Worl nearly overcame her senses. At this distance, his stink was more horrible than his ugly soul. *I should have stayed hidden with Uncle Frederic behind the throne when the King pushed me to safety. And where did Frederic go? David, oh, David!*

Sarah looked at the King. His eyes were fixed on the Deputy, his expression riveted with deadly determination. The two adversaries moved sideways around each other, creating a circle between them broken only by Sarah's fear-stiffened gait as she hung in the Deputy's clutches. Without warning, she heard Worl grunt deep in his throat and his hand holding the knife to her throat dropped away.

The next moment Sarah felt a brief sharp pain in the side of her head and then swirled down into darkness.

Jonathon

His stomach plummeted as he watched his mother slide uncon-scious to the ground.

"You hit your maam!" Snuggla squealed in Jonathon's ear. He brushed her off and looked over the parapet again at the scene below, his thoughts pounded around inside his head. *Oh God! Is she okay? Did I kill her?* His dang hand got so shaky when he saw the knife at her throat that he missed his aim. He picked up an armful of rocks, packed more in his belt pouch and turned to run back down the stairs. He yelled to Snuggla.

"Bring rocks. We're going out there!"

David

In his anxiety, David fumbled with the lock that he had practiced opening but managed to flip the hook out of its loop. He popped into the open with a yell. The King had his back towards him, so David had a clear view of the Deputy. *Better yet*, David thought, *the Deputy has a clear view of me.* He saw Sarah slide limply away from the scarred warrior's grasp. A roar bubbled up from the depths of David's gut and he released it with a bellow of pent-up ferocity. He threw the apple he still clutched in his hand and found his mark square between the Deputy's eyes. Bits of apple clung to Worl's nose and lashes. Out of nowhere, more projectiles pelted the stunned Deputy and forced him back towards the shadows. David rushed forwards to stand over his wife. Worl's eyes gaped open and his jaw unhinged in horror as he stared at David.

The Deputy backed up bit by bit, flanked by two of his men with shaky swords pointed towards David. He bellowed again at the retreating traitors and waved his hands. At the same moment, a rain of rocks out of nowhere drove the hostiles further into the shadows.

Cragmire roared an order and his loyal men grabbed Worl and his henchmen. The rest of the Deputy's minions saw the capture of their leader and dropped their swords. Worl snarled out orders, but his once-loyal followers shifted their gaze away. Only two tried to reach their leader, but they were quickly subdued and disarmed. Worl stood, arms pinioned behind his back, eyes narrowed in hatred. Not a shred of repentance in his demeanour. Some other warriors joined those who held him and looked to have been worse for their battle, their protective jackets agape and torn, their faces blackened from the fire.

"This is not over, *Crumb.*" Worl spat his venom at his half-brother. His guards led him away.

Aengus stepped forward to receive orders from his King and to see to the attendance of the wounded that littered the ceremonial site and amphitheatre. Some of the badly injured lay without their protective coats. Without the distinctive red and gold badges, the soot blackened faces made identification almost impossible. The smaller fortress San attended them all, indiscriminately. The disguised San warriors had melted into the night.

The sudden silence that trod on the heels of the cacophony of the skirmish was deafening.

It was over.

The scene unfurled in surreal folds of activity and calm, moans and brisk orders. After all the terror that the Deputy had inspired, all the stress and build-up to the ceremony, it seemed impossible that it was over so easily. No, not easily; the number of wounded belied that judgment. But the end arrived more quickly than any could have hoped for.

David knelt beside his wife and gathered her into his arms. Focused on Sarah, he heard the King, as from a distance, issue commands to secure the rebels. A dribble of blood trailed down from her temple and into her hair. Her lashes formed inky shadows on her cheek. Her pallor frightened him.

"Sarah!" he called to her, both urgent and tender. Her eyes stirred under her lids, then her lashes fluttered. David held her tightly. His hand trembled against her cheek. "Sarah, wake up! It's over! The King's safe...we're all safe."

Sarah heaved in a deep breath and opened her eyes to David's shirt collar. With a laugh more like a wheeze she pushed him back a bit to look up at him—and *screamed.*

She kicked and paddled him with panic-fuelled strength.

"Where is your head!"

"Shhhh-shhhhh!" David held on to her, "It's okay!"

Sarah stopped trying to mash her husband to pulp, but her heart still sprinted around her chest. She moved her eyes to where his face should be.

"You put yourself back in one piece, David! Right now! Do you hear?"

The hand resting on her husband's shoulder shook him with each word.

David took a breath and allowed his head to shimmer into view again, just as Jonathon had taught him.

Sarah

"I should have known you'd learned a trick from your son!" Despite her words, her voice softened. "After nearly having my throat cut by Worl, the last thing I needed was to see my husband headless!"

Her voice hiccupped into a sob.

"I'm sorry. I'm so sorry." He stroked her hair and kissed her forehead. "I needed an advantage to scare off the enemy...and it worked! I forgot about it when I saw you were hurt."

"Well, nephew," said Frederic. "A fine sight you are!"

Sarah struggled to sit up and stretched out her hand to the old man.

"Uncle Frederic, I was worried about you."

"I'm an old man, my dear, and I do have *one* talent," he patted her hand. "Survival."

Sarah felt a rusty chuckle rattle her chest at the layers of truth in his statement. The squeeze of a hand on her arm drew her attention, but she could only see the dimpled indentation of fingers on her skin. In the next moment a sound she had longed to hear made another sob catch in her throat.

"Mom?"

Sarah reached for the spot where her son must be standing and grabbed a handful of cloth. She pulled him to her and squashed him to her chest.

"Let me see you!" she demanded, the firmness in her order belied by a tremor. The air shimmered and the open circle of her arms filled with her son's sturdy body. She brushed a stray lock of hair back from his eyes and kissed his cheeks, half expecting a protest. Instead, Jonathon squeezed her back.

"I'm so glad you're okay, Mom. I didn't mean to hit you!"

"Oooh...that was you?" Sarah rubbed the sore spot and said with a rueful smile. "Knocking me out probably saved my life." Her fingers stroked his cheek. "Thank you, sweetheart."

David reached around her to touch his son and opened his mouth to add his gratitude but Frederic cut him off.

"We need to leave the amphitheatre," said the old man, "and let the King's warriors finish dealing with the traitors."

He signalled for them to get to their feet and follow him. As they approached the stone entryway, Cragmire stopped them. For one of the few times since they met, he looked Sarah in the eyes and laid a huge hand on her shoulder. His gaze expressed gratitude that she was okay. His words had a more personal agenda.

"Bring back my son."

His request delivered, the King turned on his heel to continue directing his men. He looked back over his shoulder with one last demand.

"Go to my war room."

David

David saw his son whisper to the air beside him and hold out his hand before letting it drop back to his side. He had no time to wonder further as Uncle Frederic hustled them down the maze of hallways and up a staircase to more hallways to the King's war room. The old man pulled some chairs together in a circle.

"Sit, sit, sit!" he said as he fussed around them. Sarah grabbed his hands and held him still for a moment.

"Uncle, could you please fetch my bandage box for me?"

His eyes opened wide and his mouth stretched in distress. "Oh, why didn't I think of that?" He patted her shoulder. "I'll be back in a trice, my dear."

Silence expanded in the room with the Steward's departure. Jonathon got up and circled the perimeter. David was aware of his son watching him and Sarah as they turned to sit knee to knee and took each other's hands. They stared at their joined hands for a long time before they finally looked up.

This has been so hard on all of us. Time to make things right.

Jonathan

Tears spilled down his mother's cheeks, while his dad's eyes became shiny. Words hung in the air, unspoken. Difficult words that no longer seemed to have a place between them and yet had not disappeared. His father's grip tightened on the small hands in his. He struggled as though the knot in his throat threatened to strangle him.

"I'm so sorry." His words came out in a whisper, forcing her to lean into him. "It's all my fault! Can you ever forgive me?"

"The fault isn't all on one side, honey." Sarah rested her forehead on her husband's cheek. "I have some responsibility here, too." She paused to twine her fingers with his.

"But, I should have talked to you," he said. "I should have listened. I should have—" his voice caught. "I should've been *there* for you."

Sarah let his words sink like a balm into her heart while they clung together.

"We're here now." Sarah took a deep breath. "And you'll have another chance when the doctor's results come in."

David squeezed her hands and then let go to take her into his arms.

Jonathon smiled to himself as he watched them talk. With his help, his folks had finally gotten their act together!

CHAPTER TWENTY-FOUR

Uncle Frederic returned with the bandage box and set it beside Sarah on the table. He fussed with bandages and tried to help her clean the gash on the side of her forehead. Gently, David removed the cloth from the old man's hands and took over.

"This is my job now, Uncle Frederic," he said with a smile.

The old man hovered around them, shuffling. Sarah could see his eyebrows labour with his heavy thoughts.

"What's wrong, Uncle Frederic?" she asked under the shadow of David's hand as he patted away the blood. The Steward's hands worried the edge of his tunic. His mouth worked as though practicing his words and then he peeked at them from under his brows.

"I want to come home with you."

Sarah's hand fluttered out to touch Uncle Frederic's hand, but stopped as he continued.

"The King has been my family for so long now, but seeing you all, I miss my brother!"

David and Sarah locked eyes and then broke into slow smiles that grew into grins.

"Yes!" They said in unison and stood to wrap him in a James family embrace. David and Sarah felt him relax in their arms.

"Dad," Jonathon pushed at David's elbow, "I hear a scratching at the door."

"Can you have a look at who's there, son?" David asked. Jonathon padded over to the door and opened it with a grunt. He looked over his shoulder at the others and stood back from the opening before closing it again.

"Who is it?" Sarah asked.

"I don't know. I thought I heard something, but nobody's there!" Jonathon said but he hurried across the room.

A suspicion occurred to David, and he turned his head to follow his son, who now stood by the King's large, carved chair. His son seemed to have developed a bit of a showman's flair. *What is he up to now?* Jonathon leaned nonchalantly on the arm of the chair with his hand stretched towards the cushioned seat, as though waiting for a cue.

All heads snapped towards the door as the King burst into the room with a flourish, his usual stern glare softened by a look of satisfaction. His Steward bustled forward to greet him. Cragmire glanced around at the tableau his guests presented. David and Sarah stood close together and the boy by his great chair. He strode to his healer's side and poked at the bandage on her forehead, a question in his eyes.

"I am all right, Sire."

"Good." His eyes travelled around the room. "Where is my son?"

Sarah gulped and prepared to meet his wrath.

"He is safe and on his way, Sire." She hoped.

At that moment, a cough from the direction of the big chair drew their attention. Jonathon waved his hand vigorously in the air over the cushion. A mewing sound erupted into a full wail of complaint. With robe flapping, the King rushed to Jonathon's side and froze as the air shimmered over the seat of the great chair and the stocky body of the young prince materialized. Cragmire reached down and scooped him into a fierce embrace. As a knock sounded, he turned his back to the door and looked over his shoulder. His Steward answered it and then returned to the King's side.

"A delegation of San and Maorrr are at the front gate, my Lord. What is your will?"

Sarah knew the King well enough now to be able to see his thoughts circling behind his eyes and saw when the decision was made. He gazed at the portrait of his grandfather, Cragmire the Good.

"Bring the leaders to me, here," he said and then added after a thoughtful pause, "and bring us food. I believe a feast had been prepared. Let it be served."

The King sat cradling his son. It may have been a trick of the light, but his eyes glistened as they soaked in the sight of the chattering child curled in his arms and smiling up into his father's face. Sarah longed to ask Cragmire what had happened, but part of her didn't want to break the moment—and another part still stuttered with the aftershocks of the battle. She waved to catch Uncle Frederic's attention instead. She could tell by the waggle of his eyebrows that he was hiding big news.

"What's happened, Uncle Frederic?" she whispered, her knuckles whitened in their grip on his sleeve.

"I sent for the leaders. They'll join us here."

"No. I mean what happened out there?"

Uncle Frederic fidgeted in place and glanced at his Liege.

"The San and Maorrr are gone and have taken the sacri—the San's body with them. The traitors are under guard but...well, not all the numbers match up."

"What do you *mean*?"

"Some of the wounded—the King's men—were found without their protective coats and a couple of Worl's men's coats were found discarded."

"But Worl is still in custody, right?"

"I don't know. I haven't been able to check myself, but I have sent one of the King's trusted men to check." Frederic wrung his hands.

"Does the King know?"

The Steward shook his head.

"Don't you think he should know before the leaders arrive?" Sarah persisted. "It might change how he negotiates with them." She watched anxiety and indecision waggle through Uncle Frederic's brows and she reached out to steady him. "He *needs* to know."

The King's Steward drew in a calming breath and with a brief nod turned on his heel and strode to his master's side. At the same moment he ahemmed for the King's attention, a knock sounded at the door. Sarah groaned. Timing couldn't be worse.

Cragmire gestured to his Steward to answer the door and then ordered him to pause. He turned with a request to David and Jonathon. Together, father and son rotated the chair until the tall, carved back faced towards the door. In a deep bass rumble, Cragmire issued a further order.

"Protect my son. Keep him quiet."

Jonathon piped in. "We will, sir!"

David smiled down at him. "I will help."

As the King moved towards the door, Jonathon whispered to his dad. "How did you know?"

Before David had a chance to answer, the Steward hurried to the door ahead of his King and swung the huge door wide. Then Frederic stepped through the door and disappeared behind the leaders of the San and Maorrr delegation. They stood on the threshold: Snugg, straight and stern, with his hand at his side instead of its customary place on his sword hilt; Maorla, towering beside him; both regal and soldierly. They bowed their heads as befitted leaders greeting an equal but waited to be invited into the room.

Cragmire moved a step towards them. The San leader took two steps forward and stood with ears sloping respectfully to his shoulders. The Maorrr warrior advanced one step to align with Snugg and wrapped her tail around her feet in deference to the King. The silence stretched while the leaders contemplated each other and waited for the first move to be made. At last, Snugg raised an ear.

"Good health, Your Majesty." Both ears straightened and bowed forwards as the San leader spoke. "It pleases us to see you well."

Cragmire's brow arched, but then he nodded. As he looked from one to the other of his counterparts, Sarah thought he looked strained in a way that reminded her of someone who had an apology to make but didn't know how to start. Instead, he swept his hand toward his war table and they took their seats across from each other.

"My thanks for your visit here today."

David and Sarah shifted their chairs to the exposed wall of the ancestors, where they could see each of the players. Jonathon's back was in view as he played finger games with the King's son in the curve of the great chair.

The King leaned forward with his hands on the table.

"Let us speak of peace."

David let out his breath and glanced at his wife. She had looked tense, but now she rested against him, her strength flown. For a long space of time, the torches flickered around them and the mounds of food, served by the tiny castle San, disappeared as the three leaders conferred. Their voices ebbed and flowed. Ears, tail, and eyebrows spoke as clearly as their words. Between them, two generations of hostility became transparent and trickled away into nothingness. Cragmire established his authority and intention in his rule. He laid out his plans to lead his people in a new direction, one with an emphasis on the culture and refinement of his grandfather, Cragmire the Good.

Sarah whispered into David's ear.

"Uncle Frederic told me that, in King Cragmire the First's day, these talks were common and the Grue, San and Maorrr were fast allies. He tried to teach the King the values of his grandfather without getting caught by the Queen or Worl. Maybe now with the poison cut out—"

Sarah stopped as the Steward slipped back into the room and slithered over to where they sat. Her face filled with questions and more than a trace of worry.

"Uncle," she said. "What did you find out about Worl?"

"What *about* Worl?" David intercepted her aside.

"He may have escaped!" She gripped her husband's arm. "Uncle Frederic doesn't know how to tell the King."

"There's no 'may' about it, I'm afraid. He *has* escaped!" Frederic said, his voice vibrating. "I was afraid as much when the coats were found. They disguised themselves with the red and gold badges and soot on their faces."

"You have to tell the King, now!"

"I wasn't always gutless, you know," the old man said sadly. "But I've been terrified for my life ever since Worl could throw a knife. It's a hard habit to break, but I will. I will tell the King." He raised his head towards the group gathered around the table. "Shhh, wait. The King is speaking again."

"Friends, allow me to add together our parlay." King Cragmire the Third proceeded to summarize the treaty: the Grue would cease all hostilities against their neighbours and open negotiations for trade; the San would share their knowledge and help the castle San to regenerate the gardens; the Maorrr would train a new generation of Grue masons to fix the crumbling castle and its holdings; with trade, a sharing of woven goods and valuable seeds in both directions; within the Grue gardens were some rare fruits and nuts that they once provided to the San and they could once again trade livestock with the Maorrr. "We will have schools again that will teach more than combat and revenge, a school to which all will be welcome." He turned to Sarah.

"Madam, would you help set up the school and classes for our young?"

Sarah's eyes widened to their fullest and her grip on David's arm became painful. Her brain wanted only to return home and never leave again, but the challenge of setting up a school tugged at her teacher's heart. She glanced at her husband as she struggled to find an answer. David bowed his head and spoke,

"My wife is a valued teacher in *our* village and is needed there, Sire." His eyes questioned her and received an answer. "Would it please you if we came after planting and stayed until just before harvest, in the new year, to *train* a teacher?"

The King's Steward cleared his throat. "I would be pleased, my Liege, to help with the teaching and set this library to rights again so that the children may learn. My nephew could show them a thing or two about art, too." David swallowed the chuckle that rose into his throat and merely nodded.

"But Uncle, there is still one thing to be cleared up..." Sarah hissed out of the side of her mouth.

Jonathon leaned forward and spoke to his father, and then turned and whispered to the air beside him. A few heartbeats later, a knock sounded at the door. David gave his son the wink of approval.

"Uncle," David said, "I believe there might be a message for the King at the door."

The Steward's eyebrows jerked in understanding and his mouth rounded into an "O". He trotted to the door and opened it a crack. The murmur of his voice was heard and then he closed the door and returned to the King's side. With only a slight tremble in his voice, he delivered his message.

"M-my Lord, Worl has escaped!" He paused by the end of the table and folded his hands together to keep them from wringing. "Two of his men disguised themselves with coats stolen from your warriors and attacked the guards."

Silence crackled and played against the tension in the room. The San and Maorrr leaders reflected Cragmire's concern.

"Your Majesty, we place our best trackers to your use," Snugg said. Cragmire scowled and then nodded.

"My thanks to you, my new allies." His hands fisted against the table. "This mischance affects us all, once again."

"Your Majesty," Maorla's melodious voice raised in a question. "Will your wife and son be safe?"

Cragmire turned his eyes to his Steward. "My beloved wife is still missing, and my men search for her." A wave of strain rippled across his expression. "She disappeared en route to our country estate a week ago. Only last night did we discover that she never arrived." He nodded in Frederic's direction.

"My Steward will protect my son."

To Sarah's eyes, Uncle Frederic seemed to droop at the King's plan.

"May I offer a proposal, Sire?" Maorla's tail gracefully accented her point. "Your son's education and safety could be blended if he stays with the San and Maorrr until your enemy is caught."

"His place is with me. My son would be frightened away from his people—"

Cragmire pivoted to regard his son and appeared to stop in mid-breath. His vulnerable son trilled with giggles as Snuggla and Jonathon tickled him. "Where did you come from?"

The young San stood and bowed her head so that her ears drooped below her waist.

"Your Majesty, I have watched over your son. We're good friends now."

Snugg rose and came around the table when he heard his daughter's voice.

"Are you about to get me in trouble with your Maam again, daughter?" he asked sternly.

One ear whisked across Snuggla's eyes. *At least a bit of grace to look embarrassed,* David thought. *No. Wait! Daughter?* Jonathon nodded at him and mouthed "Marly." *Ahh,* he thought as he wrapped his brain around this twist.

"No, Baba, but I heard the King say that his son would be feared with us. I wanted His Majesty to see differently."

"I understand, Your Majesty, the want to keep your son close," Snugg said. "But I know my daughter is true. Your son knows my mate, Meeri. He'll be safe with us."

"We are pleased to provide protection to your son, the prince, as well." Maorla added. "It will be our pleasure to teach him about our culture."

Cragmire sat, his head lowered deep in thought. He turned to Sarah and flicked his fingers to attract her attention. She went to his side. He murmured a question into her ear. She placed one hand on his arm and one on her heart. The King nodded. His decision was made.

"I will allow my son to accompany the San to their camp for the time of two moons. From there, he will spend two moons with the Maorrr. We will discuss further what I wish him to learn while he is under your protection." Cragmire rose and raised his hand to make his first proclamation. "The traitor, Worl, will be caught and punished. Our kingdoms will once again be safe."

Cragmire called for his guards. The first to enter, Sarah saw, was Aengus who had saved her life on the first day. The King grasped him by the shoulder and pressed him to a kneel. With a few words he created his new Deputy.

The Deputy's first report of business detailed an account from the search party. Tracks had been found outside the walls leading deeper into Grue country. His recapture was just a matter of time.

Cragmire next ordered Aengus to escort the delegation along with his son back to their encampment.

"This is an educational visit," the King said.

"We would be pleased to have you visit our Kingdoms, your Majesty," Maorla said. "There is much we can learn from each other."

"Sire?" David queried. "We should go with them as well. The portal to our home is in the San forest."

Cragmire approached Sarah. "I will miss you, my healer. I ask that on your return you pass on your healing knowledge to a successor."

Sarah felt such a confusion of emotions. She was elated, of course, that the battle was over and that they had all survived and joyful at the thought that they would soon be on their way back to the portal.

But, at the same time, she felt a surreal connection to this King and his loyal subjects. In her brief time with them she had been terrified, useful, freaked out, appreciated and now in demand. There was something exhilarating about helping to rebuild a culture. But could she get past the memories of terror that Worl had left behind?

"My Liege?" Uncle Frederic's tremulous voice betrayed his apprehension as he approached and sought Cragmire's attention. "My Liege, if your son is protected by the San and Maorrr, may I go home to my family?"

The King stopped mid-step and turned to his Steward.

"Walk with me, my friend."

He led the way to the opposite wall. All the James family could hear was his deep bass murmur.

"I wish I was a fly on the wall to hear *that* conversation!" David said.

"I can do better than that." Jonathon took out the talisman given to him by Memgarr, the Maorrr shaman. He whispered into the shell-like side and proffered it. "Put this to your ear, Dad."

David did as he was bid. Surprise lit up his face. Did it bother him to be eavesdropping? After all they had been through—not even a tiny bit. He clasped his son by the shoulder and mouthed "Well done, son!"

"What's happening?" Sarah asked.

"The King is saying that Uncle Frederic is the only one close to him who knows what things were like under Cragmire's grandfather. He needs him to help rebuild his kingdom to honour the memory of the Good King so that he may earn that title, too. He says that Uncle Frederic is too valuable to him as both his friend and his Steward. He humbly asks that Uncle Frederic remain."

Sarah observed Uncle Frederic's body respond to the King's request. His shoulders straightened and his step had spring as they walked back to stand with David and Sarah and Jonathon.

"Thank you for the services of your Uncle, my friends." Cragmire started.

From behind the King's elbow, with new confidence, his Steward interrupted.

"Give my greetings to my brother, and tell him I'm well." A slight quiver in his voice belied his brave face.

Tears brimmed in Sarah's eyes and a hiccup caught in her throat as she grabbed Uncle Frederic in a crushing hug.

"I will. I promise!"

"We'll see you again, Uncle Frederic." David added. He took his turn and folded the rumpled old man into his arms.

Jonathon had the last word.

"I'll be back, too, Uncle Frederic! I'll help with the school and the library." He glanced around at his parents. "Besides, you all need me to protect you."

—

The castle walls shrank behind them as the delegation returned to the allied encampment. The shelters had already been taken down and the fire pits filled in. One would never know that an army had been camped here for days.

David spoke with the Deputy Aengus along the way. He felt reassured that the young King would be in good hands with this warrior who cheerfully laid out his new mandate: to catch Worl; to find the Queen; protect his King and help his people, weakened by decades of war and neglected resources, to grow strong and prosperous again.

As they parted, David and Aengus grasped each other by the forearm. The warrior gave him a serious but respectful nod, and left the James family to the San.

—

Snugg, Meeri, Snuggla and Tugg gathered around one side of the flower-covered shrine of deadwood in the forest clearing while Maorla and a select few of her warriors stood on the other. Each came to say goodbye to the family that had changed their lives.

Snugg first. He gave David a soldierly salute and gripped his hand in a vise that translated his gratitude and respect. To Sarah, Snugg gave a heart-shaped flower in shades of red and pink with a deep yellow throat with one hand while the other covered his heart. He bowed low to her. He saved Jonathon for last. Snugg took out of the pouch on his belt, a medallion—intricately constructed just like David's—and placed it around Jon's neck.

Meeri came forward and draped a necklace of flowers around Sarah's neck, along with a smaller, more delicate medallion on a finely braided chain of bark. They shared a deep gaze that spoke of their experience together and as mothers of willful young warriors. Next, Meeri pressed into David's hand a small sculpture of a tree. Its shape reminded him of one of the guardian trees that lined the inner path to the stronghold gate. To Jonathon, Meeri gave a wooden carving of a San warrior oiled to a high sheen and followed it with a light tap on the forehead with her ear as she had when he tried to finesse her in the camp with a cheeky bow.

"I have one other thing for you, young warrior." Meeri turned to gesture someone forward. Through the trees, two San warriors carried something heavy in their linked hands.

Pugg.

Jonathon ran forward, his chest about to burst. Not Pugg. His breath sighed out in pain. The warriors carried a stone effigy of their fallen comrade. They placed it amongst the branches and flowers of the deadfall shrine. Tugg came forward and placed his hand on Jon's shoulder.

"My brother, Pugg," the San said, "would've been proud to see your skills in the battle. He'd be puffed to see the warrior you be now." Tugg winced with the ache of his loss and squeezed Jonathon's shoulder. "And I be proud to have fought along the way with you."

Jon turned to his father. So many words all jammed in his throat in a mass.

David's heart felt all the emotions that roiled in his son's face. He could help him get through this now.

Snuggla came forward to stand beside Jonathon. The insides of her ears glowed bright pink.

"Me, too. I'm proud to've fought at your side, Jon," She said as she gave him back the slingshot he had used in the battle. "You're one of us now, Jon," she bumped his shoulder. "A furless San!" She trilled with her own joke and then sobered. "You're ever welcome at our hearth."

"We made a good team, Snuggla." Jon twisted the slingshot in his hands. "You're a warrior, too. I couldn't have done it without you!"

With the farewells over, the allies melted into the trees and left the James family alone with the portal. There was no siren pull on this side like there was in the Home Wood, but as they sat down together beneath the shadow of the deadwood shrine, arms linked, a familiar lethargy overcame them and made their eyes heavy and limbs leaden.

Jonathon had one last thought before the portal's power overcame him.

His father wasn't the only legend in the James household now.

—

The trio supported each other across the creek in the Home Wood. Jonathon could smell woodsmoke from a bonfire. Gramp had probably finished the leaf raking that he had asked Jonathon to do last week. He knew he should feel guilty about that and maybe he would later, but right now, he felt like the promise had been made by someone else long ago.

Jon heard the songs of warblers and robins and the cheeky call of a cardinal, songs he recognized. He realized, in that surreal moment, that he had missed being able to hear and recognize the familiar sounds of his own world. As they approached the back porch, Gramp Matthew came through the screen door. He stopped short when he saw his family, his face frozen in shock. How must they look to him? They were all smudged with soot, clothes ripped, his mom looked thin and her curls tangled.

Without a word, Gramp Matthew's eyes, sheltered under bushy brows so like Uncle Frederic's, filled as he held his arms out to Jonathon. He crushed his grandson to his chest.

David could read in his father's body language the nightmarish déjà vu he must have experienced over the last three days, reliving David's disappearance as a boy. How much worse for him to miss both his son and grandson this time. Matthew didn't know that he should also have missed his favourite daughter-in-law. Sarah smiled as she wrapped Matthew in her own hug.

"Careful, kiddo!" Matthew warned with a gruffness not reflected in the embrace he returned. "You're going to break me."

Sarah stepped back and disguised a half sob with a sniff. She turned away to wipe her eyes, while David had his turn to embrace his father. He caught and held his father's sheltered gaze.

"I'm sorry we frightened you, Dad. I really am. We have so much to tell you. You can hardly imagine." David led Matthew back indoors.

Jonathon followed and then swerved into the kitchen. He put on the kettle. He had a feeling this conversation with Gramp was going to take several cups of tea. As he passed the table in the hall, he saw a mound of mail and remembered something. He dug into the pile and found the official-looking letter addressed to Mrs. Sarah James. It seemed a hundred years since Gramp had asked him to pick up the mail at the end of the lane before he left to play, little knowing that his grandson intended to disobey and follow his dad across the creek in the Home Wood. Jon took the envelope into the parlour and waited for a break in the flow of the conversation to hand it to her. Gramp Matthew, head swinging back and forth like a patron at a tennis match, sat on the sofa between Jon's parents. His waggling brows told the effort of concentration as he tried to follow.

Sarah caught her breath as the letter touched her hand as though it might singe her fingers. The return address listed Doctor Wright's office.

Her test results.

She felt David's eyes on her and met his anxious look.

"Open it." He said and moved to kneel beside her, a hand on her shoulder.

The silence stretched out. Only Matthew seemed a little puzzled by the tableau. Sarah buried her face into David's neck and handed him the letter. After a quick glance he dropped it and put both arms around her.

Jonathon picked up the single sheet and read the final word: Negative. He smiled.

Unnoticed by his parents, he took Gramp Matthew by the arm and led him back into the kitchen, sat him at the table and poured tea into a mug that read: "Old farmers never die, they just go to seed." Then he added a heaping teaspoon of honey.

"It's okay, Gramp," Jonathon said. Matthew had barely spoken a word since he saw them on the porch. He had been shaken but relieved, but after the stories they'd only scratched the surface of, he seemed now somewhat stunned. Jonathon spoke reassuringly.

"Mom and Dad are good now. And as for the rest, I'll fill you in." Jon grabbed an oatmeal raisin cookie to go with their mugs of sweet tea.

"Did you know that you're the father and grandfather of Legends...?"

The End

ACKNOWLEDGEMENTS

This book has been a labour of love and torture. It started decades ago as a short story assignment for a creative writing class at Sheridan College. The main character came back to me a few years later with more story to tell. I doodled a bit with his story, but reached a roadblock. Very slowly and with help along the way, it became apparent I was stuck because his was not the only journey. His wife and son were meant to be on this odyssey and his son intended to take over. I owe a debt of thanks to many people along the way who helped me to open up to the family's greater involvement. Tom Sawyer mentored me in an on-line course, which gave me the confidence to go back into the classroom with Brian Henry to take the story further. Through Brian's class, a group of us formed a writing group. I owe a huge debt of thanks to Judi, Toni, Jennifer and Ann for their support and encouragement. With the initial draft complete, I applied to the Humber School for Writers and received great, thought-provoking feedback from Richard Scrimger. Through Humber, I also found an editor. Valentina D'Aliesio has the eyes of a hawk when it comes to grammar, but she couples that with a fine sense for scene and character. Her help has been absolutely invaluable in getting my story to its final stage. Thank you also to the folks of FriesenPress who have taken my labour and made it into something tangible. My family have been my constant supporters, each encouraging me to "get 'er done!" so that they could read it. My husband, Pierre, has been the best, ready to listen if I became blocked or confused, supportive and always understanding. And finally to my daughter, Jennifer, who has been patiently waiting for my story to be finished so that she could hold it in her hands. Here it is!

ABOUT THE AUTHOR

Julie Whitley is a retired nurse who lives in Stoney Creek, Ontario, with her husband, mother and daughter. _Secrets of the Home Wood: The Sacrifice_ is her first novel and represents a labour of love over twenty years in the making.